P9-DTU-580

"Why are you doing this?" Sheila demanded.

"Who are you trying to punish? Yourself? Your family? Me?"

He shifted in the bed. "What are you talking about?" he snarled without making eye contact. "I'm not trying to punish anyone."

She studied the lines of his face, the deep creases gouged by age and adversity. "Aren't you? Cutting yourself off from the people who love you and the place that's a part of you. Leaving the ranch is stupid, Adam, and it's senseless."

He came close to grinning, as if this were another of their word games. "So you think I'm stupid?"

Her stoic expression did not change. "Yes."

The shock on his face told her he'd expected her to retreat into some benign statement that he was smart enough but acting foolish. As if being a fool was better than being an idiot.

"You're also a coward."

This time his eyes went wide and his jaw dropped. Coldly he rearranged the neat fold of the sheet across his midsection. "I think you'd better leave," he said in a tone that was low and rough.

She struggled to collect her thoughts, to ignore the pain in his eyes, the hurt pride, the fury generated by her insult. "No, Adam," she told him when she was sure of herself again. "Not until I've had my say...."

Dear Reader,

If you're a Texan or you've ever been to Texas, you know it's B-I-G. Really big. There are ranches that cover several counties, a few that even rival small countries in size.

So I started wondering. What if…

What if a man owned a ranch that had been in the family for more than a hundred and seventy years, a spread so big it had several villages on it?

What if he lost control of it—not through fraud or his own incompetence, but because a person he loved wanted to get even with him for some real or imagined wrong?

What if a beautiful woman was given the job of passing judgment on whether or not he should be allowed to continue managing his empire?

Well, that's what this story is all about. The First family doesn't really exist. There is no Number One Ranch. And 512,000 acres isn't the biggest ranch in Texas! But it'll do. I sure wouldn't want to be responsible for the yard work.

I hope you enjoy meeting the members of the First family. Each of them has a story to tell. So stand by for more to come.

I love to hear from readers. You can write me at P.O. Box 4062, San Angelo, TX 76902.

K.N. Casper

The First Family of Texas

K.N. Casper

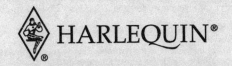

HARLEQUIN®

TORONTO • NEW YORK • LONDON
AMSTERDAM • PARIS • SYDNEY • HAMBURG
STOCKHOLM • ATHENS • TOKYO • MILAN • MADRID
PRAGUE • WARSAW • BUDAPEST • AUCKLAND

If you purchased this book without a cover you should be aware
that this book is stolen property. It was reported as "unsold and
destroyed" to the publisher, and neither the author nor the
publisher has received any payment for this "stripped book."

ISBN 0-373-70951-X

THE FIRST FAMILY OF TEXAS

Copyright © 2000 by K. Casper.

All rights reserved. Except for use in any review, the reproduction or
utilization of this work in whole or in part in any form by any electronic,
mechanical or other means, now known or hereafter invented, including
xerography, photocopying and recording, or in any information storage
or retrieval system, is forbidden without the written permission of the
publisher, Harlequin Enterprises Limited, 225 Duncan Mill Road,
Don Mills, Ontario, Canada M3B 3K9.

All characters in this book have no existence outside the imagination of
the author and have no relation whatsoever to anyone bearing the same
name or names. They are not even distantly inspired by any individual
known or unknown to the author, and all incidents are pure invention.

This edition published by arrangement with Harlequin Books S.A.

® and TM are trademarks of the publisher. Trademarks indicated with
® are registered in the United States Patent and Trademark Office, the
Canadian Trade Marks Office and in other countries.

Visit us at www.eHarlequin.com

Printed in U.S.A.

To Janet Branson, thank you for your insights.
To Connie Marquise and Lori Kerr, my thanks, as well.
To Barbara and Judge Jerry Jennison,
much appreciation, friends.
And to Mary, without whose help, guidance, patience
and inspiration none of this would have happened.

understand they'll also be sending someone out to evaluate the way the place is being run.''

Michael stared hard at his sister and turned away. He paced in the narrow confines of the cluttered living room. At last he sank into an easy chair, his hands dangling over the grease-stained arms.

''So you're taking the easy way out. I should have guessed.'' He threw his head back against the cushion, squeezed his eyes shut and opened them again. ''I know you and Dad don't get along, Kerry, that the two of you are always butting heads, and I understand why.'' He frowned at her and added softly, ''But I didn't know you hated him.''

Leaning against the edge of the bar next to the entertainment center, his sister sipped her glass of blood-red wine, apparently unmoved. ''In three months, when school's over, Brian and I are out of this dump.''

The two-story house was well built and fair-sized, hardly a hovel. She had a cleaning service come in twice a week to shovel the place out, too. Michael was tempted to tell her it looked like a slum because that was the way she chose to live. But what was the point? ''Where are you going?''

She smirked. ''What do you care?''

''About you? I don't. You can go to hell as far as I'm concerned. But your son is my nephew. Family may not mean anything to you, but it does to me.''

''Ah, sweet brotherly love,'' she taunted.

''What you've done is despicable, Kerry. You've given up your right to love.''

For a fleeting moment he saw her lips quiver before she pressed them together defiantly.

Michael rose to his feet and stared down at her. ''Next week is Dad's birthday. We're planning a big

PROLOGUE

Coyote Springs, Texas

MICHAEL FIRST TURNED to his sister with venom in his eyes. "You did what?" he demanded. His deep voice boomed off the walls of Kerry's house on the eastern edge of the Number One Ranch.

"I sold my share to the bank," she said calmly.

Michael's knuckles were white as his fingers curled into tight fists. "Just like that, without a word to anyone? If you wanted money so damn badly why didn't you give us a chance to buy you out?"

She laughed, but there was more bitterness in the sound than humor. "Believe me, you couldn't possibly have matched Homestead's generous offer."

He knew it was true. Her share wouldn't have made any difference in the family's common ownership of the ranch, but combined with the forty-five percent Homestead Bank and Trust already held, it gave them controlling interest. He was afraid to ask how many millions of dollars she'd received for her critical six percent.

He ran a hand through his thick dark hair. "You've told Dad, of course." His voice was low, filled as much with sorrow as anger.

"The bank said they'd notify him in a day or so. I

bash like we do every year. Brian is welcome." He strode to the door, tugged it open and was about to step outside, when he turned one last time to his sister. "I think it would be wise if you stayed away."

CHAPTER ONE

ALL SHEILA MALONE could see in her rearview mirror was the billowing cloud of fine white caliche dust her two-year-old Lincoln Town Car was kicking up. She chuckled, remembering the adage: "You know you're in West Texas when the directions to the house say to continue another ten miles after the pavement ends." The paved road had ended eight miles back.

She shifted restlessly in her seat. The six-hour drive from Houston had been mercifully uneventful, but she was ready for the boredom to be over. This Number One Ranch job was a godsend. She'd studied every scrap of information Homestead Bank and Trust had given her access to, and privately researched magazine articles, agribusiness journals, livestock markets and economic analyses. She was ready—she hoped.

Establishing her own consulting business had been a big gamble for a single woman approaching fifty, but specializing in farm and ranch management had been a lifelong dream, one she felt uniquely qualified to perform. She was, after all, a rancher's daughter. She'd seen the cards fate could deal, knew how pride could cloud an intelligent man's vision and how shame could eat at his soul. Maybe in coming here she could help one rancher retain control of his spread, and in doing so avenge in some mysterious way her father's bad luck and poor judgment.

Altruism wasn't her only incentive, however. Despite hard work and determination her financial position had deteriorated in the three years since she'd opened her doors. She needed this fee, by far the largest she'd ever been offered, to solve the chronic cash-flow problems she was experiencing with her struggling firm. The bank's tentative offer of a continuing oversight role in the Number One's future operations—if this initial evaluation produced satisfactory results—was a bonus that would ensure her company's reputation, growth and long-term success. Failure, on the other hand, could well destroy it.

Stone and wrought-iron gates to the interior of the mammoth ranch were spaced about two miles apart. As she approached the ten-mile point, the fifth gate loomed on her right. A call box was embedded in a rock pillar within arm's reach of the driver's-side window. She pressed the button and gave her name to a crackly voice that couldn't be identified as male or female. The wide gate swung open.

She drove another three miles over more packed caliche between budding green pastures before spying the house perched on the edge of a bluff. It didn't look especially big from her vantage point, but appearances could be deceiving in this broad, open land. Downshifting into low gear, she climbed the steep dirt road that skirted the side of the mesa.

The top was in stark contrast to the rugged prairie below. Oak, mulberry and pecan trees shaded the two-story gable-roofed house. Red-tipped photinia, purple sage and pink Indian hawthorn bushes lent splashes of color to the well-kept landscape.

After parking in the neatly bordered driveway, she alighted from the vehicle and inhaled the spring-fresh scent of the gentle breeze. She was stretching her stiff back muscles, when the front door of the house opened and Adam First emerged.

He was halfway down the concrete path before she realized she was staring. She'd seen pictures of him in *Texas Monthly*, but they didn't do him justice. He was taller than she'd expected, a couple of inches over six feet. In spite of his fifty-plus years, he still had a full head of dark hair, conservatively cut, and the lean-hipped, broad-shouldered build of a physically active mature man. What the glossy photos had totally failed to capture was the seasoned masculine power his square jaw and loose-limbed gait projected.

She extended her hand. "Mr. First? I'm Sheila Malone."

He accepted it and squeezed her fingers gently. His hand was large and had the thick-skinned texture of a working man. "Miss Malone."

"It's Mrs., actually."

"Sorry," he said, the single word laced with just enough sarcasm to make it insincere. "I suppose I should have pronounced it Miz."

She hadn't expected him to greet her with open arms—the thought sent an uncomfortably warm shimmer up her spine—but she was a little surprised by his coolness. Texans in general, and West Texans in particular, were notoriously friendly.

"It's very kind of you to invite me to stay here at your place. I didn't realize you were so far from town," she commented as he led her up the walk. Feeling foolishly self-conscious when he ignored her thanks, she added, "Lovely house."

"My father built it." He turned the knob of the ornately beveled glass front door, pushed it open and with the sweep of his arm motioned her in ahead of him. ''In the early fifties,'' he added, closing the door, ''Before the drouth.''

The drouth. She wondered if there was any other part of the country besides West Texas where this archaic word for drought was still used. Seven years of substantially below-average rainfall in the mid-fifties had turned West Texas into a second dust bowl. As a child she'd never realized she was living in hard times. It was only later when she read *The Time It Never Rained* by Elmer Kelton, a western writer from San Angelo, that she began to appreciate the disaster it had been and the stubbornness of the people who had endured it. A lot of landowners had gone under; many of those who managed to hang on never fully recovered. The Number One, among the oldest continuously operated family-owned ranches in Texas, had survived.

Why then had Adam's daughter Kerry Durgan sold her share of the spread? According to the annual reports the bank had given Sheila to review, profits had been declining over the last three years. Had Kerry calculated that the ranch was headed for bankruptcy, and she'd wanted to make her deal while she still had bargaining power?

The entrance hall of the brick-and-stucco house was large and square. A split-landing staircase ascended on the left. The wall to the right was faced with rough-cut weathered boards. A spinning wheel, blacksmith's anvil and a branding iron stood proudly before it, as well as a silver-encrusted saddle of scarred brown leather over a saddle blanket with the Number One brand emblazoned on one corner. A four-by-eight-foot oil painting behind them immortalized a small wagon train crossing an endless, sun-bleached prairie of cactus and scrub. There were mesas in the background; above them, ominous gray storm clouds. No one entering the home, Sheila realized, could forget this family's pioneer heritage.

Adam led her past the wall into an open-timbered room that rose the full two stories and ran the entire depth of the house. The furnishings were simple, heavy and very masculine. Huge picture windows at both ends of the room filled it with light.

A short round woman wearing a Mexican peasant dress appeared at the far left corner of the room. She wiped her hands on a bib apron as she approached.

"Elva, this is Mrs. Malone." Adam turned to Sheila. "Elva Hernandez is our housekeeper and the best cook on either side of the Pecos."

"I'm very glad to meet you, Elva."

The woman smiled politely as they shook hands. "Welcome, miss."

"It's Mrs.," Adam corrected her.

The silvery-haired woman arched an eyebrow quizzically at him.

Sheila glanced at her host and for a fleeting moment thought she saw humor twinkle in the corners of his gray eyes, but it quickly dimmed. "Please, call me Sheila," she told the housekeeper.

Adam rubbed the back of his neck as he glanced at the old Regulator ticking on the wall beside the stone fireplace. "It's too late to show you around today," he declared. "Sun'll be down soon. We'll start the tour tomorrow. I'll get your bags from the car and take them up to your room. We eat in about an hour, so you have time to freshen up." Without waiting for her reply, he strode to the front door.

Elva shot Sheila an apologetic smile that said he wasn't usually this abrupt. It brought scant comfort.

"He's very busy preparing for the barbecue," the housekeeper explained. "You must be thirsty after your long drive. I have lemonade in the kitchen."

"Wonderful. I'll come with you and you can tell me all about this barbecue. What's the occasion?"

Elva poured the tangy beverage into a tall glass filled with ice. "It's for Mr. First's birthday."

Sheila accepted the drink gratefully and took a long swallow before the alarm went off in her head. "His birthday?" From an article she'd read she knew the birthday of the head of the family was traditionally celebrated as a sort of founder's day. Prominent guests were invited and the entire ranch was treated to a gala western cookout. "When?"

The housekeeper gaped at her. "Why, the day after tomorrow. Didn't you know?"

Sheila closed her eyes in exasperation. "No, I didn't."

SHE WAS WAITING for him at the foot of the stairs when he came down after delivering her luggage. Sheila Malone looked nothing like his late wife. Helen had been short, brown haired and inclined to put on weight. This woman was tall, blond and slim. Helen had been a homemaker. Sheila Malone had the air of a professional businesswoman.

"Mr. First, I wish you'd told me last evening when I spoke to you on the phone that this was the week of your annual barbecue."

The waning sun slanting through the glass door behind her caught the golden-red highlights of her stylishly short hair. Like little fires, he thought.

He folded his arms across his chest. "Does it make a difference?"

"Of course it does," she responded irritably. "I'm here to evaluate ranch operations, not interfere in your personal life."

He raised an eyebrow.

"I think there's something we need to establish right now, Mr. First. If I'm going to be of any help to you, you're going to have to be honest with me. Play games and we both lose. Is that clear?"

Adam found himself enjoying the set of her jaw, the determination in her attitude. She projected strength and confidence, qualities he respected regardless of gender.

"Perfectly."

His easy agreement seemed to irritate her all the more. She took a deep breath. "I also have a business to run back home. Time is valuable, Mr. First. I wish you hadn't seen fit to waste mine."

He could have explained that he'd mentioned the ranch party to Nedra Cummings when she'd proposed this consultant's visit. The acerbic vice president for investment management had been quick to point out they were in a hurry to get started—and that it was in his own best interest to cooperate. He'd gritted his teeth at the time. Now he was more inclined to run his tongue over them.

"I'll leave tomorrow morning," Sheila announced. "I'd like to reschedule with you, however, for a more convenient time. Perhaps next week—"

"That's up to you." He dropped his arms with a shrug. "On the other hand, you're here now."

She wasn't the thirty-something he'd pictured from

her voice on the phone. Closer to his age. Surprisingly, that pleased him.

The shake of her head made her slender drop earrings bounce against the delicate skin of her neck. "You'll be tied up with your barbecue," she pointed out.

She had a beautiful complexion, clear and smooth. The laugh lines at the corners of her eyes and mouth were delicate and appealing.

"On Wednesday," he said. "One day. If you turn around and go back to Houston now you'll have lost two days." He tossed her a peppery smile. "As you say, your time is valuable."

He motioned her toward the double doors opposite the living room. "You might as well stay," he observed nonchalantly. The woman walking ahead of him into his office fascinated him. She'd been very careful to identify herself as married, but he noticed she wasn't wearing a wedding band. Did that mean she was divorced? Widowed? Or one of those liberated women who refused to wear a man's ring?

"I can give you a quick tour of the place tomorrow. Then, after the picnic, we'll explore a little more closely."

She clearly wasn't happy with the situation, but she had little choice.

"Since you're here to evaluate ranch operations—" he waved her to the leather couch and joined her there rather than take his seat behind the desk "—why don't you tell me what your qualifications are for passing judgment on how I run things."

The quick parting of her lips and the color creeping up her neck told him she didn't appreciate his choice of words, but she refused to be riled. Impressed by her self-control, Adam settled against the arm of the other end of the couch. "Tell me about yourself, Mrs. Malone."

She studied him a minute, seemingly troubled by the inconsistency between his harsh words and casual manner. In truth, the push-pull of his reaction to her mystified him, as well.

"Call me Sheila." Her voice softened and the worry lines around her mouth began to recede. He'd already noticed the intelligence in her blue eyes, but now he had an opportunity to examine them more closely. They were tantalizing. He hadn't been with a woman in a long time. It was even longer since a woman had stirred him the way this restrained female was stimulating him.

"Okay, Sheila." He smiled back. "Call me Adam. So how did you get into this management-consulting racket?"

Again he detected an impulse to snap at his uncomplimentary terminology. She crossed one knee primly over the other. Her nail polish matched her wine-colored pantsuit.

"I majored in management in college," she began, "and worked as what they used to call an 'efficiency expert' for a few years after that, until Bill and I had our son. I planned on putting my career on hold for only a couple of years, but then our daughter was born and I got caught up in being a full-time mom."

"You have two children?" He and Helen had had five and might have had more…but he pushed the memories aside.

"Just the two," she said with perhaps a note of regret. Because there weren't more? Or because they were a disappointment in some way? Because they'd interrupted her career?

"What does your husband...Bill...do?"

"He was a CPA."

"Retired now?"

"He died seven years ago."

So she was a widow. "I'm sorry," he said, and meant it. He knew what it was like to wake up alone in bed.

"By then the kids had their own lives and my time was my own." There was a hint of vulnerability, too, in the way she toyed with the shiny gold buttons on her burgundy jacket. "I went back to school, earned my master's and rejoined the business world."

"And now you work for Homestead Bank." He made it sound like a putdown, or at least a disappointment.

"They're one of my clients."

He stretched his arm across the back of the couch. "Do you enjoy the work?"

"I've been able to help people keep and improve their businesses, Adam. Contributing to their success has been important to me. I think I can help you, too, if you'll let me."

He was tempted to tell her she was too late, that the damage was irretrievably done. Would things have turned out differently had Helen lived? Undoubtedly. Or if Sheila Malone, widow, mother and management consultant, had appeared on the scene years earlier? It was an intriguing question...one that would never be answered.

"Tell me about your kids," he prompted.

"Derek's a geologist working for one of the big oil companies in the Middle East. He's still single. Melanie's married to an army captain. They're stationed in Germany.''

"Any grandchildren?"

"Two beautiful granddaughters." For the first time, Sheila's smile was completely spontaneous, revealing dimples in both her cheeks. And for a moment, Adam forgot to breathe.

"I don't imagine you get to see much of them if they live overseas."

"Not nearly enough," she admitted. "Your children live here on the ranch, don't they?"

"My eldest son, Michael, his wife and four kids have a house west of here. Kerry and her boy to the south. Gideon works at the university, so he has an apartment in town, as does his sister, Julie, who's finishing her master's in education."

He almost added that he'd had another son, a bright spark of life that had glowed and then died.

"You're very lucky to have them all so close."

He kept his face neutral as the picture of the family graveyard flashed before his eyes. A wife. A son. "Do you have any other family in Houston?"

"An aunt who lives not far from me. She's in her eighties now and still quite independent. We've developed a routine of breakfast and shopping every Saturday."

"No other family?"

"A brother in Ohio. We're originally from north of Wichita Falls, just across the Red River from Oklahoma. Still have a few cousins there, but we're not particularly close."

"Too bad."

Sheila toyed with the bracelet of silver rings on her wrist, making them jingle. She didn't like to be reminded that the tight-knit family life she'd dreamed of, with a husband, children and grandchildren underfoot, hadn't happened. Bill was gone. Kids and grandkids were scattered across the world. Instead of baking cookies, cutting out sewing patterns and reading bedtime stories, she spent her time worrying about profit and loss, efficiency and effectiveness. She envied his full rich life surrounded by the people he loved.

"I understand you don't want me here, Adam. I appreciate the situation you're in—"

"Do you?"

"Maybe better than you realize. I'm sorry my visit has to be under these circumstances."

Her self-assurance now irritated him. "If I hadn't agreed to your being here, you wouldn't be."

He gazed at the beautiful woman sitting across from him. Sending her away would mean she'd have to come back. Maybe it would be better to get this over with.

He closed his eyes and took a deep breath before opening them again. "I apologize for my rudeness, Sheila." He smiled at her wryly. "I don't usually shoot the messenger. If I haven't made you feel too unwelcome, I'd like you to stay and enjoy the barbecue with us."

"That's very generous of you, Adam, but I don't want to be a wet blanket."

"I don't think you will."

SHEILA WALKED into the breakfast nook the next morning dressed comfortably in jeans, a midnight-blue turtleneck and her old hiking boots. Simple gold studs had replaced the more ornate earrings of the previous day.

"I'd forgotten how quiet the country is," she said

as she slipped into the seat opposite her host. "And how dark."

She received the barest nod in response. The few brief moments of softening she'd sensed the evening before seemed to have melted with the light. Perhaps he wasn't a morning person, though she suspected his unwillingness to communicate had more to do with her than the time of day. She caught his sidelong glances. It annoyed her that his silent rebuke nudged her into apologizing again for being there.

"I'm sorry showing me around will take you away from your work," she commented as they left they house. "Especially with so much else going on."

"Making sure you see and understand what this ranch is all about is my work while you're here." He might as well have been talking to a ranch hand about the day's tasks. "Besides, I can still carry on business with my people at each location."

My people. It sounded paternalistic. Was it? Whole families had worked the Number One for generations. What should he have called them—his employees? Somehow that sounded worse.

She declined the hearty breakfast of sausage and eggs he'd eaten, choosing an English muffin and coffee, instead.

Twenty minutes later they were in his chopper.

"My grandfather first started using biplanes to check on roving herds back in the twenties," Adam explained as they skimmed over the rugged terrain.

Sheila adjusted her headset so her mouth was closer to the lip microphone. "Helicopters are a lot more complicated, aren't they?"

He scanned the land below and the sky around them

as he responded. "They're harder to fly and more expensive to maintain."

They rose smoothly above a ridgeline and maintained altitude as they approached the next one. "In forward flight they're about as fast as most small conventional aircraft, plus they have the advantage of being able to hover and land almost anywhere. Being able to pick up cargo with a sling—or people in an emergency—is also a big, big advantage."

Land contour was difficult to discern from overhead, but Sheila was able to distinguish low spots and creek beds by the darker patches of green and winding trails of brush. "It looks so dry," she commented.

"We're going into our fifth year of drouth."

They flew past herds of cattle, sheep and goats, circled barns, sheds and corrals, pump jacks and gas lines. Cowboys and other people on the ground waved when he flew low. He rocked the chopper in acknowledgment and gave a running commentary, spouting statistics, as they flew. She wasn't surprised that he seemed to know every tree, outcropping, fence line and windmill. This land was a part of him, rooted in his soul.

"We have slightly over fifteen thousand head of cattle," he expounded as they sped across yet another grazing area, "and nearly as many sheep and goats."

"Not much market in wool and mohair these days, is there?"

"You can thank the government for that," he replied acerbically. "They're the ones who removed tariff protection. As a result of improved trade with the Middle East and our own growing immigrant population from that region, though, there's an increased demand for lamb and goat meat. So we adjust."

Watching him check instruments and gauges reinforced her confidence in his competence. She'd always enjoyed aviation and had actually started taking flying lessons, until her husband's heart attack distracted her from that goal.

"It's a cyclic thing," Adam commented. "Sometimes all you can do is wait for the wheel to turn. The mistake, in my opinion, is to expect it to cover the same ground. The future is never like the past, no matter how fondly we may treasure it. Only the fact that we continue to make mistakes is constant."

Surprised at the note of pessimism, she glanced over at him.

"Do you know the definition of a cynic, Sheila?"

Having one's mind read was decidedly unsettling, so much so that she had to consciously put a smile in her voice. "I bet you're going to tell me."

A spark twinkled in the corner of his eye. "It's what an optimist calls a realist."

Chuckling, she considered the analysis a moment. "And you think I'm an optimist?"

His smile was friendly. "Why else would you be a management consultant?"

On that score she had to agree, but she couldn't escape the suspicion he was laughing at her.

"Where do you get the labor to deal with all this?" she asked. There were 512,000 acres to cover—eight hundred square miles of land.

"We have twenty-five families living on the ranch, each responsible for designated sectors. In my father's day we hired another hundred men or more from off the ranch. We still contract for seasonal labor, but our own people manage the normal day-to-day workload. With modern equipment and techniques, we're much more efficient than we used to be."

They returned to the headquarters for lunch, or as he called it, dinner. It was a large meal, the kind she usually indulged in only in the evening when she was dining with friends.

Adam resumed the aerial tour. By midafternoon, her long trip and restless night in a strange bed, as well as the sun streaming in the side window, had her sinking into a kitteny doze. She looked over at the man in the opposite seat.

"After the heavy lunch we had, how do you stay awake and so alert?" she asked around a yawn.

"Good genes, I guess," he replied smugly.

She regarded him with sleepy eyes. Hmm. How do you spell that, she wondered: genes or jeans?

She was jolted to attentiveness when Adam landed on a narrow pasture at the mouth of a shallow box canyon.

"This is where we'll have the barbecue tomorrow," he said through the headset as he shut down the engine.

Men stopped setting up long black cylindrical smokers and staking small mesquite logs in neat piles to watch them dart crablike out from beneath still-twirling rotor blades. Adam greeted each by name and introduced her. He was at home with these people, she realized, and they with him. That they deeply respected him was also greatly apparent.

"Pretty location," she remarked a few minutes later as they began a gradual climb toward a grove of massive cottonwood trees, a sure sign of water. He strolled over to a narrow stream, where a thin rivulet trickled between smooth gray stones.

"The water table's down," he muttered, as much to himself as to her. "This creek is fed by underground springs. It should be running hard this time of year."

Sunlight danced on the crystal brook and the lily pads in the pool farther downstream. "Did it go dry in the fifties?"

"No. But I don't remember it ever being this slow." Worry darkened his eyes. "If it dries up, we're in real trouble. These are the headwaters of the Coyote River."

"What will you do?"

He shrugged fatalistically. "Same thing other ranchers are doing. Sell livestock. We can bring in feed for them in bad times, but there's no way to truck in enough water to keep them alive, not for the numbers we have." They proceeded up the hill. "Consumers may enjoy the low prices for a while, since we'll be flooding—no pun intended—the market with cattle for slaughter, but a few years down the road, when herds have been nearly wiped out and the appetite for beef had been whetted—oops, no pun again—prices will skyrocket. It's that cycle again."

Then she saw the house on the side of the hill and her heart stopped. It didn't much resemble the one she'd been born in, where she'd spent her most formative years, but it had the same aura. For a magical moment she was coming home to a world that had felt safe and secure.

This building was abandoned and had been for a long time, based on the red-budded trumpet vines twisting and curling around the wooden porch columns. The single-story building was set high on a stone foundation. Its long gabled roof sagged in the middle. Old-fashioned shutters covered the windows.

She gazed with acute sadness at the derelict house. This had been someone's home. People had lived and loved here, had experienced hopes and dreams.

"This is the home place," Adam explained. "Built by my great-grandfather over a hundred years ago. It was a vast improvement over the simple log cabin he'd grown up in."

"Is the cabin still in existence?" Her voice was almost a whisper.

She'd seen the primitive dwelling her grandfather had been born and raised in, a cross between a log cabin and a sod hut. She could still recall the expression on his weathered face when he talked about his parents settling on what was then still inhospitable frontier. She wished she could have met those stalwart pioneers, who valued independence above comfort and the achievements of hard work over the softness of luxury. She remembered, too, the sadness in her father's eyes years later when they went back to the same spot after the flood to find nothing left. It had been an omen, though she hadn't realized it at the time.

Adam shook his head. "Washed away in the flood of 1882. That's when he built this house. The family lived in it until the fire in '51. My father designed the new house, the one we live in now."

"This is lovely." She drew closer.

It wasn't nearly as imposing as the current ranch house, but where the newer one had mass and an almost pretentious sophistication, this one had charm.

"Is it safe to go inside?"

He slanted her a forlorn smile. "'Fraid not. The roof and floor on the right are rotten. The kitchen and dining room were on the left. That's where we had the fire."

They walked around the back. There was another porch, but this one had been partially enclosed—probably, based on the size of the windows, to create a bathroom when they installed indoor plumbing.

"I've considered restoring it," Adam remarked, "but it's a little too far from the ranch headquarters to use for guests. I could rent it out to hunters, I suppose, but that would be for only a few weeks a year. Doesn't seem worth the expense. Now—" he looked at her unhappily "—the decision isn't mine to make."

"You don't kill messengers, remember?"

He offered her an apologetic smile.

She studied the crumbling building. "It must have been beautiful when it was in use," she mused, unwilling to face the pain she knew she would see in his eyes. "The porch, shaded by the huge old trees…I bet it was cool in the summer."

Without conscious thought, he took her hand and led her around the ruin. For a moment, they strolled like lovers in a private park, before he released her.

"I can picture young children scampering around the corners," she continued dreamily, "playing hide-and-seek in dappled summer sunlight. Their parents and grandparents sitting in rockers in the evening after all the chores are done, grabbing those few precious minutes of relaxation and calm before bedtime and the dawn of a new workday."

He smiled at her and her heart melted in spite of herself. Had he lived that life here as a kid?

"You called it the home place," she reminded him. "Was this part of the original acreage?"

He nodded. "My great-great-grandfather purchased sixty thousand acres from the Spanish government in 1820. Six years later, Mexico won independence from Spain. In 1836, when Texas fought its own war of independence from Mexico, he was killed in the Battle of San Jacinto."

She knew the history by heart, but she relished hearing him tell it. There was pride in his voice, respect for the past.

"His son," Adam continued, "my great-grandfather, took over the ranch, added more land and later served in the legislature of the old republic. He was killed in the Civil War, or as Granddaddy would say, the War Between the States. Till the day he died he insisted that since Texas was a sovereign nation when it joined the Union, it damn well had the right to secede."

Sheila laughed. "I'm a native Texan, Adam. You don't have to convince me. My grandpa referred to it as the War of Northern Aggression. He left me his stash of Confederate money."

He smiled distantly, then grew somber. "Every generation of Firsts has increased the size of the ranch, my father included. The drouth of the fifties damn near destroyed us. Dad had two choices. Sell out at depressed prices or borrow on the land and hope he could pay back the loan. He chose the latter."

Adam stooped to pick up a stick, then tested its strength between his strong hands.

"Dad refinanced the loan several times, trying to forestall the inevitable. We hadn't yet found oil. He'd drilled a few wells, but they all came up dry. In the end he had no choice but to give the bank a forty-five percent interest in the ranch."

He threw the stick with a sidearm motion that had the force of anger, a man swinging out at fate. "Five years later we did hit oil and gas, but it was too late. The bank refused to renegotiate. The drouth had broken. We were operating in the black again, and they had no reason to give up a profitable investment." Bitterness crept into his voice. "Since then, they've collected the original debt, plus interest, many times over.''

A sharp gust of wind came up and swirled around them, reminding them there was still a remnant of winter's chill in the February air.

"We'd best be getting back," he said. "It'll be dark soon."

Even in her light wool sweater Sheila shivered as they started making their way, side by side, to the helicopter. Glancing over, Adam saw her cradle her arms below her breasts, hugging herself against the biting blast.

"You're cold," he said with concern. Moving closer, he spread his arm around her shoulders and drew her into his side. The snug warmth of his embrace, meant merely to harbor her against the north wind, stirred a strange remembrance in her, the sensation of being protected, even treasured. It had been so long since a man had held her, she reminded herself, that the desire curling through her was simply an overreaction. This man meant nothing to her, and she meant nothing to him. Yet she had to resist the temptation to wrap her arm around his waist and rest her head against his chest.

He escorted her to the passenger side of the aircraft. Was it her imagination that he hesitated before letting her go? That he pulled her tighter for a fleeting moment before releasing her? That the hand holding hers lingered longer than necessary as he helped her up into the seat? That just before he closed the door she saw something in his glance to match the sudden, urgent ache inside her?

CHAPTER TWO

SHEILA SPENT the evening in her room on the telephone. Her first call was to her aunt in Houston.

"I'm in Coyote Springs this week, Mildred."

"Coyote Springs?"

"In West Texas. I'm at the Number One Ranch. I told you about it."

"Of course. I must have been having a senior moment. I remember now. That real big ranch."

"I expected to be back Friday evening, but something's come up and I won't be getting home until late Saturday afternoon or evening."

"What you're telling me," Mildred said lightheartedly, "is we won't be going for our usual Saturday breakfast and shopping."

"I'm sorry. I know you were looking forward to the sale at Neiman Marcus."

Following an automobile accident ten years ago in which she had been cited as at fault, Mildred had given up her car, claiming she had no right to be driving in the heavy traffic of Houston. Mildred was mentally alert but physically rather frail. Sheila played chauffeur a good deal of the time.

"Oh, fiddlesticks," the octogenarian said. "There'll be other sales. Besides, I rarely buy anything."

Neither did Sheila. Mildred's retirement plan had taken a severe beating in the twenty-five years since she'd retired from a large insurance company. She wasn't destitute, but she wasn't nearly as flush as she once had been.

"No, but window-shopping is fun." Sheila wasn't in the position to make many purchases beyond the necessities these days, either.

"How is your meeting going with...Mr. First? Wasn't that his name?"

"Yes. Adam First. I'll tell you about it when I get back. How about brunch on Sunday and then shopping?"

"I'd love to, but it's the second Sunday of the month," Mildred reminded her. "I have brunch with the ladies' circle after church, and then we play canasta all afternoon."

Many of her aunt's friends were passing on, but Mildred maintained a routine that kept her active and socially in touch. "How about I come over in the evening, then? I'll pick up mu shu shrimp at the Mandarin Star on the way."

"Oh, dear. Helga and Jim invited me to their house for dinner."

Sheila laughed. "This doesn't seem to be our weekend, does it?" She was disappointed. She enjoyed the time she spent with her father's sister and had come to value the woman's opinions and counsel, as well. "Can I make an appointment to call you during the week?"

Mildred's chuckle was filled with warmth and solicitude. "Let me check with my social secretary. Ah, yes, I think I have a few minutes available. Anytime Monday through Friday from 7:00 a.m. to about 11:00 p.m., if that would be convenient."

Sheila hung up a minute later. Her second call was to her business associate, Jonas Elling.

Her current fiscal strain wouldn't be so bad, she mused, if she had only herself to worry about. After all, her kids were grown and making their own way in the world. She did employ a small office staff, but most of them were young enough to find other opportunities if she closed her doors and put them out of work. Her real concern was Jonas.

An old family friend, he'd also been her mentor at Crowder and Breckenridge Consultants, Inc., her former employer. Jonas had been the one person she could count on for straight talk and sound advice. He and his wife, Catherine, had also been her emotional anchor following Bill's death, the friends who'd become a second family after her two children returned to their own lives overseas.

Last year, C&B had downsized, and fifty-nine-year-old Jonas found himself redundant six months before he was eligible for retirement. He'd come to Sheila and explained his dilemma.

The settlement package the international corporation offered him was paltry and would be quickly eaten up by his wife's medical bills. Catherine had cancer. The only hope for her recovery was for medical insurance to pick up the astronomical expenses for her treatment. With a preexisting condition, however, there was no way he could obtain coverage on his own—even if he'd been able to afford the premiums. Jonas pointed out that Sheila's insurance carrier was the same as C&B's. If she put him on her payroll, she could transfer him to her group policy without a break in coverage. Sheila had no qualms about hiring him. Jonas was good at what he did and could significantly bolster her business.

Unbelievably, six weeks later, C&B expanded into

Sheila's chosen field and became her chief and most formidable competitor. If Malone Economic Consulting and Services went out of business now, not only would she be bankrupt and her people unemployed, but Catherine Elling would probably die an early death. She couldn't let that happen.

Jonas answered the phone on the third ring.

"How's Catherine?"

"She's sleeping," he said softly. Sheila could hear the click of a door closing. "She had a treatment today, and that always knocks her out." The advanced chemotherapy Catherine was receiving had left her hairless and severely sapped of energy. "The doctors seem very pleased, though. They're saying now they think she has a better-than-even chance."

"That's wonderful news." Sheila wondered if it was true. In her experience, doctors sometimes sugarcoated the severity of conditions. Patients just as frequently heard only what they wanted to hear or avoided asking the questions that would give them bad news. "Hang in there, Jonas, and when Catherine wakes up, give her my love."

"I will. Sheila, I don't know what we would have done without your help..."

"As Aunt Mildred would say, fiddlesticks. You and Catherine were there for me when Bill died. I'll never forget that."

After a short pause, Jonas cleared his throat. "You didn't call to rehash old conversations. How are things in West Texas?"

"Dry."

"Does that refer to the man or the weather?"

Sheila couldn't keep from chuckling. "I hadn't thought of him that way, but now that you mention it, it's an apt description. As you can imagine, he's not overjoyed at my being here, but he's at least trying to be civil. I've run into a little snag, though.'' She told him about the upcoming picnic. ''Since I'll be losing Wednesday, I plan to hang around until Saturday and leave around noon.''

After another brief hesitation, Jonas said, ''We received an answer from Cathgart today.''

Sheila had a sinking feeling. ''They turned down our proposal, didn't they?''

''I'm afraid so. I made a couple of phone calls. C&B underbid us—again.''

Damn. Sheila had been hoping to get the electrical company's management-services business. A few long-term contracts would help stabilize her financial position.

''What are the prospects of a continuing relationship with the Number One?'' Jonas asked.

''I don't know yet, but if the bank keeps us on, I'll probably have to set up an office here.'' Sheila wondered what Adam's reaction would be to that. ''Cummings is good at dangling the carrot, but I get the distinct impression she's on a power trip and that the deal is contingent on my telling her what she wants to hear. Maybe I'm wrong...''

''I don't think you are. I've checked with some of my sources. She's known in banking circles as the 'battle-ax.' So beware.''

''THE BARBECUE DOESN'T officially start until noon,'' Adam said the next morning at breakfast, ''and I have chores to attend to in town before then. You indicated yesterday you wanted access to some of our records.

I've set them out in the office. You can review them while I'm out.''

''That'll be fine, Adam. Thank you.''

''My son Michael will pick you up on his way to the home place. It'll give you a chance to see some of the ranch from ground level for a change.''

She continued to feel uncomfortable about imposing herself on the ranch festivities, especially since her presence appeared to be diametrically opposed to the family's interests. But she'd apologized once; she wasn't going to do it again.

''If you're still having qualms about imposing,'' he commented as he chopped off a piece of sausage with the side of his fork, ''forget them.''

Adam First seemed to have an uncanny ability to read her mind; or was her wariness that transparent?

''You came here to find out how this ranch runs,'' he went on. ''It runs on people, Sheila. Come meet them…unless you're afraid to,'' he added with a touch of humor.

''Afraid?''

''Why else would you want to avoid a party?'' He took a perverse satisfaction in watching her squirm.

''I'm here to evaluate—''

''Relax, Sheila,'' he cut her off. Her reluctance to attend the celebration was probably as much to spare him embarrassment as it was to avoid her own. ''You're my guest. We're simple country folks out to have a fun day. Join us and enjoy it.''

Simple country folks. Sheila had no illusions that people were simple. Adam First certainly wasn't. He was complex, intelligent and aloof—except when he'd put his arm around her to shield her against the cold wind. Then he was unexpectedly warm and disconcertingly intriguing.

Michael showed up promptly at 11:30. Adam's eldest son was as tall as his father but more sturdily built. He wasn't by himself. Sitting in the back seats of the white Suburban were four children and an auburn-haired woman with hazel eyes and a ready, friendly smile.

"I'm Clare, Michael's wife," she said after Sheila climbed into the front seat.

Her husband closed her door and circled the hood of the vehicle.

"This is our son, Davy—" Clare continued.

"Mom," the boy objected in an annoyed singsong.

"Excuse me," Clare said with a mother-to-mother sidelong glance at Sheila. "This is Dave."

Michael resumed his place behind the wheel and they were under way. Introductions continued. Dave was ten and his three sisters, Sarah Jean—they called her Sally—Kristen and Beth Ann were eight, six and four, respectively.

Sheila found the air of normalcy unnerving. They were treating her like a distant cousin or a maiden aunt.

"No school today?" she asked as Michael turned to the right at the base of the mesa.

"They get to skip a day for Grampa's birthday," Clare explained. "All the other ranch kids take off, too."

The scene at the home place had undergone a massive change since Sheila had been there with Adam the day before. Now it resembled a fairgrounds. Two large tents had been set up, one with long tables for food, the other with a bandstand and dance floor. A country-and-western group was already playing a bluegrass tune. Pearl-gray ribbons of smoke trailed from steel barbecue pits, filling the air with the sweet, rich aroma of slow-burning mesquite.

"There must be five hundred people here!" Sheila exclaimed.

"About that," Clare agreed. "We supply all the meat. The rest is potluck. If you like home cooking, you're in paradise."

A young man and woman hurried to the Suburban as soon as Michael stopped on the periphery of the chaotic parking area. Most of the vehicles were pick-ups, though there were a few sedans and an occasional luxury car. While Clare and the kids unloaded boxes and baskets from the back seat, Michael introduced his sister Julie. Blond, blue-eyed, petite and full of energy, she thrust her hand out. "Welcome to the Number One."

Michael introduced the young man. "Sheila Malone, this is my brother Gideon."

He was lighter in build than his elder brother, blond rather than dark-haired, but with the same air of male confidence. The rugged good looks Michael had inherited from his father had been transformed to smooth-cheeked, almost beautiful handsomeness.

"He's not very smart," Michael taunted, "but we keep him around because he's so cute."

Gideon's pale-blue eyes narrowed as he shot his brother a withering glance and a sharp elbow to the ribs. Michael backed off in time to avoid contact, his face glowing with satisfaction.

"Don't mind him," Gideon told Sheila as he shook her hand. "He's just jealous 'cause my pickup's newer than his." He put his arm around a raven-haired woman with deep-brown eyes who had quietly followed at a reserved pace. "This is Lupe Amorado. She works with me in the kinesiology department at the college."

Lupe greeted Sheila and introduced her two children, a boy around Davy's age and a girl a couple of years younger. Both Miguelito and his sister, Teresita, had the strikingly dark good looks that spoke as much of American Indian as Spanish blood.

A minute later, the kids went yelling off to join their friends.

"Dad told us last week you were coming," Gideon said as he grabbed a cooler from the back of the Suburban and thrust it at his brother.

"He's probably giving you a hard time," Julie added as she struggled with a couple of large quilts. Sheila relieved her of one; Lupe grabbed the other. Julie snagged a pair of pillows.

"Don't worry, he'll mellow," Gideon assured her. "His bark is usually worse than his bite."

Sheila raised an eyebrow and gave him a nervous smile. "Usually?"

"Well, sometimes."

Sheila knew of Adam's reputation for having a temper. She also realized the few snide comments and the occasional note of sarcasm she'd been subjected to hardly qualified as a bark, much less a bite.

"That's encouraging," she commented wryly.

Gideon dumped a case of soda on top of Michael's cooler. "There you go, bro. Now, don't drop it."

Turning her head, Clare announced, "Here's Brian."

Sheila spun around and watched a new, bright-red Mustang convertible roll to an abrupt stop and a teenage boy jump over its door. He wore a black baseball cap backward, baggy knee-length shorts, an oversized tank top and expensive running shoes, open laces trailing dangerously. She gauged him at about sixteen. He wasn't as tall as his uncles and had the rangy build of a still-growing teenager.

"Hey, Brian. You came after all." Gideon stepped forward and put his arm around his nephew's thin shoulders. "I was going to give you a lift, but when I phoned your mom she said you'd decided not to show. Come meet our visitor."

The young man looked about as unenthusiastic as a patient getting a shot in an undignified place.

"Mrs. Malone," Gideon said, pretending he wasn't dragging the kid along, "my nephew Brian Durgan."

She recognized the last name. This was the son of Adam's daughter Kerry, the one who'd sold her share of the ranch. Sheila wondered if the boy's mother would show up.

"Hello, Brian." She offered her hand from under the colorful quilt she was holding.

For a moment she thought he was going to refuse to take it, but a word in his ear from his smiling uncle seemed to convince him to play along. He accepted her hand.

"I'm here for just a few days," she said, trying to sound upbeat. "I hope you don't mind my crashing your party."

His hazel eyes were wary. "Whatever."

"Come on, let's get you something to drink." Gideon put a vise grip on Brian's neck and steered him toward the soft-drink stand.

After helping Adam's family get settled and meeting a dozen people whose names she had no hope of remembering, Sheila slipped away to wander around the huge campground. She couldn't remember the last time she'd been to a big-ranch barbecue. Growing up, she'd loved such occasions: the Fourth of July, graduations and anniversaries, weddings, even funerals. She'd expected to spend a lifetime surrounded with this sense of community, this atmosphere of wholesome pride. She'd taken for granted that she'd be one of these hardworking people, struggling with Mother Nature on a daily basis, respecting her, fearing her, yet loving her deeply.

Sheila also knew that these simple people, as Adam called them, could be full of surprises. Behind the West Texas twang and scuffed boots, there might be a cowboy who spouted Shakespeare by heart. A wrangler who had a degree in linguistics and spoke half a dozen languages fluently. A blacksmith who'd known the last six governors on a first-name basis. A campfire cook who had attended the Cordon Bleu in France. Looking around, Sheila wondered who among the people gathered here, most of them in blue jeans and cowboy shirts, might be millionaires and philanthropists. Undoubtedly, there were a few.

There were also the traditional events: horseshoes and washers for the older folks. Softball for those a little younger. Flag football for the twenties crowd and soccer for the teenagers, as well as a three-legged race for the preteens. And drought or not, a trench had been dug and flooded to make a mud bath for the losers of the tug-of-war. Later, too, she was told, there would be a jalapeño-eating contest.

Adam was standing under a live oak tree, cowboy hat in place, a beer can in one hand, the other fingertipped into the pocket of neatly creased jeans. He fit in perfectly with the men gathered around him, yet something about him was unique and made him special.

Maybe they showed him deference because it was his party, but she didn't think so. Adam First would stand out in any crowd.

He interrupted their laughter and beckoned her to join them, then introduced her as a guest from Houston. The incomplete accuracy, rather than the whole truth, was certainly easier for both of them to finesse in the company of the ranch hands, state representative and judge who tipped their Stetsons to her. But the implication, the pretense that she was a welcome friend, made her feel like an imposter, a fraud. She wasn't one of them, an ally and supporter in a difficult time; she was an agent of the forces that wielded power over their host.

"I ran across a tourist the other day," Adam recounted. "He wanted to know if we get much rain here."

Everyone snickered.

"'You familiar with the Bible?' I asked him. He said he was. 'Then you remember the story about it raining forty days and forty nights.' He nodded. 'Well,' I said, 'we got a trace.'"

After the laughter died down, Sheila inquired how long they thought the drought would last.

"Till the next rain," seemed to be the consensus.

She matched their banter for another minute or two, all the time glancing at Adam, trying to gauge his attitude, his reactions. He slouched on one hip, took a perfunctory sip of beer and watched her, his eyes smiling, but he gave very little away. Finally, she excused herself and left them.

Back at the family campsite she found Clare and Michael soaking up soda that had spilled on a picnic table. Sheila picked up some paper napkins and pitched in.

"What do you do here on the ranch, Michael?" she asked to make small talk.

"I keep the books." He swiped at the sticky liquid dripping off the edge of the table. "I'm also a stock contractor. I furnish bulls and buckin' horses for rodeos." An engine's distant whine had him straightening abruptly. He spun around, stiffened and cursed.

A shiny new and very expensive foreign sports car was approaching the campgrounds, kicking up a trail of dust behind it. The yellow sportster slid to a halt. When the dust cleared, a woman clad in tight-clinging jeans and snug tank top got out and walked toward the center of activity. People stopped what they were doing to gape at her. Those in her path backed off as if she were a princess—or a plague.

"I told her to stay away," Michael muttered through clenched teeth. "Damn her to hell."

It didn't take much for Sheila to figure out Kerry Durgan had arrived.

ADAM WAS TALKING to Judge Mayhew, exchanging quips and good-natured razzing about their high-school exploits and capers, when he realized something had changed. Suddenly the activity around him subsided and the assembly grew apprehensively silent. He spun around. Kerry was approaching him, her long raven hair tangled by the breeze. In her right hand she carried a box wrapped in silver paper, with an elaborate gold bow.

People stared at her, some with their mouths hanging open. They obviously hadn't expected to see her here and were shocked that she'd dared to show up. Though he had never said anything to his friends, somehow word had gotten out that she hadn't told him of her plans to sell her share of the ranch, hadn't even had the decency to tell him after the fact. She'd left that painful task to her brother. Adam could still visualize the contrition in Michael's eyes when he broke the news—as if he were somehow responsible for not keeping his sister reined in.

Adam's first reaction had been disbelief, followed by panic and denial. There had to be some mistake. Then the letter had come from Homestead Bank and Trust notifying him the First family was no longer the majority shareholder, that they had acquired controlling interest in the legendary Number One.

Only then had come the blinding rage, abject depression and finally, inevitably, searing pain. He'd considered telephoning his daughter, stopping by her house, ranting at her, telling her what an ungrateful, selfish person she'd become, that her mother would be ashamed of her, that he certainly was.

He'd done none of those things. Instead, he'd quietly waited with an aching heart for her to come to him. Waited in vain. There'd been no call, no explanation, no apology.

Apparently, she'd chosen this public occasion to face him.

How beautiful she was, he thought as she made her way toward him. Tall and willowy, with Helen's fine features and pale-blue eyes, his black hair. Did she sing anymore? He couldn't remember the last time he'd heard her sing. She used to have the most delightful voice, clear and sweet, with that tearful hitch in it reminiscent of Patsy Cline and Connie Francis. In high school she'd seriously considered becoming a country-

and-western singer—until she'd become pregnant by that son of a b—

Adam pushed the memory aside. Now was not the time to relive old mistakes, hers or his.

She walked through the crowd, her head held high, waving to people, calling out greetings to a few of them by name. She received mumbled responses or blank stares in return. She laughed, and the tree-dappled sunlight glinted off her designer dark glasses.

"Happy Birthday, Daddy." Her voice was a little too loud, too theatrical, an entertainer inviting the entire assembly to witness her performance. Straight-armed, she thrust the gift out to him. "I brought you a present."

Reluctantly, he reached out and accepted the box. "Thank you, sweetheart." He wanted to smile, but his face muscles refused to cooperate.

"Aren't you going to open it?" she asked, her tone unctuous, almost childlike. Uneasiness and a sense of foreboding coiled around him.

Michael appeared at her side. "I told you to stay away."

"Buzz off, big brother," Kerry snarled, giving him a dismissive glance before turning back to her father.

Adam gazed at the cube-shaped box he was holding, then carefully searched the wrapping for a seal to break.

"Don't worry about the paper," she snapped. "I can buy you all the fancy paper you want now. Just open the damn thing." She snatched it out of his hands, viciously tore off the heavy paper and thrust the white cardboard box back at him.

Michael seethed. "Kerry, you're drunk."

She leered at him, mean eyed. "I told you to get lost."

"You're coming with me." He clasped her above the elbow.

"Keep your hands off me." She twisted out of his grip and turned back to her father. "Why don't you open your present, Daddy?"

Adam blinked slowly, noticed Sheila on the outskirts of the crowd gathered around him, and realized he felt nothing, that his mind and body had gone numb. Mechanically he opened the box, and found a large velvet-covered jeweler's case within. He pried the lid up. A gold Rolex watch winked up at him. The face was studded with tiny diamonds for numbers.

He concentrated on his daughter and for a moment saw the little girl who'd hand-printed a birthday card with crayons on construction paper and had beamed at him proudly, eager for his approval. But she wasn't a little girl anymore, and he couldn't throw his arms around her and hug her to his chest. The sweet child smell had been replaced in the grown woman with the miasma of expensive perfume and the reek of stale whiskey.

"Now you'll always know what time it is, Daddy." She tore off her glasses and glared at him with belligerent, slightly bloodshot eyes. "You'll always know it's too late."

Michael clamped her shoulder heavily. She wriggled, trying to escape it, but when she couldn't, ignored it and went on in a taunting, lilting tone.

"Too late because I'll be gone and so will Brian. You won't be able to preach or lord it over us much longer." She giggled. "You won't be able to lord it over anyone or anything, because you won't be in charge anymore. I took care of that, Daddy."

Her brother spun her around at the same time he raised his other hand. Several people sucked in their breaths in anticipation of his slapping her hard across the face.

Adam's arm shot up. "Let her be."

A self-satisfied smirk hardened her mouth. Once again Kerry faced her father. "Aren't you going to thank me for your present, Daddy?"

Everyone waited. Michael muttered something in Kerry's ear, but her attention was riveted on her father.

"Oh, my baby," Adam said in a soft voice that sounded strangled. "I'll do one better than that. I'll forgive you."

Kerry's mouth clamped tight as she watched him place the expensive timepiece on the picnic table behind him, turn and walk away.

CHAPTER THREE

WITH HEADS BOWED in embarrassment, people parted to let Adam pass. Michael once more gripped his sister above the elbow. This time when she struggled to get loose, he tightened his hold painfully.

"You're hurting me," she complained as she clawed at his clenched fingers.

"Not nearly as much as I'd like to," he hissed into her ear.

Brian shot out of the crowd. "Leave my mother alone," he demanded, and tried to pry his uncle's fingers away from Kerry's arm.

The boy was no match for the man, however, and Michael used his free hand to shove the teenager aside. Brian stumbled back, caught himself, adjusted his stance and with lowered head charged forward, fists upraised in attack. His other uncle grabbed him from behind and lifted him bodily off the ground.

"Take her home," Gideon said to Michael as he encircled his kicking and cursing nephew in a bear hug. "Calm down, Brian," he growled into the boy's ear. "No one's going to hurt your mom, but she doesn't belong here, and she's too drunk to drive."

"Leave her alone," the child cried helplessly as Michael hauled his profanity-sputtering mother away.

Clare followed her husband and helped him force Kerry into the rear seat of the Suburban. Everyone stared as Clare grabbed her sister-in-law by the hair, yanked her head back sharply and whispered something in her ear. Kerry stopped resisting, though her face remained a mask of menacing fury.

SHEILA OBSERVED the episode with alarm. Kerry Durgan was a hellcat; there was no question about it. Her concern, however, wasn't for the daughter but the father. She watched with a breaking heart as Adam moved off, face blank, away from family and friends.

The crowd that had quietly gathered dispersed now, shaking their heads and talking in muffled tones.

"Shouldn't someone go after your father?" Sheila asked Julie.

The younger daughter stared at the Rolex nestled in the plush velvet case, but didn't touch it. "Dad'll be all right," she muttered, and turned away. "He needs time alone right now is all."

Sheila wasn't so sure. She'd been close enough to see the agony in the man's eyes as he faced his drunken, vicious child. Not certain she was doing the right thing, she followed him.

Adam mounted the hill leading to the old house.

"I know this is none of my business," Sheila said softly as she came up behind him, "but will you tell me what's going on? Why is your daughter so... angry with you?"

He snorted. "It's no secret." He removed his hat and wiped the sweatband with the handkerchief he'd pulled from his back pocket. "You can get an earful from just about anyone here, so you might as well hear my side of it first."

Sheila trailed beside him toward the derelict building.

"Kerry was always a little wild. Her mother was able to keep her in check, but I couldn't. I didn't really have any trouble with the boys, but the girls...I lacked Helen's subtlety and...I almost want to say deviousness." He picked up a stone and rubbed it for no apparent reason other than to keep his hands busy.

"I know what you mean," Sheila said sympathetically. "With Derek a blunt decree and an equally straightforward explanation usually kept him on the straight and narrow. If he screwed up, he almost always took the consequences without complaining. Melanie was another matter altogether."

"In what way?"

Sheila flashed a grin. "Logic didn't always work with her, and a onetime explanation was never enough. She'd explore every possible angle and nuance of a situation, then revisit it over and over." She shook her head in amusement. "Used to drive me crazy, but there wasn't any alternative if I wanted to get my thoughts across."

Adam nodded. "I see your point. Maybe patience is a better word, then. Helen had a way of bringing people around. I've always been, well, blunt—the proverbial bull in the china shop. There's right and wrong. I don't have a whole lot of tolerance for things in between, for rationalizations and little white lies."

Maybe he lacked subtlety with his daughters, but he was a caring man. Sheila had listened to him talk with his ranch hands, sometimes in English, sometimes in Tex-Mex Spanish, about their spouses and children, about aging parents, recent illnesses in the family and the kids who'd gone off to college, the military or other professions.

"Teenagers can be pretty good at playing mind games," she consoled him.

He grunted. "Kerry was a sophomore in high school when her mother died. The following year—she was sixteen—Craig Robeson invited her to the junior-senior prom. I liked Craig. He was a bit of a nerd, I guess, but he was well mannered and a nice enough kid." They skirted a massive cottonwood tree. "I had no qualms about Kerry attending the prom with him."

Adam's features hardened with what Sheila assumed was the memory of an old anger. "I didn't know Rafael Durgan would show up." He clenched his hands into fists. "You've seen the type. Skintight jeans, leather jacket, long black hair, dark eyes—"

Sheila smiled. "Every adolescent girl's fantasy of dark and dangerous."

The lure of the bad boy, the forbidden. Her own daughter had gone through a similar stage. Fortunately, the only such characters Melanie met were in magazines, so she'd never had the opportunity to act out that particular fantasy.

"He was that, all right," Adam agreed. "Durgan wasn't exactly welcome in polite society. His father was in prison for the second or third time, and his mother…well, let's just say she had a fondness for male companionship. Rafe himself had had a tangle or two with the law, underage drinking, smoking pot, an occasional fistfight, that sort of thing."

They resumed their climb in the shade of old trees toward the burned-out house.

"At the dance, Kerry ditched Craig and left with Durgan. Three months later she told me she was pregnant." Sadness and disappointment softened Adam's face. "Durgan, of course, was the father. As you can imagine, I was furious. I swore no grandson of mine was going to be a bastard and threatened to have Durgan arrested for statutory rape if he didn't marry her.''

"Not an auspicious beginning for marital bliss," Sheila noted.

"Bliss it certainly wasn't. Kerry had been a good student up until then, but she dropped out of school in her senior year a couple of months before the baby was born."

A woodpecker hammered out its staccato tattoo somewhere off among the budding foliage to the left. "I didn't like Durgan. I don't deny it. But I swear, Sheila, I tried my damnedest to get along with him. Built them a house here on the ranch, offered them both special tutoring so they could finish high school and go on to college. I wasn't completely surprised when he turned me down, but I was disappointed when Kerry did. Her explanation was that her place was home with her husband and kid. I couldn't argue with that, but I also figured Durgan knew he couldn't make it in school and talked her out of going back because he was afraid she'd show him up. Anyway, I gave him a job working with the ranch hands, stringing fence and anything else that needed doing."

Adam settled on the ground under an oak tree and with an outstretched hand helped her sit down beside him.

"But the marriage didn't work." Sheila brought her knees up and rested her arms on them.

"It lasted less than three years." He leaned back on his elbows, but the tension in his posture indicated he was far from relaxed. "Kerry, Rafe and the baby didn't come to the headquarters for dinner one Sunday, so I stopped by their place the following afternoon to see how they were. I figured Brian had a cold. What I found..." He sat up and took a deep breath. "She had a black eye and a cut lip."

Sheila closed her eyes, but couldn't shut out the image.

"I went ballistic," Adam said in a hard voice. "I brought her and Brian over to the headquarters, then tore out after her husband. Michael had just graduated from college that spring and was working on the ranch for the summer before going on to graduate school. Kerry managed to get hold of him somehow, and thank God for that. If Michael hadn't pulled me off that piece of scum when he did, I might have killed Durgan."

Personal violence and vigilante justice weren't methods Sheila approved of, but she wondered how she would have reacted in Adam's place.

"Kerry got a divorce," Adam said, "and Durgan left town. A couple of years later we heard he was killed in a high-speed car chase with the police."

"Sounds like your daughter was well rid of the guy," Sheila commented.

The crowd down below had resumed its festivities. She could hear the singer in the band doing his rendition of a George Strait tune.

"You'd expect so, wouldn't you? To hear Kerry talk about it..." He paused. "I know this sounds crazy, but I think she actually loved the miserable bastard."

"In her own way, maybe she did, but she was still better off without him."

Adam shook his head. "I don't understand it. It doesn't make any sense to me. All I know is that she's never forgiven me. That's what this is all about, you know. Payback time."

"Why now? What's happened recently to make her do this?"

He lowered his head contemplatively. "Six months ago my son Stuart died."

A chill rippled down Sheila's spine. She reached over and placed her hand over his. "I'm sorry, Adam. I had no idea."

"He was the youngest, just twenty-one."

No parent should ever have to bury a child, she thought, and ached for the man sitting beside her. "How did it happen?"

"He'd graduated from college with a degree in electrical engineering and was on his way to Dallas to take a job with a computer company there. It was late at night, rainy. A truck coming from the other direction crossed the line and hit him. He was killed instantly."

Sheila brought her hand up to his shoulder. "Adam, I'm so sorry."

He didn't pull away from her touch. If anything, he leaned into it. "I owned thirty percent of the ranch. Each of my kids had five percent. The bank held the other forty-five. After Stu was killed, his five percent was equally divided among his four brothers and sisters and me."

"So they each had six percent." It didn't take a mathematical genius to figure out what happened next. "And Kerry sold her share to the bank."

He nodded.

"Combined with their forty-five percent," Sheila concluded, "it gave them—"

"Controlling interest."

That explained a lot. Nedra Cummings, the bank's vice president, had intimated this wasn't a friendly takeover, but Sheila had assumed Kerry's decision had been strictly business, not a personal vendetta.

They sat in silence for several minutes. Finally, Adam adjusted his Stetson and climbed to his feet. He helped Sheila up and led her back to the valley, where friends and neighbors waited. No one would mention the incident that had just transpired; they would discreetly avoid any mention of Kerry. Instead, with broad smiles and cheery phrases, they'd focus on how much fun it was for everyone to get together, how great the food tasted and how much they needed rain.

Before he fully realized what he was doing, he reached out for Sheila's hand. Surprisingly, he felt comfortable with the impulse, maybe because she'd listened to him patiently without passing judgment. At least not in so many words. These last years had been lonely in a way he was only now beginning to comprehend. The Old Testament was right. It is not good for man to be alone.

He'd been thinking a lot about Sheila Malone since she showed up the evening before last. He'd had a few lady friends over the years since Helen died, a few dates. None of them had ever gotten to the serious stage or occupied his thoughts the way this woman did.

Was he mistaken about her, too, or did he see in her eyes something akin to what he was feeling? She was even more alone than he. Her husband of twenty-something years was dead and the children they'd brought up had moved away. At least he still had four of his kids close by and five grandkids to pamper.

Maybe if circumstances were different, Sheila Malone, he mused to himself, *maybe then we really could help each other.*

"I GAVE YOU a quick overview the other day," Adam said Thursday morning. "Now let's look at details. You up to horseback riding?"

She gaped wide-eyed at him over the rim of her coffee cup. "Horseback riding?"

"You do know how to ride, don't you?"

"Of course I know how to ride. It's just that it's…well, it's been a while."

"Don't worry," he said with a crocodile smile. "It's like riding a bicycle. You never forget."

She lowered her cup to the saucer. "I'm afraid it's not my memory that'll be taking the beating."

He chuckled. Picturing her hips swaying in the saddle wasn't at all hard on the imagination. "We'll mosey along nice and easy."

Twenty minutes later they were mounted, she on a quarter-horse paint, he on a larger dappled gray Thoroughbred. His breeding stables were a couple of miles away. True to his word he set a leisurely gait, and she found herself relaxing in a way only horseback riding could generate, a pace that harked back to a time when life was slow enough to allow contemplation.

When she was a girl, she'd ridden out like this with her father. Across open land under a clear sky. They'd check herds, inspect fence lines, gates, cattle guards. Sometimes they'd talk, but mostly they'd go about their tasks with a minimum of words. Being in each other's company was enough.

Now, as she and Adam plopped across a muddy stream, she stole a glance at him, tall and straight in the saddle. He was very much like her father—proud, determined, hardworking. Her dad would have liked Adam. They would have shared the kind of friendship two men can have because they understand and respect each other's pride.

It had been many years since she'd been in a horse barn, but the scents of hay, leather and animal were as familiar as the smell of bacon frying on a Sunday morning, and as filled with nostalgia. Her father had loved horses. She'd spent many a pleasant hour in their old wooden barn grooming slick coats, cleaning stalls and nursing the inevitable cuts and sprains. She regretted not having passed those simple pleasures on to her children, an omission that made her feel a guilty pang of disloyalty.

She took in the size of Adam's facilities. The three huge stone buildings would have made her father's stable look like poverty row. There were six sturdily reinforced stallion stalls on either side of a wide aisle, then what appeared to be a tack room and an office facing each other. Beyond them, well lit by skylights, was a long row of conventional stalls, presumably for geldings and mares. Everything was glowingly spotless.

Her job, unfortunately, wasn't to admire but to evaluate.

She cast a critical eye on the shiny brass plate of the nearest stall. "You have a lot of capital tied up here."

"Of course we do. Quality costs money. We also take care of what we have."

If she was an *efficiency expert,* she should know that.

"Labor-intensive," she muttered.

He wasn't going to let her rile him. He wouldn't jump at the bait. He was damn proud of the care he gave his horses and what they had given him back. He walked to the nearest stall and rubbed the nose of a black stallion.

"We've had three high finishers in the Breeders' Stakes series."

First Endeavor was a magnificent Thoroughbred with intelligent dark eyes and a remarkably laid-back disposition.

"How many horses do you have altogether?" she asked.

"At the moment we're standing six stallions and a herd of fifty broodmares, both quarter horse and Thoroughbred. In addition, we have another seventy-three working horses available for resale."

"What are you doing with your young stock?"

Adam kept watching her as she looked around. She was trying to concentrate on the facilities, but he didn't miss the sidelong glances at the animals. "We keep some," he responded. "The others go to the yearling sales."

She inched over and ran her hand along the neck of the stallion. She was comfortable around horses, though she claimed to have not been around them in many years. The contradictions in this woman fascinated him.

"A lot of old Kentucky horse-breeding families are going bankrupt," she observed.

"And the price of quality stock is higher than it's ever been," he countered without a pause, as if he'd been anticipating her approach.

"The market's poor and getting worse."

"The market's high and getting higher," he rebutted.

"Horses aren't a very good investment these days."

"And the world is going to end tomorrow."

She glared at him.

He glared back.

"You've been in the red for three years running." She stroked the firm flesh just below the stallion's shiny mane.

"And before that I was in the black for seven." He enjoyed their battle of words, but this wasn't a game. They were discussing a matter he took very seriously. "There's always a market for good horses, Sheila, both for ranch work and competition."

She nodded, but he could see she wasn't convinced. It annoyed him, but he held his tongue.

Since the next stop was twenty miles away, they left their mounts at the stable. He took one of the new pickups, fully equipped with automatic locks and a CD player, to drive her to the farmland where they raised cotton, corn, alfalfa and coastal hay. The fields were beautiful in their early-spring colors.

"We irrigate when we have to, but groundwater, with all its salts and minerals, is noticeably inferior to rain. That's why I've been cloud seeding. The improved harvests more than compensate for the few extra bucks it costs, not to mention the advantages it has for the water table."

The process of injecting moisture-laden cloud formations with carbon dioxide to precipitate rainfall had been around for decades but was still a contentious issue. It didn't always work, and when it did, no one could prove conclusively that it wouldn't have rained if the seeding hadn't been done to begin with. And the few bucks he was referring to, according to the fiscal report she'd read, amounted to a quarter of a million dollars.

She gave him a disapproving shake of her head. "There's a lot of controversy over cloud seeding, whether it really works or not."

"Only in the minds of people who don't know anything about it," he grumbled back, making no effort to hide his contempt.

That day and on Friday they stopped off to eat "dinner" with two different families. Each greeted her with warm hospitality, though she felt sure they knew she was a representative of the bank. Aside from asking her impressions of the enormous spread and how she enjoyed the food at the barbecue, however, neither questioned her reason for being there.

"Who pays the utilities for ranch families?" she asked late Friday afternoon when they were on their way back to the headquarters.

"They do. Each house is separately metered."

"What about maintenance?"

"They do their own. I pay for the materials, of course."

"And if they want to expand or improve their houses?"

He leveled his eyes at her. "We usually cut a deal, Sheila. I pay for all or most of the materials, if they want to add a room, for example. They do the work. The same goes for upgrades to permanent fixtures such as plumbing, siding or roofing. Now, if they don't like the color of the carpet and want to replace it, they pay for that themselves."

"You're very generous," she told him. "Some would say too generous."

"Who?" he challenged. "Pinstripes who've never gotten their hands dirty?" He took a deep breath. "Trust me. My people work hard for what they get."

SATURDAY MORNING Sheila sat at the table by the bay window, sipping coffee, determined to sample just enough of the egg burrito Elva had served to not offend the woman. This past week she'd eaten in quantities she hadn't consumed since she was pregnant with Melanie. Worked it off, too. Not only hadn't she put on a pound according to the scale in the guest bathroom, she'd actually lost one. But if she continued to chow down like a cowboy while spending most of her time sitting at a desk in Houston, she'd have to widen the doorways before long. Better start now on cutting back.

Over the past two days she'd ridden horseback, walked miles and talked incessantly. She and Adam had argued about everything, from how often vehicles should be traded in to charging his vaqueros, the people who lived on the ranch, rent. They disagreed on just about every subject, too, yet there had been times when they laughed, shared companionable meals and a few quiet, contemplative moments. It was during these days that they seemed to draw closer. As friends. Or potential friends.

"Thank you for a wonderful week, Adam." She smiled as he looked up from the local newspaper folded beside his plate. "I came here to work, but I have to admit to feeling guilty. I've enjoyed myself, your company and the generous hospitality everyone has shown me."

It was true. The constant activity and especially the company of an intelligent, occasionally testy, but always honest man had made what could have been a very tense situation into an adventure. The whole family—with the exception of Kerry and her son—had shown up for dinner the evening before to say goodbye.

"What did you say to Kerry," Sheila had finally gotten around to asking Clare when they were helping

Elva clear the dinner table, "that made her calm down in the car?"

Clare grinned. "I told her that Michael, for all his posturing, was too much of a gentleman to actually hit her, but that I wasn't a gentleman, wasn't a blood relative and that I would have no qualms about beating the crap out of her in front of all her friends."

Sheila stopped in midmotion and raised her eyebrows. "Did you mean it?"

Clare smirked. "We'll never know, will we?"

"I'm glad your appetite's improved," Elva said now, breaking into Sheila's thoughts. "Another burrito?"

Looking down at her plate, Sheila almost gasped. It was empty. *I'd love one,* she was tempted to say. "I better not, but I'll take some more coffee."

She caught Adam smiling at her. "What's so funny?"

"I just enjoy watching you fight with yourself. You know darn well you want another burrito. Why don't you have one?"

This mind-reading ability of his was unnerving. "Because I have to go back to Houston, where I don't ride horses or climb mountains."

"Maybe you should move to a place where you can."

"Like here?" The words had popped out before she'd thought about their implications. If the question was a proposition, who was propositioning whom?

His smile broadened. "That's a thought."

He reached across the table and rested his hand on hers. "I've enjoyed having you here, Sheila. I've enjoyed your company. I hope you'll come back and let me take you out riding again."

A nodule of something resembling fear formed in her chest. She wanted to return, to spend more time in this man's company.

Unwilling…no, afraid…to pursue the notion, she removed her hand from under his and switched topics abruptly. "I'll be writing my preliminary report next week, Adam, and forwarding it to the bank. Of course I'll send you a copy of it."

Her sudden change of subject and withdrawal irritated him, reminding him of the reason for her being here. "Are there going to be any surprises?"

She shook her head. "That doesn't mean you'll agree with everything I write, but I don't think there'll be anything you can't live with. My bottom-line recommendation is unequivocally that you stay on as general manager."

His chest heaved as he took a deep breath in frustration. "We may have lost controlling interest, but this ranch is still my family's heritage." He picked up his coffee cup and brought it to his lips. "Thanks for your endorsement, though. I appreciate it."

Did she detect an undertone of sarcasm in his response?

"Adam, you've done a marvelous job running this ranch. Under other circumstances I would say to carry on exactly what you're doing, but we have to be realistic. Homestead is in a position to dictate, and at this early stage they're strongly, very strongly, inclined to exercise it, if only to show they can. With that in mind, I think you have to face the fact that some changes will need to be made. I'm going to suggest adjustments I believe will improve the profitability of the ranch but that won't disrupt the core of your operations. Bending a little now will prove your flexibility in their view and make them a lot more amenable to your staying in charge.''

She watched anger skitter across his features, darkening his eyes, closing his face. Being cast in the role of supplicant hurt.

"Please understand, Adam. This is my job.''

"Of course I understand.'' This time he didn't try to hide his sarcasm or the anger beneath it. "You're just doing your job. It doesn't matter that it doesn't make sense, doesn't improve anything or that you don't believe what you're spouting. You're just doing your job,'' he repeated, "telling your employers what they want to hear.''

A SPECIAL DELIVERY arrived by courier the following Saturday morning, a copy of Sheila's sixty-seven-page report on the operation of the Number One Ranch. Adam settled into the easy chair in his office and began reading.

In spite of the way they'd clashed on almost everything, she said some very complimentary things about the ranch, about the quality of the people he had running it, about its organization and efficiency. He began to relax. Maybe this wouldn't be so bad after all.

There were pages and pages of statistics. He skimmed over them, assumed they were accurate and moved on.

Finally, he came to attachment one, the list of specific recommendations for improving cash flow and cost of operations. At first he saw nothing to be concerned about. He'd agreed that more modern, more durable and lower-maintenance plastics should gradually replace wooden fencing; that they should explore a series of underground cisterns for storing water.

He didn't agree with her on downgrading trucks and tractors to less expensive models, but he figured he could show the bean counters at the bank that it was a false saving. Cheaper models didn't last as long and required higher levels of maintenance.

He certainly disagreed with her about downsizing and gradually eliminating racehorse breeding. True, the program had lost money in the past couple of years, but in the long term it was solidly in the black. He was confident he'd be able to successfully oppose the proposal.

He felt less confident about her recommendation regarding cloud seeding. She wanted to eliminate it altogether. He was convinced that would be a mistake. But fighting it would mean trying to prove a negative— a waste of time. She said he'd have to bend if he wanted to win the Homestead's support. Maybe this was an issue he should bow to with the hope of later converting them to his way of thinking.

Suddenly, his muscles tensed and he sat bolt upright.

She wanted the bank to charge the vaqueros fair-market-value rent for the houses they occupied.

He stared at the words. She'd said there would be no surprises. She'd lied.

CHAPTER FOUR

THE BIG QUESTION in Sheila's mind was whether Adam could swallow his pride and accept the bank's leadership and direction in running the ranch. She considered the improvements he'd made on the huge spread in the twenty years since his father died and the personal interest he took in the people who worked for him. But it was the remembered glow in his eyes when he gazed across a sweeping pasture to the rolling hills on the horizon that told her his giving up leadership voluntarily wasn't likely.

She'd just closed out the Web site Gideon had designed to advertise Number One stud services, when her door flew open.

Her head shot up. The ranchman himself stood looming down on her. Her pulse quickened. "Adam, what are you doing here?" The words tumbled out in a breathless rush.

"Mrs. Malone, you have some explaining to do."

"Do I?" She knew why he'd come, why he was so angry. From the moment she'd written the report she'd known this confrontation was inevitable. She gestured toward a chair. "Would you care to sit down? I made a fresh pot of coffee a few minutes ago." She started to get up. "Can I get you some?"

His attention didn't waver or his expression soften. "You lied to me."

It might as well have been a slap. She could feel the sting warming her cheeks. "I beg your pardon?"

"You lied," he repeated no less sharply. "You said there wouldn't be any surprises—" he held out a rolled-up copy of her report "—and that we'd discussed all your recommendations."

She was forced to angle her head up as he hovered over her desk. "There isn't a single item in the report we didn't discuss."

"You didn't tell me you were going to recommend—"

"I never told you what any of my recommendations would be." She rose to her feet and stood squarely in front of him, her desk separating their hips but their noses practically touching. "If you recall, I also said you probably wouldn't agree with all my conclusions."

"You blindsided me, Mrs. Malone."

Her heart thudded. All she could see was his angry face glowering menacingly at her. His words hurt, maybe because in a hidden part of her conscience she agreed with him. He'd been right at their last parting. She didn't like some of the recommendations she'd made, and he didn't know how many times she picked up the phone and started to call him—to prepare him. He'd been correct, too, when he pointed out that her allegiance had to be to the people who were paying her. Not to Adam First. She had a job to do, a business to run. Not just livelihoods but lives depended on her success.

Besides, her approach was in his own best interest— just as the changes people had advised her father to make had been in his.

"I don't work for you, Mr. First. I've been engaged by the Homestead Bank and Trust."

His fists were pressed to the surface of her desk and the veins in his neck bulged. His stormy gray eyes narrowed as he repeated, "The Homestead Bank and Trust."

Silence hung between them, charged and dangerous. Finally, he straightened, turned his back, took a pace toward the door and spun around again.

"How could you possibly recommend I discontinue cloud seeding in the midst of a drouth?" he asked in a low, mocking tone. "What stretch of logic, Mrs. Malone, led you to advise selling horses that have the potential to earn far more than their keep? And what—" his voice was raised again "—what in the name of all that's decent drove you to suggest I charge my ranch hands rent for the homes they live in?"

She opened her mouth to try to explain, but he cut her off before any words had a chance to come out.

"Do you charge your staff for the use of their offices?" He scanned the room. It wasn't plush by any means. She'd softened the angular lines of what was one meager step above utilitarian furniture with strategically placed plants. The artwork on the walls, though tasteful, was not original.

"It's not the same and you know it." Her voice trembled. In fact, her whole body shook, and a part of her detested him for making her feel so unhinged. "Besides, this is a preliminary report. I'll explain my reasoning in greater detail in the final version."

"I see. Your mind is made up and now you're chasing after facts to justify it."

"If you recall, I questioned you at some length on the matter of cloud seeding. Your bottom-line response—"

"Bottom line," he spat out in contempt. "It's always the bottom line, isn't it?"

"Was that anyone who disagreed with you was stupid and—"

He slammed his palm down on the simulated-wood Formica desktop, making her jump. "I never said anyone was stupid. I said people who opposed cloud seeding usually didn't know what they were talking about." He leaned forward and lowered his voice. "Obviously, I was right."

She kept herself from sputtering, but just barely. "I also pointed out that racehorse breeding in other parts of the country was in serious trouble and that you'd lost money for the last two years."

His eyes narrowed. "You seem to have very conveniently forgotten that this isn't a short-term investment but one that in the past has earned us a high reputation. The name *First* means something, Mrs. Malone, but of course, you're only interested in today's *bottom line.*" He tossed back his head in disgust. "Go on. What about housing?"

"As for charging rent for your workers' houses, I also quizzed you extensively about the arrangements you had with them. If you think back, you'll recall I told you I felt you were being overgenerous."

"Felt?" he asked with raised eyebrows. "Now, there's a solid criterion for running people's lives. I wonder how you're going to *feel* tomorrow. As for overgenerous, if you'd listened to me—before you passed judgment—you would have heard me tell you the people living in those houses worked damn hard for their benefits. Including the stereo-equipped trucks and tractors you're so eager to take away." He straightened and spread his arms. "It's nice and comfy in here, isn't it? Pretty plants you have hanging in your windows. The background music in the front office is classy, too." He stuck his face within an inch of hers, so close she could smell the woodsy scent of his aftershave. "Do you suppose y'all deserve creature comforts more than people who work by the sweat of their brows?"

Her heart was pounding now, whether from his words or the closeness of his body she wasn't sure. "I'm perfectly willing to discuss these subjects, Mr. First, but don't patronize me, and sinking to personal attacks won't get us anywhere. I never said your people didn't deserve comforts. I said cutting back on luxuries might be a way of lowering costs."

He gave her a twisted smile. "I certainly wouldn't want to offend you, so please don't take this personally, lady, but you don't know what in the blue blazes you're talking about."

She plopped down into her chair. "This isn't getting us anywhere, Adam." She sounded exhausted.

He lifted an eyebrow and studied her. "You're right. Grab your purse. We're going for a ride."

She tightened her grip on the armrests. "The hell we are." Leaning back in her chair, she lifted her chin and glared up at him.

He dropped into the cushioned chair beside her desk and spread his long legs out in front of him. "Sheila, you really tick me off." His tone was lowered, but hardly calm. "Why couldn't you be up-front and honest with me?" He waved his hand in a familiar, dismissive gesture. "I know. Your allegiance isn't to me, though I seem to recall something about your wanting to help. I guess you didn't really mean that."

The disappointment in his voice came closer to reducing her to tears than all the shouting.

His remarks had offended her. He should be gratified. Wasn't that what he'd wanted, to lash out and hurt? He exhaled loudly.

"I owe you another apology, Sheila. I'm sorry for coming on so strong."

She uncrossed her arms. The eyes studying her were as deep and fathomless as the hot West Texas summer sky.

"What *are* you doing here, Adam?" She relaxed her face muscles. "If it was just to yell at me—"

"I had a meeting all day yesterday and early this morning at A&M. About livestock breeding," he added. "We finished a little while ago. I thought I'd come and explain to you what's wrong with your report—over lunch."

A tickling sensation curled in the pit of her stomach. Hunger pangs probably, rather than a reaction to the lopsided, self-deprecating grin he gave her. "You have one hell of a way of asking a lady out."

He emitted a self-mocking chuckle. "You're right." He pulled his feet under him, stood up, removed his Stetson and placed it dramatically over his heart. "Mrs. Malone," he intoned formally, "would you do me the honor of joining me for lunch?"

How could a woman stay mad at this man for very long? Still, a lady wasn't supposed to fall prey to a handsome male's charms too quickly.

"I don't know." She demurred. "I have a very busy schedule." She reached forward and flipped the page on her desk calendar. It wasn't necessary to look up to know he was staring at her—and smiling.

"Where do you propose we go?" she asked.

"Back to College Station," he said, referring to the town where Texas A&M was located. "I flew the Cessna."

Judging by the way he'd barged in on her, there was more to this than his wanting her company over a noon meal. The university was a hundred miles to the northeast, not exactly down the street from her Houston office. Well, there was one way to find out.

"That means I'd be gone all afternoon." A slightly extended lunch hour was manageable, but taking the rest of the day on such short notice meant inconveniencing clients. She pressed the button on her intercom. A female voice responded.

"Leah, would you ask Mr. Elling to come to my office, please."

A minute later there was a tap on the doorjamb. Adam swiveled in his chair and rose.

"Jonas," Sheila said, "come in. I'd like you to meet Adam First. Adam, this is Jonas Elling, my associate and the guy who taught me everything I know."

The man stepped forward with a wide smile. "She's exaggerating, of course." He extended his hand. "I'm very pleased to meet you, Mr. First."

He was a few years older than Adam, several inches shorter, had shaggy gray-brown hair and a potbelly.

"Please, call me Adam."

"Adam's in town for the afternoon," Sheila explained, "and we need to spend some time going over the report on the Number One." She fingered the day planner on her desk. "Cafferty's coming at 1:30 and Shultzbach at 3:00. He'll probably be late—"

With a casual shake of the head, Elling said, "Not a problem. I'll take care of them." He turned to Adam. "I know the decisions you're being asked to make aren't easy, but I think over the months— and, I hope, years—ahead, you'll find Sheila's a tremendous asset in helping you meet your business goals.''

Adam's eyebrows rose. ''Months and years ahead?'' He shot daggers at Sheila. ''I thought you were performing a onetime evaluation.''

''I am,'' she assured him, but he could see discomfort in the glance she quickly shifted toward the other man. ''If we're successful in helping you through this initial transition, we hope to continue advising you…''

Anger pulsed through Adam. Another deception. She wanted to keep her hooks in the Number One. He managed to keep his voice level. ''Advise me or the bank?''

''If you'll excuse me…'' Elling began. Adam had the distinct impression Sheila's associate realized he'd said too much and was eager to escape. Elling moved swiftly to the door and turned back to his boss. ''Oh, Sheila, I meant to tell you, Catherine has an appointment tomorrow morning. I'll try to come in…''

''Stay with her, Jonas. That's your place.''

''I'll make it up to you. Thanks.'' He ducked out the door.

''What was that all about?'' Adam asked after Elling left.

''His wife is taking chemotherapy at M. D. Anderson.''

Adam's temper collapsed. By the time he'd taken Helen to the prestigious cancer-treatment center in Houston, it had been too late. The information also explained the sadness and worry Adam thought he'd seen in Elling's brown eyes. ''I'm sorry.''

Five minutes later Sheila shut off her computer, rose from her desk and unhooked a light jacket from the coat tree in the corner behind her. The early-March weather was warm, but the breeze was cool. Adam held the jacket for her. It flustered her as she slipped into it that she was so conscious of his hands brushing her shoulders.

He took her by cab directly to the airport. During the drive, they talked about the continuing drought in West Texas. Exactly what this excursion was all about still wasn't clear, but she doubted it had anything to do with lunch. She could be patient when she had to be. Wait and see was obviously the only game in town.

The taxi dropped them off at the private aircraft side of Hobby International Airport, where his twin-engine airplane sat fueled and waiting. A few minutes after tower clearance they were airborne. Less than forty-five minutes later, Adam landed at Easterwood Airport on the west side of the Texas A&M campus.

"Do you come to College Station very often?" she asked as they pulled out of the parking lot in his rental car.

"Two, three times a year. I've been breeding Santa Cruz cows with my Longhorn/Brahma–cross bulls for the past five years. The Department of Animal Science here has been running a study on them. It's still a little early for a conclusive analysis, but the preliminary tests are positive for both higher meat grade and yield."

They talked a few minutes more about breeds, breeding and the changing taste in beef and other meat products.

Texas A&M sprawled over a square mile of open campus, most of the buildings modern, the grounds immaculately maintained. Adam stayed on University Drive, then turned right onto Wellborn Road. The tall square Albritton Bell Tower, with its beautiful carillon, loomed on the left. He took another right onto a broad tree-lined avenue leading to a four-story gray concrete building.

The Kleberg Center, one of the major cattle and livestock research facilities in the country, had high wide windows shaded by louverlike awnings of the same gray concrete. The few trees around it, mostly live oaks, didn't reach past the second story. Low-growing, dark-green junipers hugged the building's base.

The center was named after Robert Kleberg Jr., the great-grandson of Captain Richard King, founder of the famous King Ranch. Once the largest privately owned ranch in the world, it had contracted in size in the past few years, as its owner sold off some of its non-Texas holdings in Florida and Australia. Nevertheless, it was still a formidable enterprise, covering more than fifteen hundred square miles of the Texas scrubland south of Corpus Christi—a landmass larger than the state of Rhode Island and more than half again the size of the Number One.

"Ever been here?" Adam asked after parking in the lot to the west of the entrance. They were walking up a wide promenade that led to the building's central atrium. In a little garden alcove to the left stood a two-thirds-life-sized bronze statue of a man astride a horse. Robert Kleberg had established the first new breed of cattle in the United States.

"A few times," she replied, holding back a threatening frown.

"There's something here I'd like you to see."

Had Sheila known this was where he planned to bring her, she would have found an unbreakable appointment. She had a good idea what he had in mind. Awareness of what she would show him in return brought a heaviness to her heart. Keeping these thoughts to herself, she remained silent.

He led her through the sunlit atrium to a hallway on the left that led to a staircase. Its enclosure, as well as the walls on the lower level, were lined with polished pine placards. The top row identified the 254 counties of Texas. Below each were the brands found in each.

Adam didn't descend, however, but went to the left of the head of the stairs, to the "Brands Book." It was a mammoth, six-inch-thick, dark leather-covered volume containing most of the state's brands, their dates and the signatures of their founders. The pages were yellowed with age and use.

With care he turned the heavy vellumlike pages to the West Texas section of the book. Many of the brands recorded there had long since disappeared, but one of the earliest was still in existence. He pointed to the stylized *f*.

"This brand has been part of Texas history for more than 175 years, Sheila," he said in a tone rich with pride. "It was here before Mexico won its independence from Spain, before Texas was established as an independent nation, before it joined the Union. The First brand survived the Civil War and every war, fire, flood and drouth we've experienced since then. I don't intend to see it disappear."

She bit her lip and wished the sudden lump in her throat didn't ache so much. She'd heard similar words and sentiments as a child, in the wake of disaster. Unable to speak, she turned several pages of the massive tome to the Texas counties along the Red River, which separated Texas from Oklahoma and pointed with a shaky finger to another brand. £.

"My maiden name was Pounder." Her voice was a

croak. She cleared it. "Our brand wasn't quite as old as yours, but it was around for over a century. My father was sure it would last forever, too, Adam, but it's gone now. It exists only in history books." She traced a finger along the edge of the pages. "And here."

Fighting the tears that suddenly loomed, she moved away from the pedestal supporting the huge volume and studied the brands cluttering the walls. Memories ripped through her like a flood through a narrow canyon, churning, tearing and rushing on. She found the pound sign. The sight of the brand blurred her vision, threatening to crack her tenuous composure. She'd never forgotten the symbol, but at least she'd been able to push it to the back of her mind.

A moment passed before she realized Adam had moved up beside her and another few seconds to notice the First brand on the wall only a few feet away.

He curled his hand around hers, the tender warmth of his touch nearly bursting the floodgates of her emotions. "Will you tell me about it?" he asked quietly.

"Yes, I think I should," she replied in a voice that sounded squeaky to her. "Maybe then you'll understand." She bit her lip and lowered her gaze. "Can we go somewhere?"

He cupped her elbow gently, protectively. "Of course. I did promise you lunch, after all."

The closeness of his body sent heat waves through hers. She remembered his sheltering her in his arms at the home place and had to fight the urge to lean into his chest once more. Until they were outside in the clean whispering breeze of early spring, she wasn't sure her legs wouldn't buckle out from under her. He didn't try to invade her thoughts as they strolled back to the car. Unlocking the passenger door, he saw her in, then circled the front of the vehicle and slipped behind the wheel. Still he remained silent as he drove conservatively to a grill across from a strip mall a few blocks away from the university campus. It was early afternoon on a weekday. The place was nearly empty.

She ordered Hawaiian chicken salad and hot tea, he a club sandwich and coffee.

"I had no idea bringing you here would upset you," he finally confessed.

She tried to smile. "I didn't, either." Without thinking she reached across the table and placed her hand on the back of his—to reassure him he'd done nothing wrong, she told herself. But her pulse leaped when he reversed his hand and clasped her fingers in his. "It shouldn't have. You'd think after all these years…"

The waitress brought their food. With unsteady fingers, she drizzled dressing over her salad. He removed frilly toothpicks from his triple-decker. Delaying tactics.

She bit into a tiny tomato, chewed and swallowed. "We lived outside Wichita Falls. Our place was called the Pound Sign, like the brand. It wasn't nearly as big as your spread, only five sections. My great-grandfather bought it before the Civil War."

He grinned. "The War Between the States."

She smiled back weakly.

He stroked her fingers. "The War of Northern Aggression."

Her smile strengthened. "We raised some cattle. Dad earned decent money in the good years, but there were as many bad years as good and the vagaries of weather and the market always made it chancy."

She removed the tea bag and squeezed in lemon.

"Dad managed to get us through the drought of the fifties, but it left us deeply in debt."

Adam nodded. The same drought that had forced his father to sell a share of the First Ranch and sown the seeds of its downfall.

"In 19 and 60," she said, reverting to a form of expressing dates her father and grandfather had used, "we were hit with a double whammy. First a tornado, then a flood. The twister ripped directly through our place and wiped out half the town. When it was over we were not only left with dead cattle, but all our buildings were either damaged or destroyed. What the wind didn't get, the rain and flooding that followed did."

The sadness in her words, the note of forlorn despair, had Adam reaching anew for her hand. She gave it to him willingly, gratefully. He'd witnessed a twister or two and enough flooding to know how physically devastating each could be. People were able to replace possessions, but it was the loss of a sense of security that sucked the peace and confidence from them. Sheila Pounder Malone, it seemed, had experienced that loss of faith and hope.

"Surely you got government assistance."

She grimaced. "A grant that was too small. A low-interest loan that wasn't enough to cover even a part of our outstanding debt, and a lot of promises that were either kept too late or not at all."

The waitress stopped by with a steaming coffeepot. "Refill, sir?"

Adam smiled up at her. "If it's a fresh pot. Wine may improve with age. This black stuff doesn't."

She pulled down the corners of her mouth, her eyes showing embarrassment. "Sorry. I'll brew a new batch." She picked up his cup and left.

"Go on," Adam urged.

After a moment's pause, Sheila continued. "Dad could have survived it if he'd been more flexible." She peered directly at the man sitting across from her. "He wanted things to go back to the way they were, Adam. He refused to see times had changed. Markets had changed. The economy was moving in a different direction."

Adam knew what was coming. "He lost the ranch."

Sheila took a deep, shuddering breath. "On July 5 of 19 and 63, the bank foreclosed. Ironic, don't you think? The day after Independence Day."

He didn't miss the bitterness in her question, the pain that after nearly forty years still tormented.

"We moved into town. Mom got a job as a clerk at a local food store. Dad worked at the grain elevator. He died three years later." She ran her finger along the rim of her cup. "The doctor said it was a heart attack, but Mom and I knew it was really a broken heart." She paused, fighting to keep her precariously balanced emotions in check.

"I'm sorry," Adam said, the words inadequate. Yes, men could die of grief. He'd thought such notions silly when he was younger—or took them as a sign of weakness. He knew now that even the strongest men had breaking points. Lord, how he knew.

"A hundred years of work was gone," Sheila murmured.

He understood what she was telling him, that he was making the same error, that the world around him was bigger and more powerful than even the Number One. That he had to bend or break.

"I loved my father," she said, raising her head. "He was strong and gentle and kind. A hard worker and a generous neighbor." She smiled wanly at Adam. "You would have liked him. He did his best to provide for us. He made mistakes, but neither my mother nor I ever blamed him for what happened. He carried enough guilt for all of us."

The waitress reappeared, proudly presenting a full glass pot of coffee and a clean cup. She poured and placed the cup on the table.

"Thanks." He offered her a wry grin and watched her leave. He paid no attention to the steam rising from the black brew. "You were saying…" he prompted.

"I was just starting high school when Dad died," she went on. "I decided the best way I could honor him was to help other farmers and ranchers do a better job of managing their places." She chuckled softly and attempted a sip of tea. "You accused me of being an idealist, remember? I guess you were right."

He skimmed his thumb delicately across the back of her hand. "I think your father would be very proud of you."

She folded her lips between her teeth and for a moment her breathing snagged. "I'd always been a good student," she continued, soothed by his touch and the sympathy in his gaze. "I enjoyed learning new things."

"And didn't want to let him down."

He understood. It gratified her that he did.

"I managed to get a scholarship here to A&M."

Surprise crinkled the corners of his eyes, his reaction bringing her a giddy pleasure. She grinned. "I majored in ranchland management."

This time when his eyebrows rose, she found herself actually laughing.

"I worked in a county extension office for several

years,'' she told him, the seriousness of a few moments before slowly fading into playful delight. ''That's where I met my husband. After Bill died, I came back here, earned my master's degree and went to work for Crowder and Breckenridge, a large consulting firm. It didn't take me long to realize I'd been independent too long to knuckle under to other people's rules and standards. I quit C&B and have been on my own for the past three years.''

She paused, suddenly solemn again, pursed her lips and twisted her cup on its saucer.

''Adam, I hadn't intended to go into all this with you. But since you took me to that building, it seemed the right thing to do.'' She leaned forward now and met his eyes earnestly. ''I beg you, don't make the same mistakes my father made.'' She interwove her fingers with his. ''For all his good intentions, he failed because he refused to see what was happening around him, refused to accept reality. You don't own the Number One outright anymore, but you can still run it. It can still be a part of you, and you a vital part of it.''

ADAM CONCENTRATED on flying during the trip back to Houston. He understood where Sheila was coming from now, why she seemed so set on making profit the focus of his ranch operations. He couldn't argue with her logic; a business that didn't make money was bound to fail. Nor could he deny the ravages of her personal experience.

But, he wanted to tell her, he wasn't her father. He wasn't spurning the world around him. He was very much aware of reality. He, too, had made a study of the marketplace. Hadn't he adjusted by breeding better cattle, leaner meat of higher quality? He didn't disparage her academic credentials, either. They were impressive and useful tools, but a ranch was more than a business, and the most valuable lessons of all were those learned in the school of hard knocks.

Somehow he had to make her realize she wasn't seeing the entire picture.

It was late in the afternoon when they arrived at Hobby. Airline traffic was heavy, but from his low-altitude flight path, he could see ground transportation was even worse. He landed and went with Sheila into the small waiting room attached to the hangar where he'd parked his plane.

"Hey, Gus," he called to a large, heavyset man in his forties who was sitting behind a high counter in front of a Plexiglas scheduling wallboard, "You have any vehicles available for rent?"

The man looked up from the *People* magazine he was reading. "Got the old Celica, if you aren't worried about fancy."

"It'll be fine. Just need it for a couple of hours."

"Adam, you don't have to drive me," Sheila protested. "I can get a cab from here. There's no point in your bucking the traffic both ways." She held out her hand to him. "It's been a good day. I'm glad you came."

He ignored her farewell gesture. "You're going home with the guy what brung ya," he informed her with a wink.

She laughed. "I don't know if I should take that as a compliment or a threat."

He wouldn't be taking her home, of course, but back to the office so she could pick up her car. What was her home like? he wondered. What would she say if he told her he wanted to go there with her?

He waited until they were bumper to bumper on I-10 before he broached the subject that had been bothering him since they'd left her office.

"Elling's remark about future work at the Number One...what was that all about?"

Sheila shifted in her seat before responding. "This is a onetime evaluation I'm performing, Adam, but Nedra Cummings at the bank says that if it goes well, she'll consider asking me to perform evaluations on a quarterly or semiannual basis."

"And you want that?"

"Of course. It would mean steady work." She said it lightly, but he could hear the steel underneath. "Continuity of oversight is to your benefit, as well."

Only if I get along with the overseer.

So it was to Sheila's advantage to give the bank what they wanted. Nothing new or particularly sinister there. Every business sought to satisfy its customers. He thought about her office. Tasteful, but nothing fancy. Was she a minimalist as far as the work environment was concerned? He mentally shook his head. She obviously wasn't frivolous, but she didn't strike him as a person who would economize on things she could afford. Sheila Malone had class. Which led him to the logical conclusion that she couldn't afford anything better than what she had.

"There's Thoroughbred horse racing at Turf Paradise in Phoenix this weekend. Would you care to go with me?"

Was he asking her out on a date? "I assume you have horses running."

"A couple of them. If you're going to get fully involved in checking out our operations, you might as well start now."

"So this is a business trip," she concluded, disappointed.

The statement, or was it a question, had his mind and his imagination churning. He hadn't intended his invitation to be personal, at least not consciously, but he'd already gotten personal at the home place, when he'd pulled her body close to his. He studied her face, but her bland expression didn't tell him which side of the line she was on.

"It could be a little bit of both," he suggested.

She didn't respond directly. "When would you want to leave? How long would we be gone?"

"Just the weekend. The races are Saturday and Sunday. I thought I'd pick you up here on Friday afternoon. We'd fly out to the ranch for the night and then leave for Arizona first thing Saturday morning. You'll be home by Sunday night."

She pursed her lips in thought. "I usually let everyone go early on Fridays and close down the office myself around 4:30." She paused. "I'll bring a suitcase to work with me. That way we won't have to stop back at my place before we leave."

CHAPTER FIVE

FOR THE NEXT FEW DAYS, Sheila was annoyed with herself. Adam's invitation to accompany him to Phoenix shouldn't prey on her mind. She'd been to the popular Arizona racetrack several times. On a plain northeast of the desert city, it had a striking view of the Superstition Mountains. When their kids were young, she and Bill used to take them camping and fishing there. Just this past winter she'd visited friends in Sun City, so there was no reason for her to be constantly thinking about the upcoming trip.

Except...in those quiet moments when she allowed herself candor, she knew it wasn't the snowbird vacation spot that was occupying her mind, but the man she was going with. In the seven years since Bill died, she'd accepted an occasional dinner date from men she knew. The evenings had ranged from pleasant to dull, but they'd never gone beyond the friendly good-night-kiss stage. Her body might sometimes want more... She chuckled. *Be honest, Sheila. You mean sex.* But she'd made love to only one man in her life, and he was gone. Physical needs aside, she'd never sought another man.

Until now. It disturbed and excited her to think she was actually contemplating Adam First in a sexual way. When he'd touched her at the home place, he'd stirred something inside her that had driven out all thoughts of Bill Malone. Later, of course, she'd suffered a wave of guilt when she realized that the moment Adam's arms encircled her, her memory of her late husband had been blocked out.

Now she was going to fly off with Adam First to his ranch, then to the races—like a couple of jet-setters. This wasn't in character with the sensible and serious Sheila Pounder Malone who'd been the faithful, devoted wife and mother. Yet she couldn't deny that the prospect of sleeping under the same roof again with Adam First made her blood thrum with nervous anticipation.

There was a dark side, though. She might be fantasizing about the social aspects of the upcoming adventure, but she had to remember this was essentially a business trip. They would have to discuss Adam's management of the ranch, and she knew in her gut it would be a wedge between them.

He thought he was different from her father, that he was smarter, more flexible, but he wasn't. Not really. She'd heard echoes of her dad's pride when Adam recounted the history of the Number One. She'd seen the same self-confidence in his stance when he looked out across the sweeping plains of the ranch he loved. Such men didn't bow. They didn't bend. They broke.

SINCE IT WAS Friday evening, Gideon and his sister were home for the weekend. The warmth of their greeting for Sheila reminded her how far away her own family was. The four of them ate in the breakfast nook off the kitchen.

"I hear Brian got himself into more trouble yesterday," Julie commented as Elva loaded the table with a platter of baked chicken with cilantro, cream gravy and succotash.

"He used to be a pretty good kid," Adam bemoaned. "Until this past year." He addressed Sheila. "Cutting classes, flunking tests. He'll probably have to go to summer school."

Gideon dotted his salad with homemade croutons and passed the bowl to his sister. "Last week he wrecked his Mustang."

Sheila shot Adam a startled glance. "You didn't say anything about an accident. Was anyone hurt?" she asked the group at large.

"Thank heavens for air bags." Julie scooped succotash onto her plate. "He walked away without a scratch, but the car was totaled."

"What happened?"

"Speeding, of course," Adam interjected with disgust.

"He was outside city limits on Prairie Dog Lane," Gideon elaborated as he filled a pool in his mashed potatoes with cream gravy. "There's a sharp curve at the base of a crest. He miscalculated, swerved off the road and sideswiped a telephone pole."

Sheila hesitated to ask her next question since it was none of her business. "How did your sister take the news?"

"Better than I expected," Gideon said. "Michael told her to make Brian use the school bus for the rest of the semester."

"She agreed?" Sheila was surprised. Her impression of Kerry had been of a selfish woman who indulged her son with expensive gifts but enforced no discipline.

"Michael is the only one Kerry seems willing to

listen to, maybe because they're closest in age, less than two years apart.''

"Except at the birthday party," Julie commented. "Still, I think she tries to be a good mother.''

Sheila watched Adam during the exchange. He wasn't saying anything, but he was listening, as if he were trying to gain some new insight. Perhaps he was. He wasn't one to give up easily, even on his recalcitrant daughter. Kerry had hurt him deeply, yet at the barbecue, when she'd calculatingly insulted him in front of all his friends and neighbors, he forgave her. Sheila wondered if she could be as loving and generous had one of her children humiliated her so ruthlessly.

"So what happened yesterday?" she asked.

Gideon buttered a biscuit. "He got caught smashing windows in the principal's office. While the police were questioning him, he admitted he was the one who broke into the girls' locker room last week, too.''

Adam shook his head. "You know, under other circumstances I might see a glimmer of humor in this adolescent behavior. When I was his age antics like that would have resulted in paying for the damage, apologizing to the principal and the girls at an assembly and performing janitorial work around the school for a month. Then—'' he held up his fork like a scepter ''—then, when I got home, my father would have me doing every dirty chore around here for the next three months.''

"Gee, Dad—'' Gideon eyed him with a fatuous grin ''—I didn't know you were such a hellcat. I bet you even stuck the girls' pigtails in the inkwells.''

"Smart-ass. I'm not that old.'' He couldn't help chuckling, though. "Now, be quiet and eat your vegetables or I'll make you go to bed without dessert.''

Dessert turned out to be apple crunch.

It wasn't until after Sheila had excused herself and gone upstairs for the night that Gideon found his father in his office. He threw himself into the chair across from the desk and stretched out his long legs, fingers interlaced across his flat belly.

"Is this getting serious, Dad?"

Adam crooked him an eyebrow. "What are you talking about?" As if he couldn't guess.

"I've never known you to bring a woman home before. I'm not saying I don't approve or anything—"

"Sorry to disappoint you," Adam said, "but there's nothing going on between—"

His son had an impish expression on his face. "Then you're the one who should be disappointed. Sheila's a good-looking woman. She's unattached, too."

Adam felt his cheeks getting warm. This was hardly a conversation he ever expected to have with one of his kids. "We're going on a business trip."

"Sure, Dad." Gideon rose from the chair. "Whatever you say."

"It is."

"Okay." Gideon raised his hands. "I just wanted you to know I like her and so does Julie." He moved to the door, then spun around. "Now, if you need a few tips on how to woo the lady, I'd be glad to give you some pointers."

"Gideon," Adam warned with a scowl.

"Oh, and by the way. I know you've been out of circulation for a while, so maybe we ought to talk about safe sex—"

He escaped, laughing, just before a giant eraser bounced off the door frame.

THE SKY WAS a cloudless cerulean blue, the air delicately warm on this sunny day at the races. A festive
attitude imbued horses and grooms, owners and spectators. Excitement and a good-natured impatience ani-
mated the crowd eagerly queuing up to lay their money
down at the betting windows.

"How many of them really expect to win?" Sheila
mused out loud as she and Adam walked arm in arm
through the jostling crowd.

The jubilant atmosphere had infected him, too, especially in the company of the beautiful woman by his
side. He laughed.

"All of them, of course. Some of the more realistic
ones might be willing to admit they're merely paying
to have fun—"

"But they still harbor the secret fantasy that they
can beat the odds big-time and become the envy of
their friends."

"Exactly." He grinned, entranced by the glow he
saw in her eyes. "Are you willing to take a chance,
Sheila? Gamble on coming out a winner?"

"Of course," she replied automatically, then paused,
hearing another question within the question. Smiling
mischievously, she patted his cheek with a gentle tap.
"Even middle-aged businesswomen have fantasies,
you know."

For a moment they stared at each other, each strain-
ing unsuccessfully to completely suppress a smile. Neither of them said another word as he escorted her to
one of the waiting lines.

He watched her peruse the racing form, intrigued by
the faint pursing of her mouth, by the way her tongue
softly, slowly, stroked her upper lip. She didn't seem

intimidated by the form's length or coded annotations of information.

"Have you been to the races before?" Why hadn't he thought to ask the question sooner? His mind, it seemed, had been on other matters.

"A few times," she replied, her head bent over the newsprint. "Betting is fun—" she glanced up soberly "—but I'm not addicted. I stop when I run through the small amount I budget, and I have no qualms about quitting when I'm ahead."

"Smart lady."

She preceded him to the window and bought half a dozen tickets, two on his horses, three on very long shots and one on a favorite. He bet on his own horses, of course, and some of the favorites in other races.

They strolled through the paddock area, appraising the young stock. They were all spirited, some with a wild look in their eyes, others with an almost refined eagerness.

"You said you have two horses running here," she reminded him. "Out of how many?"

"About thirty-five that are old enough to race. Not all of them have the hearts of competitors, though."

"Less than ten percent," she murmured.

He didn't want to argue with her or defend himself, but he wasn't going to let her challenge go unanswered. "Might I remind you that one good purse by a single horse will keep all of them in hay for a year?"

When she had no comeback for that, he took it as an incentive to go on.

"I have fifteen at home that are in training, and ten broodmares in foal." He regarded her critically. "It's not as if the others are worthless. As I think I pointed out once before, there's always a market for good horseflesh."

"Adam, you old son of a gun," a man bellowed from behind after slapping him on the back hard enough to knock him forward. "I wondered if I'd see you here. Can't stay away, can you?"

Sheila pivoted and recognized a man who towered at least half a head above Adam and weighed over three hundred pounds. His smooth round face had the glow of a man who enjoyed who and where he was.

"Apparently, neither can you," Adam rejoined with a grin. He turned to Sheila. "I'd like you to meet Caleb Hawkins. Sheila Malone."

"Hello, Cal." She offered her hand and had it immediately swallowed up in a thick-skinned ham of a grip.

"It's always wonderful to see you, Sheila, but I have to ask what a beautiful woman like you is doing here with this ugly old goat?"

"Hey, who are you calling old?" Adam rejoined.

Cal's compliment warmed her, but Sheila also noted genuine fondness in the way he insulted Adam. "Learning about racehorses."

"From him?" Cal guffawed. "Adam doesn't know a horse from an armadillo."

"Look who's talking," Adam retorted. "Cal here raises jackasses and tries to palm them off as horses."

The huge man grinned. "Almost whupped you last year, little guy."

Sheila chortled. Only someone the size of Cal could call Adam a little guy.

"Almost only counts in horseshoes, my friend," Adam reminded him. "It's the critter wearing the shoes we're wagering on."

"Now he tells me," Cal huffed as he winked at Sheila.

"I gather you two know each other," Adam remarked curiously...or was it with a hint of jealousy?

Cal grinned at her. "This lady is brilliant, my friend," he said sincerely. "If she gives you any business advice, take it. She did a rundown of my operation a couple of years ago and really turned it around. I've got a lot to thank her for." He lifted her hand and planted a kiss above the knuckles. The unexpected gallantry had her blushing.

"See y'all later at the clubhouse?" he asked Adam.

"You bet. I may be a bit late, though. You know how the paparazzi can't seem to get enough pictures of winning owners and their champion steeds."

Caleb roared with laughter. "Hey, Rocko," he called out to someone else in the crowd, and moved off.

"Is it true that you helped him?" Adam asked.

"He was on the brink of bankruptcy when he called me in."

"So you have experience in the field of horse racing, yet you recommend I phase out my stock," he commented, confused by her conflicting standards.

"Oh, my evaluation wasn't on his hobby of raising Thoroughbreds but on how he was running his heavy-equipment business."

Before Adam could comment further, he was greeted with more backslapping, handshaking and good-natured banter as they moved through the fenced-off area where animals were being pampered and groomed.

"They've all got different personalities, don't they?" Sheila noted as they passed a roan that kept raising and lowering its head, as if to say, *Yep, I'm going to win. I'm going to win.*

"Just like people," Adam agreed. "No two are the same, and like people, looks can be deceiving. The ones that seem the most laid-back are often the most aggressive on the track—refusing to let another horse get ahead of them—while those that can't stand still often can't get their acts together, either. You can almost feel their frustration, like teenagers unable to figure out what to do with the energy building inside them."

"Kind of like Brian," Sheila observed, but didn't dwell on the comparison. "Of course, those same clumsy adolescents are sometimes in their best form when they're on the athletic field."

"Exactly. There's no predicting. That's what makes a horse race," Adam agreed. Just then a trumpet call over the speaker system announced the first race was about to start.

NEITHER ADAM nor Sheila had bet on the initial two races. It didn't keep them from enjoying the competitions, however. Sheila yelled and cheered, urging on whoever seemed to be in second place. Adam found himself torn between watching the Thoroughbreds flying at a dead gallop and observing Sheila's breasts shift erotically as she raised an arm and clenched her hand to encourage the steeds on.

First Lady placed in the third race.

"Not bad for her initial time out," Adam crowed.

"She earned me six bucks." Sheila beamed.

Her long shots didn't pay off in the next two races and the favorite pulled up lame in the one that followed. First Endeavor ran in the seventh. The four-year-old had done well in some of the smaller local competitions but never made it on the major tracks in Louisiana or Texas.

"Something in the air east of the Pecos, I guess," Adam opined. "But that's okay. He's still got a couple of good years of track time left, then he gets put out to stud."

Sheila frowned, though her eyes were laughing. "Poor baby."

"Hey," Adam rejoined with an ironic shrug, "we all have to contribute to a better world."

"Yeah," she replied straight-faced. "I wish him every success."

The shiny black stallion came in fifth in a field of nine.

"Better luck next time," Caleb shouted from two boxes over.

"Tomorrow's another day," Adam shot back with good humor.

"We all have our bad days," Adam philosophized a minute later as he tore up his ticket. "Wait until tomorrow. First Addition runs in the afternoon."

Sheila had the big winner in the last race, an absolute long shot. Cal Hawkins's Tickler's Fancy paid 25 to 1.

She waved the hundred-dollar bill under Adam's nose as they sauntered from the payout booth to the parking lot. "Dinner is on me."

"You're my guest," he countered.

"Well, I'm reciprocating your generosity out of the kindness of my winnings. I know a nice little French restaurant—"

"French?" he asked.

She wound her arm around his before responding. "I know it's not the home cooking you're used to. Not exactly low fat, either. Everything is made with real butter and lots of heavy cream, and I'm afraid there won't be any barbecue—''

''Do they have *ris de veau?*''

She stopped short, causing him to jerk around off balance. ''You like sweetbreads?''

He nodded sheepishly. ''As well as brains and eggs, except that Elva won't fix them for me. Claims they're real high in cholesterol.''

Sheila laughed. ''She's right.''

''Actually, I think it's handling them she objects to.''

''Some people are squeamish,'' she observed, though Elva didn't strike her as one of them.

''You won't tell her, will you?''

She snickered. ''And get put in the doghouse along with you? Are you kidding? Besides, I'm not one to kiss and tell,'' she added, conscious of the meaning of the words only after she'd spoken them.

They'd reached the car, which was all but hidden between a large van and a gooseneck trailer. He turned her to face him, his wrists draped on her shoulders. ''I'm glad to hear that,'' he murmured just before he brought his mouth down on hers, before she had time to protest.

Not that she had any desire to resist. She'd been wondering what it would be like to kiss him. After all, it had been a long time since anyone had kissed her...with passion.

No, she decided as she brought her arms up to circle his neck. She didn't have to wonder anymore. Adam First was one hell of a kisser.

IT WAS TOO EARLY when they arrived back at the hotel to go to dinner. They could have gone to one of their rooms, of course, and followed up on the experience in the parking lot. Adam was definitely tempted, but awareness that neither of them was quite ready yet for the next step persuaded him to resist making the suggestion. Instead, they proceeded to the cocktail lounge and had a single glass of wine.

They didn't say much, yet there was no strain in the silences that interspersed their brief comments about the races, the loveliness of the weather, the excitement of the day. It amazed him how comfortable they were with each other. To anyone passing by, Adam realized, they probably appeared to be a contentedly married couple on a holiday.

They weren't, of course. He didn't, couldn't, take Sheila's company for granted. Every moment he was with her seemed special, alive, charged with an electricity that heightened his awareness of his body's responses in a way he hadn't experienced in many years. She made him feel young, vibrant…and let's face it, horny.

She glanced over at him, and he only then realized he was smiling.

"Penny for your thoughts," she said.

"Uh-uh. These are worth a lot more, more than money can buy."

There was amusement in the quizzical expression she bestowed upon him. Could she read what he was thinking? The notion, rather than being intimidating, pleased him enormously.

He looked at his watch. "Do you want to change for dinner?"

"If you don't mind," she replied, her eyes still leveled on his.

He rose from his seat and stepped behind her chair to ease it out. She gathered her purse, stood and turned to face him.

"Thank you for a wonderful day, Adam."

A sly grin creased his face. "It's not over yet."

They walked hand in hand out into the lobby and crossed it to the bank of elevators.

"I'll meet you downstairs in an hour," he suggested when they came to her level. Having made her hotel reservations long after his own, their rooms were not on the same floor. "Will that be enough time?"

"Perfect," she said as she stepped out.

He watched her walk down the corridor a moment before he pressed the button and the door closed. Yes, he was definitely feeling young.

LE BEAU CIEL, which the locals called the Bow Seal, was within walking distance of their hotel, which pleased Adam. He looked forward to walking her "home" in the moonlight. What would happen after that he couldn't predict, though he could certainly conjure up a few ideas.

The restaurant was small and intimate. The beautiful sky its name referred to was apparently the one at midnight when stars twinkled like diamonds on black velvet, for the place was dark and romantic.

"Excellent," Adam said as he perused the long, leather-covered menu by the glow of the shaded candle in the middle of their table. For a modest inducement, the maître d' had shown them to a corner booth that afforded total privacy. "They have braised sweetbreads as an appetizer." He smiled at her. "Share them with me?"

The softness around her eyes, the tug at the corners

of her mouth told him neither of them was thinking about food.

"I guess I can sample a little bit without suffering a major coronary."

"What else would you care for?"

She pursed her lips. "*Coq au vin,* I think. Chicken is always good for salving lingering pangs of conscience. You?"

"I'm less virtuous. *Steak au poivre.*"

"A meat-and-potatoes man."

"Mostly. Red wine or white?" he asked.

"Since my chicken is cooked in red wine sauce and you're having beef—" she gave him a crooked Lucy Brown leer "—let's go for the red."

He order a Chateauneuf-du-Pape.

The stroll back to the hotel after dinner wasn't quite as romantic as Adam had envisioned. The moon wasn't full and the evening was too young, for a continuous stream of traffic clogged the main drag, fouling the night air with exhaust fumes. The pounding beat of hard rock coming from a teenage nightspot disturbed the serenity he'd hoped for.

He took the elevator to the sixth floor and walked her to her room. As she fumbled in her purse for her key, he asked quietly, "Are you going to invite me in for a nightcap?"

Her movements slowed. She found the plastic card and held it firmly. "Not tonight, Adam."

He gently turned her around to face him, curled a finger under her chin and raised it to exactly the right angle for him to bring his mouth down to hers. She accepted his kiss, responded to it, then pulled away and lowered her head.

"Adam, I care for you." She kept her voice low

because she was nearly breathless. "I think you know that." She put her palm on his chest. His heartbeat was as thick and measured as her own. "But I'm not ready for this yet." She looked up, her eyes cautiously meeting his. "I don't think either of us is."

He wanted to protest, but she put a finger to his lips to silence him. "There are still things we have to discuss, issues we have to resolve—"

"The ranch..."

She nodded. "That's part of it." She studied the passion in his gaze, the frustration. "Please don't..."

He scooped her up in his arms. His mouth this time was less gentle, more urgent. As their tongues whirled and danced, yielded and savored, she began to have doubts. Regardless of what her mind said, her body wanted more.

He broke off the kiss but continued to hold her. "I know you're right," he murmured in her ear. Finally holding her away, he smiled forlornly at her. "Damn it."

Had the light been better in the tiny alcove outside her door, he might have seen the moisture pooling in the corners of her eyes. He slipped his hold from her forearms to her fingertips. "Sleep well."

She watched him walk down the hallway to the elevators and doubted she'd sleep at all.

FIRST ADDITION missed third place by a nose in the opening race the following afternoon. Sheila wavered between consoling Adam and keeping silent, opting for the latter when she saw the disappointment on his face.

Caleb Hawkins grinned from ear to ear as he moved out of his box to join Gandy Dancer in the winner's circle. "Better luck next time," he boomed to Adam as he passed. "Against someone else."

"Congratulations, Cal. Dancer ran a good race. I'd keep him if I were you."

Admiring him for his good sportsmanship, Sheila wrapped her arm around his.

"I'm sorry," she commiserated.

He shrugged philosophically. "You win a few, lose a few."

There were three more races. Sheila hadn't picked any winners today, not even a two-dollar show.

"I suppose Addition's poor performance this afternoon confirms your opinion that I shouldn't be in horse racing," Adam kept his eyes forward as he wended through traffic on the drive back to the hotel. They'd checked out that morning, but since the hotel was between the racetrack and the airport, they'd left their luggage there.

"I've nothing against horse racing, Adam." She didn't like kicking him when he was down, but he'd asked for truth and she was determined to give it. "If you can afford it. My reservation is that at this point I don't think you can. The arguments you have for pursuing the venture are valid, or would be under other circumstances. I just consider it unwise to tie up capital and other resources on something that's so unpredictable. You have too many irons in the fire."

He listened to her words and considered them carefully before replying.

"Seems like a catch-22, doesn't it? If I concentrated on livestock, you'd say I have all my eggs in one basket. If I diversify, you maintain I'm spreading myself too thin."

"I can understand how you might feel that way," she agreed.

"Can you?" He hated the frustration he could hear in his voice. But, damn it, he was frustrated. In more ways than one.

She turned sharply to him. There was loneliness in his voice. Sadness. She understood both. The time they had spent together had been...pleasant. Not full, not complete. Yet part of the satisfaction had been in the subtle promise of more, of better, of sharing intimacies they both needed, perhaps even deserved.

He reached across the narrow space between their bucket seats and squeezed her hand. "Could be we both have things to learn," he said, his voice suddenly thick.

"Maybe we do."

It was a few minutes past five o'clock when Adam landed at the ranch. Their plan was to grab a quick bite while one of the hands refueled the aircraft, then he'd fly her back to Houston. He started to unload his baggage from the plane and was surprised when he looked up and saw his eldest son approaching.

"Uh-oh." Adam eyed him suspiciously. Michael had other things to do besides mope around the hangar waiting for his father to land so they could unload luggage together. "What's up?"

His son stood in front of him, fists shoved in his pockets. "We have a problem."

Adam gave him a silent glare. "I've already figured that much out. Now, what is it?"

"It's Brian, Dad. He was arrested."

CHAPTER SIX

ADAM'S MOUTH had become a thin line. Sheila could feel the stunned rage emanating from him and wouldn't have been surprised to hear him explode, but he didn't. Instead, he asked in a low, simmering tone, "What happened? What was he arrested for?"

"Drunk driving."

Adam took a deep, patience-begging breath. "Let me see if I have this straight. Last week he totaled the brand-new Mustang his mother bought him and got cited for reckless driving, and now he's been arrested for driving under the influence."

"Was anyone injured?" Sheila asked.

"No."

"Thank God for that, at least," Adam intoned. "I'll meet you up at the house."

Michael watched his father pick up the bags and cart them, stiff shouldered, toward his Jeep in the corner of the hangar.

"I'm afraid you're about to see another downside of the First family." With that, Michael strode to his car.

Sheila had to take several running paces to catch up with Adam. He seemed oblivious to her presence as he slid onto the front seat, his knuckles whitening when he gripped the spindly steering wheel. He'd already turned the key and rammed the gearshift lever into first by the time Sheila climbed into the passenger side.

She'd hardly clicked the lap belt in place when he popped the clutch and they leaped into forward motion.

The engine screamed before he rammed the transmission into second gear. Again the light utility vehicle bucked in its skidding advance.

Sheila gripped the frame of the windshield for stability and half turned to the scowling driver.

"If you're going to help and not get us both killed," she warned him sternly, "you'd better slow up and calm down, Adam."

He ignored her at first, then inhaled deeply, let the air out and pulled his foot off the gas pedal. The Jeep slowed, but he was far from composed. She could see the vein on his neck throbbing.

"Kerry's the one who should be coming to me for help." There were anger and bitterness in his words and beyond them a deeper hurt. "Damn it, if she were a decent mother, Brian wouldn't be getting into all this trouble."

"I'm not sure that's completely true," Sheila replied. "The children of good parents sometimes go astray. But the one you have to focus on now is Brian, not Kerry."

"Thank you for the lecture, Sheila, but I don't need you or anyone else telling me what my family duties and obligations are." He pressed down again on the accelerator as they climbed the steep roadway to the nearly dark house at the top of the mesa.

"Adam, I'm on your side."

He halted in front of the breezeway that separated the three-car garage from the kitchen. After dousing the lights and turning off the ignition, he rested his arms on the steering wheel, laid his head on them for a moment, then straightened. "I'm sorry, Sheila. I shouldn't be snapping at you."

She suspected the calmness in his voice was taking every ounce of his control to maintain. She placed her hand on his. His fingers were hard, knotted with tension, hot with anger.

"I'll check on flights from Coyote Springs while you and Michael talk."

"No, don't." There was a note of panic in his order, his request. "I'll take you home...or have Michael fly you, but...I'd appreciate if you'd stick around." He smiled wanly. "Maybe you can help me keep this damn temper of mine in check."

Michael's Suburban pulled up behind them, making them aware of their closeness, their touching. Instinctively, they drew apart and dismounted from their respective sides of the vehicle.

Elva opened the kitchen door before they reached it. She obviously knew about this latest family crisis because concern rumpled her brows. She was reserved in her greeting, though Sheila sensed genuineness in her welcome as they exchanged brief hugs.

"Have you eaten?" Elva asked when Michael followed them inside. "I made enchilada pie. It'll only take a minute to heat up."

"Not right now," Adam said as he relieved Sheila of her jacket and hung it on a peg by the laundry room. "How about you?"

"Maybe later." Sheila briefly curled a hand over his, feeling the tension beneath the skin.

"Coffee, then?" Elva asked, and received a nod from all three people.

They sat at the kitchen table, father and son facing each other, Sheila between them.

"Okay. Now, tell me what's going on. When was Brian arrested?"

Michael hooked the handle of his thick china mug. "Last night."

Adam cursed. "So Kerry did buy him a new car after all. I figured she would. Didn't take her long. The boy'll never grow into a man if she keeps giving him every damn thing he wants."

"As a matter of fact, she didn't," Michael replied. "He was driving his buddy Benjy's T-bird."

"What exactly happened?" Sheila asked.

Michael slurped coffee. "A deputy sheriff pulled him over on the lake road for driving erratically. He smelled liquor on their breaths and ordered Brian to perform the usual physical-coordination tests—which he failed miserably. The deputy then administered a Breathalyzer. He failed that, too. Both kids were taken to the Juvenile Justice Center and charged with under-age drinking. Brian was also given a ticket for DUI. The cops called Benjy's father and Kerry. She called me."

"Why didn't you notify me?" Adam demanded.

"There was nothing you could do from Arizona, Dad," Michael reminded him reasonably. "I was here. I took care of it."

With a deep breath of frustration, Adam asked, "Where's he now?"

"Home. They released him in his mother's custody."

Adam gritted his teeth. "You should have told them to throw him in the tank. A night in a cage with a bunch of drunks puking all over themselves might have shown him where he's headed if he keeps this up."

"Dad, he's only sixteen."

It was the wrong thing to say. Adam slammed his fist on the table, making the cups bounce and coffee spill over. "He's old enough to take responsibility for his actions. We're not talking about childish teenage pranks anymore. If he drinks and drives he may not live to be seventeen. I don't ever want to stand over another open grave, Michael, and I don't want to contemplate the lives he might destroy with his own."

Sheila pressed her eyes closed and shuddered.

"His mother's been a real good example for him, hasn't she?" Adam added with biting sarcasm.

Sheila reached over and touched his wrist in a calming gesture. "What happens now?" she asked Michael.

"He has to appear before Judge Mayhew tomorrow morning at ten," Michael said. "The sheriff says he could be sent to juvenile...prison."

"He won't." Adam was adamant, but distracted. His mind raced.

He and Ronny Mayhew had gone to school together. Ronny had sold real estate for years, gotten actively involved in the chamber of commerce and finally run for justice of the peace some ten or twelve years ago, even though he wasn't a lawyer. Adam had strongly supported him. Mayhew had been unopposed in the last two elections. Ronny, his wife and children had come to Adam's birthday party.

"Have you or Kerry talked to Mayhew?" he asked.

Michael shook his head. "She's hoping you will."

"Well, I won't."

Michael's jaw dropped. "Dad, I know you and Kerry don't get along—God, that's an understatement—but don't take it out on Brian."

Adam went very still, except for his eyebrows rising

and his jaw setting. "Is that what you think I'm do-ing?"

"Why won't you speak to Mayhew? I know you're friends."

"Because it would be unethical. Ronny's a tough, no-nonsense judge who doesn't believe in kid gloves, but he's fair and reasonable. He's also honest. If I ap-proach him now, he'd recuse himself. I don't want him to do that."

"But…you said he's tough. He might send Brian away…as an example—"

"I also said he was reasonable." Adam's voice had softened.

"What will you do?" Sheila asked.

"What I have to." He refused to elaborate.

Adam's heart ached. If Kerry had been the one to come to him about Brian, could they have put their history aside long enough to focus on her boy's wel-fare? Or did she think he wouldn't give her his help? Is that why she sent Michael? Was she afraid he would rebuke her for not being a good parent? Oh, he would want to, but the irony was that he hadn't lectured to her in years. All the recrimination she thought she heard from him came from her own conscience, not from his mouth.

"Go home," he instructed his son. "I'll see you, Kerry and Brian at the courthouse tomorrow at nine-thirty. We'll discuss this further then."

Michael pushed back his chair and rose slowly. "Thanks, Dad. Someday Kerry'll thank you, too."

Adam watched him leave, then muttered, "But it won't be tomorrow."

He turned to Sheila. The weekend hadn't gone the way he'd hoped or planned. "I'll ask Elva to pack some sandwiches and we can eat on the plane. Sorry for the delay." He rose from the table and picked up his half-empty coffee mug. After placing it in the sink, he leaned against the counter. The wind had ruffled her hair. And he had an urge to smooth it. He could imagine his hand lingering on the side of her face, absorbing its warmth, her mouth turning and kissing his palm.

"It's so late, Adam." She squirmed self-consciously under his gaze—but held it. "Maybe it would be better if you let me stay overnight and have someone drive me to the airport in Coyote Springs in the morning—"

Sheila once again sleeping in his house. He pictured her curled against him under the sheets, her soft skin warm, inviting. A wave of desire pulsed through his body and clawed at his insides, begging for release.

"Would you be willing to stay an extra day or two?" he asked uncertainly. "I can fly you back early Tuesday morning."

He wanted her to stay, and so did she, but she also had a business to run.

They were within inches of each other. He had only to put his arm out to touch her. Her lips were slightly parted, her chest moving in slow, tense breaths. His hand rose and was about to caress her cheek, when Elva bustled in from the laundry room with a stack of folded dish towels.

"I...uh...I'll call Jonas," Sheila said hurriedly, "and see if he can take charge of things tomorrow."

SHEILA WENT to the room she'd been given on her previous visit and phoned Jonas.

"I thought you'd be back tomorrow," Jonas said, "so I set up a second meeting for you with Cosgrove

Tuesday morning at nine o'clock. Do you want me to postpone it till later in the day?''

She thumbed through her day planner. There were already three appointments that afternoon. They could be reshuffled, but it would inconvenience a lot of people. Not a good way to instill confidence in clients.

Cosgrove Enterprises was a fledgling software company with great ideas and not an ounce of business sense. The president of the company was a twenty-four-year-old computer geek; most of his employees were even younger. Not a huge account, but one that was growing and showed potential for more business.

''Is there any chance you could take it?'' she asked.

Jonas hesitated. ''Catherine has an appointment at M. D. Anderson Tuesday morning.''

''How is she?'' Sheila asked.

''Everybody says she'd doing fine, but she's awfully tired. No appetite at all.''

''Poor thing.''

''I can see if they'll postpone the appointment for a day.''

''No, don't do that.'' She had been knocking around a notion in her head ever since her initial discussions with the pierced-and-tattooed programming genius. ''What would you think about Amy working with Cosgrove?''

Jonas's laugh carried an undertone of relief. ''I think it would be a perfect union. She's on their wavelength. Frankly, I don't have a clue what they're talking about half the time. In fact, I was going to suggest Amy, but...''

''Whew.'' Sheila chuckled. ''I thought it was just me.''

She also wished he'd made his recommendation earlier. She had no doubt Jonas was worried. His wife's medical condition was stable but precarious. Even though he didn't have direct access to Sheila's business records, Jonas had been in management consulting long enough to figure out that the firm wasn't in tiptop financial condition. Fear of making a mistake and further jeopardizing his employment and medical insurance for his wife seemed to have robbed him of the aggressiveness that had been one of the reasons she'd so gladly hired him.

"I'll call her and set it up. You take care of Catherine. And Jonas...take care of yourself, too."

Sheila called Amy at home. The young woman jumped at the opportunity to honcho her first independent assignment and was bubbling over with ideas.

"I'll have them approach their financial structure like one of their mind-bending games," she said.

They talked for a long time, going over details. Even without files at her fingertips, Sheila was able to recall enough of the small company's operations to help her assistant work out a strategy and plan of action. Helping start a new career gave her a satisfying feeling.

Behind the young woman's bravado, however, Sheila could also hear a hint of anxiety. Rather than giving Sheila doubts about the wisdom of her decision, though, it encouraged her. Fear of failure was a good incentive for thorough work. Amy would do fine. Sheila hung up the phone a few minutes later.

What about herself? Had fear of failure caused her to be as overcautious as Jonas? Had success with Homestead meant so much that she was telling them what she thought they wanted to hear, rather than what she really believed? The problem was that Nedra Cummings had made it clear she expected changes at the

Number One that would increase its profits. Telling her Adam was doing an excellent job and should be allowed to continue without interference or adjustments sounded like a whitewash. Without some concrete recommendations for change, hiring Malone Economic Consulting and Services would appear to be a waste of money. Did that mean Sheila had betrayed Adam for her own profit?

She wished Jonas was bolder. Maybe it was time for her to be more bold, too. And honest.

"DON'T BOTHER with those, Elva. I'll wash up," Sheila offered when the cook started clearing dishes from the table. Her enchilada pie had been spicy and delicious, but in spite of their not having eaten since noon, neither Sheila nor Adam had made much of a dent in the large casserole.

Exhaustion showed on the housekeeper's face, but she marshaled her strength. "You're a guest. This is my job."

Adam glanced at the clock over the dining-room door. "It's after eleven, Elva. I'm sorry we kept you up so late. We'll make sure everything gets put away."

When the housekeeper tried one more time to resist, he rested his palms gently on the back of her shoulders and steered her toward the back door. "Go to bed, Elva, and sleep well. We'll see you in the morning."

Sheila called out a good-night as she turned the faucet and began running water into the sink.

Adam joined her. They worked in silence. Twice when he reached for a cup to dry it, Sheila's hand brushed against his. Flint striking steel. Sparks flared inside her and each time her breath caught in her throat. She glanced up and saw the challenge in his eyes. Her fingers fumbled in the soapy water. Spoons clattered as she set them in the rack, then nestled perfectly inside each other.

At last the utensils were put away, the coffee mugs suspended on their hooks. Sheila spread the wet dish-cloth across the sink divide and Adam hung the damp towel on its bar.

He encountered no resistance when he touched her shoulder and spun her around to face him. His fingers moved across her collarbone, up her neck, along the base of her jaw. Balancing her chin on the tip of his knuckle, he tilted it up as his mouth swept down to capture hers. She snaked her arms behind his back, stimulated by the assault on her senses, the heat and strength of his body. He pulled her snugly into a tighter embrace.

"We're alone," he whispered hoarsely into her ear.

She rested her head against his shoulder. "So we are."

"Just you and me," he murmured.

He kissed her again and she felt the warmth of his tongue flood her and burgeon into heat.

"It's time to go to bed," he said softly.

Adam flipped light switches, bracketed her shoulders and led her to the stairs. She leaned into his solid mass, clutched his narrow hips and the sinew of muscle be-neath his shirt. Even with his support, her legs were unsteady as they mounted the steps.

They bypassed her room. Her heart was racing as he ushered her into his, then gave it a practiced shove. It swung closed with a well-oiled click. The only light came from a bedside lamp.

Turning her in his arms, he stroked her back. Her delicate smile as she gazed up at him deepened the laugh lines radiating from the corners of her eyes. Rather than detract from her appeal, they added allure. Blue met gray.

The kiss this time wasn't sweet but passionate, filled with aching need and unbearable want. It would be impossible to say who was the aggressor, for they were matched forces now, inciting, overpowering, conquering, surrendering.

"Are you sure?" His voice rumbled precariously, balanced on the edge of control. She wouldn't be here if she wasn't, he told himself, but he had to ask.

Insinuating a painful distance between them, she caged his face between her hands, smoothed the creases time and sun had graced him with, played over the silvery stubble of a long day's growth and looked into the depthless recesses of his eyes. What she saw there melted any chance of resistance.

Her lips curved as she held his steady gaze. "As sure as I've ever been about anything in my life," she told him. On tiptoe she kissed his mouth.

Strong but suddenly unsteady fingers traced her outline, neck, shoulders, arms, waist, then rose to possess her breasts. Their warm fullness threatened to short-circuit his entire nervous system.

Sheila's vision faded and she bit her lip against the sensations ripping through her. Her breathing halted as he fondled her silk-covered flesh and ran trembling fingers across rough peaked nipples. The fire he was igniting made her weak. It also made her impatient. She couldn't flee the conflagration building within her and had no desire to. Instead, she added to it by touching him.

Dragging her hands through the graying hair of his broad chest, she gloried in the hammering of his heart beneath the still-firm flesh. Reflexively, he contracted his belly as her palms glided down to his belt. As she undid the large silver buckle, she watched his face transform into a tense mask of wonder.

The dam was broken. Within minutes they had stripped each other of outer garments. He stood before her in bulging briefs, the soft light of the dim lamp shadowing the formidable contours of his work-hardened body. She faced him in panties and bra, her soft curves and lines highlighted into enticing peaks and valleys.

He trailed his fingers along the satiny material, setting off tiny explosions in their wake. He reached behind her back and released the clasp. His tongue against his upper lip, he stripped the barrier from her burning skin. She drew in her breath at the sudden freedom, at the look of passion in his eyes as he stared at her hard, tingling nipples.

''You're beautiful,'' he murmured as he brought his mouth down to one erect bud and gently rolled it between his teeth.

She should protest. She wasn't young and supple. She wasn't beautiful. Yet, at that moment, as she arched against the flicking playfulness of his tongue, he made her feel vibrantly youthful and infinitely desirable. She loved him for that precious gift.

She combed her fingers through his dark hair, aware of the dampness between her legs as he suckled her breasts. He straightened, moved her to the four-poster bed. He yanked away the covers and turned back to her. Slowly he slid her panties off her hips, down her legs. She stepped out of them and lay, vulnerable, waiting for him. Lips clenched between his teeth, he removed his last piece of clothing and suspended himself over her. The crinkly curls of his chest hair teased, tortured and tantalized her as they brushed her sensitized nipples.

"I need you, Sheila," he whispered in a voice gruff with passion. "In my life and in my bed."

"I'm here," she muttered as his fingers probed and parted. Her heart hammered. From the words or the actions, she couldn't be sure. Only one thing was certain. She wanted him as much as he needed her. She wanted him inside her, a part of her.

ADAM LAY by her side, facing her, his hands sandwiched prayerfully under the pillow. As if he were aware of her gazing at him, his lashes fluttered and a smile spread across his features. He reached over, feathered his fingertips down her cheek.

"I just had to make sure you're real," he said in a sleepy murmur.

She rotated toward him and stroked the sandpaper stubble of his jaw. "Very real."

Their eyes danced and his tender caress slipped down her neck on its way to her breast. The alarm clock buzzed. He hadn't wanted to set it the night before but couldn't take the chance of oversleeping.

"Come on," he said after snapping it off. "I'll let you wash my back."

"Pig," she responded, crossing her arms defiantly over her naked breasts.

His gaze shifted to her nipples peeking through the crooks of her arms. They instantly hardened. He grinned. "I didn't say I wouldn't wash yours, did I?"

She glanced at the clock on the bedside table, then at the man standing naked in front of her. They'd do more than wash each other's backs if she joined him.

"You better go ahead," she urged. "You're going to have a busy day today."

"Still won't let me act like an irresponsible young buck, huh?" He turned toward the bathroom door.

"Irresponsible? No." Her eyes twinkled. "Young buck? Hmm. That was quite a performance you put on."

He laughed this time, and she could hear the pride in it. A young buck didn't show the patience and control he'd demonstrated last night. Or the expertise. Young bucks had sex. He'd made love.

She settled back against the goose-down pillow. She'd never experienced a man's body the way she'd experienced his. She thought for a moment of Bill. They'd loved each other deeply, devotedly. She had no complaints, no regrets, no misgivings. But Bill had never carried her to the heights Adam had led her to. Was it the novelty of being with a different man? The thrill of the forbidden?

She didn't think so. The sensations hadn't been new but more intense. This union hadn't been a thrill but a fulfillment. Forbidden? She'd never been unfaithful to her husband. Remarkably, she didn't feel unfaithful now. She felt happy.

SHEILA HAD NEVER BEEN in a courtroom. She found the one assigned to Justice of the Peace Ronald P. Mayhew smaller than those portrayed on television, but it still evoked the sense of order and dignity the administration of the law demanded. The lower walls were wainscoted in cocoa paneling, the unadorned plaster surfaces above them were painted a flat cream color.

The judge's raised bench facing the double entry doors dominated the room. Directly behind it was the

Seal of the Sovereign State of Texas, flanked by cer-
emonial flags fringed with gold tassels: the Stars and
Stripes on the visitors' left, the Lone Star on the right.

Also on the right was the jury box, two tiers of hard
wooden chairs behind a carved rail.

Adam, Michael and Sheila took places in the middle
of the churchlike pew immediately behind another low
barrier that separated the court proper from the visitors'
gallery. Brian and his mother sat forward of it at a long
table on the left side, facing the bench. Across the aisle
at a similar table, a middle-aged man, representing the
juvenile division of the district attorney's office, fiddled
with papers.

Constable Maurice Jones, slender and fortyish, stood
by the judge's chamber door on the left. He sported a
western shirt, pressed jeans and cowboy boots, only his
silver badge and hip-holstered sidearm indicated his
role as bailiff.

Judge Mayhew entered, wearing the traditional black
robe of office.

"All rise," Jones called out.

Everyone stood up in place, though Kerry had to
nudge her son to do so. He complied without enthusiasm.

With broad, heavy shoulders and a shiny clean-
shaven head, Mayhew was an imposing figure behind
the high dais. His chestnut-brown face was smooth and
unsmiling.

He gathered his voluminous robe under him as he
slid into his high-backed leather chair and swiveled
around to face the assembly. "Please be seated."

Sheila was instantly drawn to the man, partly because of Adam's praise for him the evening before, but
also because she saw in his piercing coal-black eyes

both strength and intelligence. There was no doubt he was in charge.

He'd carried a blue folder of papers with him and took a moment now to review them.

"Will the defendant please rise?" Though Mayhew didn't seem to raise his deep voice, it filled the room.

Brian stood up, again without haste.

Adam had invited Sheila to attend his meeting with Kerry, Brian and Michael in the lobby of the courthouse half an hour earlier. There had been enough electricity in the air to set off a small nuclear device, and Sheila had held her breath during most of the confrontation. Kerry, to her credit, had kept her mouth shut. She hadn't thanked her father for coming, but behind the cold facade, Sheila thought she detected an unspoken gratitude that he was there.

"Were you drinking and driving?" Adam had asked his grandson.

The boy held his ground. "I only had a couple—"

Adam cut him off. "I'm not interested in excuses or explanations, Brian. Just answer the question. Were you drinking and driving?"

Brian's hard, belligerent eyes held a sneer. "So?" If he thought his tough-guy attitude would intimidate his grandfather, he was very much mistaken.

"You broke the law. That makes you a criminal. When the judge asks you for a plea, you will tell him you're guilty and you—"

"But—" Kerry started to object. Her father's glare stopped her. She dropped her gaze instantly. He turned back to the boy.

"I'll do what I can to keep you out of jail, but I can't promise anything. And I'll only speak up on your behalf if you own up to what you've done."

Brian looked at his mother. She nodded unhappily.

"Agreed?" Adam asked.

"Yeah, I guess," he snarled.

Adam eyed him sternly.

"Okay," the boy conceded.

Obviously not pleased with his grandson's attitude, Adam nevertheless softened his words to a more sympathetic tone. "You're not going to get off scot-free, son. What you did was wrong and dangerous. My advice is to be polite and respectful to the judge if you want him to deal leniently with you."

"Brian will," Michael assured his father, though there was no sign of it at the moment from his nephew.

Mayhew now studied the defendant for several seconds. "Mr. Durgan, you are charged with illegally consuming alcohol and driving a motor vehicle while under its influence. How do you plead?"

CHAPTER SEVEN

BRIAN SLOUCHED indifferently on one hip, making no attempt to mask his disdain for the situation he was in. Adam, sitting in the gallery behind him, shook his head in disapproval.

"Guilty, I guess."

Mayhew cocked a black bushy eyebrow and glared at him. "You guess." He pursed his lips. "Don't you know, young man, if you were drinking and driving?"

Brian didn't answer immediately, and Mayhew didn't press him.

"Or were you so drunk you can't remember?"

Sheila saw the corner of Brian's mouth twitch and could almost read his mind. Maybe if he said he didn't remember…but then he realized that wouldn't work. If he said he couldn't recall, he'd be admitting he was drunk, and he wasn't old enough to drink.

"Mr. Durgan," the judge rumbled, "you don't seem to appreciate the seriousness of the charges brought against you. You stand accused of underage drinking, then getting behind the wheel of a motor vehicle and driving it recklessly."

"I wasn't driving reckless," Brian argued, his denial filled with self-righteous indignation.

His Honor's firm expression hardened. "You haven't been charged with reckless driving," he conceded. "But if you weren't driving erratically—reck-lessly—why were you stopped by the police?"

Brian exhaled sharply through his nose but said nothing.

"I asked you a question, Mr. Durgan. I require an answer."

"I don't know," Brian said a little too loudly, his tone this time betraying more fear than anger.

"I think you do." Mayhew continued to stare silently at him, until finally Brian lowered his head. The judge then shuffled through the papers before him and lifted one.

"To make matters worse, you mouthed off at the officer who apprehended you. Now you stand before me and belligerently shrug off the charges brought against you."

Judge Mayhew reverted to silence once more, giving the accused an opportunity to comprehend his situation and amend his attitude. It didn't happen.

The judge shook his head and addressed the juvenile officer sitting across the aisle. "Mr. Cantor, does the defendant have a record of other offenses?"

Looking somewhat rumpled in a blue suit, Cantor stood up, his fingertips splayed on the papers on the tabletop.

"Yes, Your Honor, he does. He has been reported for truancy from school six times since the beginning of this semester, and he was picked up last week breaking windows in the school. He has admitted further to breaking into the girls' locker room on a previous occasion. In addition, he was ticketed for reckless driving a little over a week ago as a result of a one-vehicle accident in which he totaled his car."

Mayhew glared at Brian. "Mr. Durgan, whether you

know it or not, you are in very serious trouble. Do you have anything to say for yourself?''

Apparently deciding it was time to switch tactics and play the stoic martyr, Brian straightened and stared straight ahead. ''No, sir.''

''No remorse, either, it would seem.'' Mayhew waited for some response but got none.

''Very well,'' the judge said. ''Mr. Durgan, your driver's license is hereby suspended for a period of two years—''

That got Brian's attention. His head shot up. ''Two years?''

''I will reconsider the suspension after one year if you have met all the conditions of your probation.''

''Conditions?'' Brian was wide-eyed. ''Probation?''

''You will make full restitution for the expense of repairing the windows you broke in the school. I understand the damage is estimated at $350. In addition, you will pay a fine of $500 for underage drinking and another $500 for drunk driving. You will also be required to take the defensive-driving course before your license is reinstated, and you will pay all court costs and fees.''

Brian looked over at his mother. After all, she was loaded now that she'd sold her share of the ranch. But Kerry, head lowered, only bit her lip.

The judge didn't miss the silent plea. ''Get a job, young man, and work for the money. It's your fine, not your mother's, not your grandfather's. I expect an accounting from you of the source of the payment. A photocopy of the paycheck stub will suffice. In addition, I'm directing that you be placed for the next thirty days in juvenile detention.''

''No,'' Kerry moaned. ''Your Honor, please—''

"That's not fair," Brian objected. "All I did was have a couple of beers."

The judge glowered, but before he could say anything, Adam rose in place behind his grandson.

"Your Honor," he said respectfully. "May I address the court?"

Mayhew continued to stab Brian with narrowed eyes for a moment before softening his expression and recognizing Adam. "Mr. First."

"My grandson has made mistakes, and he understands he must make restitution for them."

Kerry, who'd been facing the judge, suddenly turned to her father. Her expression asked what he was up to.

Adam ignored her and went on. "I'll see to it he earns the money to pay for the damage he's done and the fines you have imposed. I also ask Your Honor's indulgence in not sending him to juvenile hall but releasing him in my custody. He will reside with me at my home on the Number One."

"What are you doing?" Kerry hissed.

"Trying to keep your son out of jail," Michael grumbled across the bar to her. "Shut up and let him."

"Mr. First," Mayhew said, "if you will assure me that your grandson will work for the money he needs to discharge the levies imposed by this court and will abide by a curfew from 10:00 p.m. to 7:00 a.m., I will waive the juvenile-hall requirement." He refocused on the defendant.

"Mr. Durgan, in exchange for your liberty, you will clean bar ditches four hours a month for the next six months—"

"You want me to be one of those dorky trash stabbers in green-and-white T-shirts and orange vests?" Brian was appalled.

"Mr. Durgan, I warn you. Watch your language and the tone of your responses in my courtroom. Interrupt me again and I'll hold you in contempt of court. That means jail time, young man." He paused for emphasis. "You will have a chance to speak when I am finished, when I tell you you can speak. Is that clear?"

"Yes."

"Yes what?"

Brian seethed but seemed to finally realize he was powerless. "Yes, sir."

A muted sound came from behind him from his grandfather.

"Yes, Your Honor," Brian reiterated.

"Just so you understand the severity of underage drinking, let me warn you that if you are caught consuming alcohol in any form during the period of your probation, I will order you confined to a substance and alcohol abuse treatment center for therapy."

Brian's eyes glazed over, and he finally dropped his hostile demeanor. The judge above him seemed totally unmoved by the boy's apparent change of heart.

"Mr. Durgan, you have spent a few hours in our Juvenile Justice Center. Let me assure you, it was paradise compared with what will be awaiting you if you fail to meet the spirit and letter of the conditions of your probation. You will report once a month to your probation officer. Do not leave this county without his written permission. Violate any of these provisions only once and I will send you to the Texas Youth Council in Bronte or Goldthwaite. Don't let the name fool you, son. It's prison." He paused again to let the word sink in. His tone remained as hard and unyielding when he continued. "There won't be any private rooms and the view from the windows, if there is any, will be of brick walls, chain-link fences, barbed wire and armed guards. If you like, I'll arrange for you to visit one of those facilities, so you'll know what you can look forward to if you continue on the path you've thus far chosen.''

Brain started to speak but then just shook his head.

''Mr. Durgan, do you understand the conditions of your release?''

Brian nodded once.

''Speak up.''

''Yes, Your Honor.''

''Your grandfather is sponsoring you. He's giving his word to this court that you will behave yourself. Because of his reputation as an upstanding member of this community, a man of integrity, I am willing to temper your sentence. But rest assured, sir, if you fail in your obligations and thereby disgrace yourself and your grandfather, I will come down on you in the hardest possible way. Is that clear?''

''Yes, sir…uh…Your Honor.''

''Do you have anything to say to this court?''

Brian thought a moment, trying to figure out what was expected of him.

''No, sir, except thank you, Your Honor. I'll do my best.''

''This court is adjourned.'' The fall of the gavel this time echoed like the clap of doom.

Kerry, Michael and Sheila stood as the judge stepped down from the dais and exited through the door by which he'd entered.

Brian was tight-lipped, his eyes red and watery. His mother hung her head, her expression mournful. She appeared to be on the verge of tears herself. Adam waited until the man from the district attorney's office had gathered his papers into his portfolio. Nodding solemnly to Adam, Mr. Cantor left the room.

"Pack up his things," Adam directed his daughter. "I'll see you at the ranch headquarters in an hour."

"The hell you will," she snapped. "You did a real fine job with your friend the judge today, but I'll take it from here."

Adam grimaced. "This isn't a game, Kerry. I gave my word to the court and so did Brian. He'll stay with me, or he'll go to jail. Is that what you want? Do you hate me so much you'd do that to your own son?"

"You bastard," she screamed, causing the heads of several courtroom people to stop and stare.

Michael's head shot up, and he looked around in a moment of panic. "Lower your voice and watch your mouth," he warned between clenched teeth.

"You'll do anything to get back at me," she snarled at her father. "Even steal my kid."

Taking a deep breath, Adam started a slow count to ten but didn't get past two. "This has nothing to do with you and me or getting even. You're the only one who seems bent on doing that."

"Adam." Sheila touched his arm. Perhaps they needed to have it out, but the county courthouse wasn't the right place.

"Dad." Michael seconded her caution.

"All right." He continued to glare at his daughter. "Just get his clothes together."

Kerry boiled, her lips compressed, her hands balled into fists.

"He'll be there," Michael agreed, then hustled his sister and her son down the aisle to the entrance.

Sheila waited until the double doors closed behind

them before speaking. "Brian's going to be a handful. He's not a happy camper."

"He's not supposed to be." Adam's words were uncompromising, but she could see a sadness and compassion in them she doubted either his daughter or grandson would be able to recognize. "He needs to learn his actions have consequences."

"Tough love."

Adam picked up the Stetson he'd placed on a neighboring chair and examined the brim. "At this point in his life, Sheila, it's the only kind he understands."

They walked toward the doorway at the back of the room.

"He's sixteen," Adam pointed out. "The records of all this will be sealed, and they'll stay that way if he keeps his nose clean. At seventeen, he'll have an open file as a juvenile offender. In twenty or thirty years, it won't matter, but in the near term it could keep him from getting a job—at least, a decent one."

Adam held the door and followed her into the hallway. People were milling around, all with somber countenances. The courthouse wasn't a carefree place.

"Do you think I'm doing this to punish Kerry?"

"Of course not," Sheila assured him, "and hopefully someday she'll come to understand that. In the meantime, Brian needs a positive male influence in his life, someone who can guide him on the confusing journey to becoming a man."

Adam laughed sardonically. "Right now, I'd say he hates my guts."

"ARE YOU up to a leisurely horseback ride?" Adam asked after lunch. Michael had taken Brian to school and would pick him up after class. "We need to talk."

Sheila knew this conversation was coming, that it was overdue. He'd made a few general allusions to her report, but they'd silently conspired to avoid discussing its details. They'd brought enough other baggage with them. Emotions. Wants. Needs. They'd spent their time exploring those, while this critical piece of luggage sat in the corner, waiting to be opened.

His eyes were dull gray now, giving nothing away. But the cool facade didn't fool her. Beneath the controlled exterior lay lingering anger and hurt pride.

She nodded. ''Yes, we do.''

It was one of those idyllic days when the breeze was so gentle it caressed the skin with the delicate, fragrant scents of budding wildflowers. The air itself felt alive and happy in the warm rays of brilliant sunlight. Adam and Sheila walked their horses at a comfortable pace, not following any roads or recognizable paths. The silence between them was punctuated by the muffled clop of horses' hooves on grassy earth and the occasional chirping of birds.

''I still don't understand how you could make the recommendations you did, Sheila. You grew up on a ranch. You've toured this one with me.''

''Adam, please remember I'm on your side, but let's face facts—''

''Facts?'' he snapped. ''The fact I see is that if your suggestions are implemented, this ranch will be ruined.''

''You're exaggerating.''

''Am I?'' He glared over at her, then looked straight ahead to collect his wits. ''You want to discontinue cloud seeding in the middle of a drouth.''

''If cloud seeding worked,'' she reminded him, ''there wouldn't be a drought.''

"Very slick, Sheila. Is that the kind of stupid logic—" He caught himself, and closed his eyes in a silent prayer for patience. "We have a drouth because rain clouds have not come our way. The point of seeding is to get the ones that do pass through to drop their moisture on us, not just blow over."

"I know what cloud seeding is all about, Adam," she retorted with annoyance.

"Do you? Then you're a hypocrite for proposing it be discontinued."

The lethal jab had her chin jutting up. "The problem," she countered evenly, determined to remain professional, "is you can't prove its effectiveness. We've been over this before, Adam."

She'd hoped she could make him understand where she was going and why. "I told you I'm on your side and I am. If I were evaluating this operation for you alone, I'd advise continuing what you're doing. It's your money. Spend it as you deem fit. But it's not your operation any longer, Adam. As much as I wish it were, it's not. Other people have the final word now and those people want change."

"To prove they're in charge."

"It's an ugly truth, but truth nevertheless."

He took in a chestful of air and forced it out through his nose. "So instead of helping me continue to do what you admit is right, you're giving them what they want. So much for honesty and being on my side."

His bitter words sliced into her like a sharp blade. Speechless, she felt them twist inside her, making her heart ache. This proud leader who had never had to answer to anyone but his own conscience was now being put in a position of subordination.

"You said once that I'm an idealist. I wish it were

true." She softened her voice. "I'm a realist, Adam." Getting no response, she added, "And if you want to survive, you damn well better become one, too."

For a moment he almost wanted to laugh, but at whom, at what? She had her version of reality; he had his. He turned to study her. The distress he saw tightening her features tore at him.

They plodded along in silence for several minutes. He pointed with a leather-gloved finger to a roadrunner streaking across their path.

"You've seen what the vaqueros do," he finally said. "I don't have to tell you it's not a forty-hour, Monday-through-Friday job. It's seven days a week at all hours of the day or night."

She was tempted to remind him that salaried people frequently worked long, irregular hours, too, but realized it couldn't compete in his world with slogging, physical labor.

He led her up a rugged incline, the eroded remnant perhaps of an ancient butte. At the crest Adam paused and peered out over the pale-green plain that stretched before them. Tiny fossils and seashell encrusted in the rocks around them attested to the fact that a million or so years ago this land had been underwater.

"They birth cattle, sheep and goats," Adam continued, referring to his ranch hands, "and take responsibility for the well-being of thousands of head of livestock. They do carpentry, plumbing, vehicle maintenance and string miles and miles of fence every year. They fix windmills, rain or shine."

She didn't need his preaching or his explanation of what ranchers do. Her father had climbed windmills, trimmed horses' hooves, mended fences, repaired the family washing machine and reshingled the roof. It was a full life. Part of the appeal and the challenge was that no two days were ever the same.

"You think they get a bargain in not paying rent for the houses they live in," Adam went on. "That they're pampered because they drive around in air-conditioned vehicles with CD players."

He was doing a good job of putting a guilt trip on her by parroting selected words and phrases she'd used in her report. Shame put her on the offensive, when what she sought was conciliation. "I didn't say they were pampered."

He neck-reined his horse to the south. "You call yourself a realist. Let's consider the real impact if these proposals of yours are implemented."

They came up to a fence and followed it on their right to a gate. Leaning over in the saddle, he unlatched it; his horse nudged it open and proceeded through. Sheila followed and Adam again secured it without dismounting.

"If you want to take away the vaqueros' perks," he stated, "you'll have to relieve them of some of the chores those *luxuries* pay for."

He headed toward a distant conical hill. Sheila stayed by his side. "Perks are gratuitous," she pointed out, "not payment for specific services."

He ignored her. "We can hire veterinarians to birth our livestock," he offered. "Shall we put a licensed vet on the payroll? It'll take more than one or two, you know. Closer to ten considering the size of the herds we have. I don't think they'll work for thirty or forty grand a year, do you?"

She heaved a sigh of exasperation. "Probably not."

"So let's round it off at half a million dollars in extra payroll expenses. Contracting out for fence repair and replacement seems feasible,'' he speculated, as if he were actually considering it. "Do you suppose it'll be cheaper and easier to schedule than having my men do it as opportunity permits?"

The sarcasm was thinly veiled but unmistakable. She shot him a killer look, but it didn't seem to slow him down.

"Shall we call out a well-maintenance company every time a windmill goes clunk or a pump motor freezes up?" The question was rhetorical, since he didn't give her a chance to answer. "You're talking about a couple hundred dollars in service fees to change a belt that costs fifty bucks. How timely do you think repairs will be when the guy from town has a hundred-mile round trip? And what about the cattle those wells support?"

He paused and looked over at her this time, giving her an opportunity to respond. When she didn't, he went blithely on.

"Then there are the animals themselves. What do you propose? That we move whole herds to other pastures while we wait for repairs to be scheduled and performed? How? By horseback, or do we contract for large semis and pay for the additional fuel and time?"

They skirted the east side of the cone. Only then did Sheila recognize the ridge behind it. She knew where she was and where he was taking her.

"Some of those things can be done," he told her. "In fact, some of them are being done right now on a piecemeal basis."

She found her tongue. "Such as?"

"We have a vet—more than one, actually—on retainer for emergencies, but we don't call him out every time a horse needs a tetanus shot. He instructs our ranch hands on procedures, gives them the vaccine and they administer the injections. The vet also does the artificial insemination on our horses since they're in manageable numbers and are more high value.''

"Makes sense."

"I thought so," he commented smugly. "We occasionally hire people to build fences, too, when our own people are backlogged and we need the work done immediately. But it's the exception rather than the rule, plus it's an added expense. Same goes for windmills and pumps.''

She drew a deep breath. "Are you finished?"

"Not quite."

They arrived at the top of the hill overlooking the home place. The hidden valley below was lush compared with the sparsely vegetated prairie they'd crossed. What a paradise this oasis must have been for the settlers who made it this far 180 years ago.

Adam led the way down the steep slope to the grove of ancient trees and the still-flowing stream that made the difference between life and death in this rugged yet delicate land. They dismounted not far from the old ranch house and dropped the reins, knowing the horses wouldn't stray far.

"The biggest thing you're missing, though, is the pride and spirit of teamwork my people have in the Number One.'' He guided her through the woods encircling the house. His tone was less strident now but no less forceful. "Take away what you call the perks and luxuries the vaqueros get,'' he said, "and you'll turn this into a union operation where three people are needed to change a lightbulb—a mechanic to open the casement, an electrician to replace the bulb and a supervisor to watch them do it. That'll destroy this ranch, Sheila. I know it and you know it.''

A part of her conceded he was right. "That was a nice little speech you just gave, Adam.''

There was hesitation in his smile. He didn't seem to know whether to thank her or be on guard. Choosing the latter, he remained silent.

"Here's mine," she said. "While everything you've mentioned is true, it doesn't change the fact that you'll have to adjust the way the Number One does business if you want to stay in charge.''

"If I make the changes they want, I won't really be in charge, though, will I?''

"Now, who's being slick with words?" She shot a scathing smirk at him. "You said the one constant in our lives is that we make mistakes. Well, maybe I've made a few in my report, but with the kind of arrogance you've just demonstrated, you're committing an even bigger blunder, because you have more to lose.''

It was a calculated slap to his ego. She only wished she could feel some sort of satisfaction in watching the smug expression slide off his face.

"The bank's in charge, Adam," she reminded him. "They'll change things with or without you.''

"Regardless of right and wrong.'' He didn't seem to know if he was asking a question or answering one.

She could see the urge to violence in his granite eyes, in the set of his jaw and the tightening of his fists. She also saw the ache of helplessness against a power he couldn't control.

He paced back and forth. "When is your final report due?''

"In another week.''

"Then you have time to correct the record."

In other words, the ball was in her court.

ADAM BEGAN to question his own wisdom in inviting Sheila to spend another day with him. Their lovemaking the night before made him want her now more than ever, but Brian's presence in the house meant they wouldn't be sharing the same bed tonight.

The first serious confrontation with his grandson came the next morning. Adam and Sheila were at the kitchen table, working on their second cup of coffee, having already eaten their breakfast with the first.

"How's Brian going to catch the school bus?" Sheila asked. "We're several miles from the nearest gate." She grinned sardonically. "Surely you won't make him walk."

"I explained to him that having his license suspended means he can't drive on public roads. He can still drive on the ranch. It's private property."

Brian dragged himself, sleepy eyed, into the kitchen at 7:00, after Elva had called him twice. He was already running fifteen minutes late. Typical, Adam thought. Of his five children Gideon alone had been a morning person. But then, Gideon was perpetually "up"—until he collapsed. Then he crashed, totally and completely.

Wordlessly, Brian navigated to the key rack by the mudroom door and grabbed the keys to the new Dodge four-by-four.

"Take the F150," Adam told him over the rim of his coffee mug.

Brian spun around, ready to fight. "That old Ford? It's all rusty and dirty and smells like sh—"

Adam brought his fist down on the table, rattling

mugs, before his grandson had a chance to finish the word. Caught off guard, Sheila jumped. Elva continued to wash dishes, undisturbed by the outburst.

"Watch your language, young man. There are ladies present." He glowered at the insolent youth across the room. "As for the truck's being dirty and smelly, you're absolutely right. So when you come home from school this afternoon, I want you to wash it and clean it out."

"Have one of the hands do it," Brian muttered.

Adam raised his brows and narrowed his eyes. "You are one of the hands." He gave the news a moment to sink in. "And let's get something straight right now, boy. You don't give me orders. If you live to be a hundred, you'll never give me orders." He unclenched his fists and flattened his palms, fingers splayed, on either side of his coffee cup. "Is that clear?"

"Yeah."

"I didn't hear you." Adam's voice went up a notch.

"I said yes," Brian answered back.

"Yes what?"

The boy tensed, paused, considered. "Yes, *sir*," he snarled.

Adam studied him hard. "That's a little better. For now. Next time we'll work on your attitude." His glare didn't waver as he let the words sink in. "I'll inspect the truck before supper." He took a sip of coffee, then added almost casually, "And Brian, if it isn't done right, you'll do it again—before you eat. Is that clear?"

Tight-lipped, the boy managed a grudging nod.

"Now, sit down and eat your breakfast."

Brian took a seat between his grandfather and Sheila. Elva placed a bowl of Cap'n Crunch in front of him.

He pushed the cereal away. "I don't want this crap."

Elva's mouth fell open. She dropped her hands to

her sides, clearly baffled. "I asked your mother and she told me it was your favorite."

"Fine." Adam rose briskly from his chair and before his grandson could reconsider, he picked up the bowl and dumped its contents in the garbage can at the end of the counter. "Now, go get your books."

Brian stared at him, stunned that someone would actually let him go hungry. Sensing no retreat on the part of his grandfather, he looked at Sheila, but she denied him eye contact as she sipped her coffee. Clearly, she wasn't going to intercede for him. With a huff, he stomped out of the room.

"I'm sorry, Elva," Adam said. "I'll have him apologize later."

"It's all right. He's just upset."

"No, it's not all right. And he's going to be a lot more upset before this day's out."

Brian returned with his backpack.

"Do you have money for lunch?" his grandfather asked.

"Yeah."

Adam eyed him critically, waiting.

"Yes, sir."

"How much?"

"Enough," the boy answered flippantly, and moved toward the door.

Adam marginally lowered his head, pursed his lips and sucked in his cheeks. Slowly he said, "I asked you how much."

Brian half turned. "Enough for lunch, okay?"

Adam said in a very patient voice, "I'll ask you one more time, Brian. How much money do you have with you?"

Anger and rebellion streaked across the young man's

smooth face. He hesitated before finally answering. "Maybe fifty bucks."

"Give it to me." The order was issued in a level voice, but there was no hope of compromise in it.

"What the hell for? It's my money."

Adam extended his hand. "Fork it over."

Sitting at the table, her fingers bracketing her coffee mug, Sheila watched the power struggle between the two males. Elva, back at the sink, also observed the exchange. Brian glanced from one woman to the other. His face reddened and with his jaw clamped shut, he reached behind him and pulled his wallet out of his left hip pocket.

Adam relieved him of it, squeezed its two halves, went into the bill compartment and removed the cash. "How much is lunch?"

"A buck and a half." The teenager's voice was taut, seething.

After removing two dollars from the wad of bills, Adam put them in the wallet and returned it to his grandson.

Brian jammed it back in his pocket. "What about the rest of my money?"

"Don't worry. It'll be safe. I won't steal it."

Blood boiling, Brian spun on his heel and stomped through the mudroom and out the door.

Adam watched him go, stepped over to the key rack and returned to the middle of the room.

The back door flew open and Brian returned.

Grinning, his grandfather asked lightly, "Forget something?"

The boy glared. "Uh...the..."

"Here you go." Adam tossed him the Ford keys.

With unconscious grace, Brian snatched them out of the air.

"Have a good day," Adam said as the boy did an about-face and stormed out. The window in the kitchen door rattled when it slammed.

"I'm glad he didn't break the glass," Adam remarked to Sheila as he sat again at the table across from her. "Cleaning it up would have made him miss the bus, and then I would have had to drive him to school myself."

Sheila's expression didn't quite hide a smile. "Now, that would really make his day. Icing on the cake, so to speak."

They heard the truck crank for several seconds and finally start up. Its wheels spun on the gravel as it pulled away.

Grinning, Adam sipped coffee. "Hmm. Cold."

He rose and went over to the sink, poured the dregs down the drain and refilled the mug at the coffeemaker. Before sitting, he pulled out the wad of paper money he'd slipped into his pocket and deposited it on the table. He resumed his seat and counted it out. One hundred twelve dollars.

"Why so much?" Sheila asked, baffled. "You don't think…" She didn't want to finish the sentence.

"Drugs?" Adam's forehead was wrinkled with alarm. "God, I hope not. Michael assures me he's clean, thinks drugs are for losers. I hope he's right."

"What else were you looking for in his wallet?" Sheila inquired. "I saw you examining it."

Sharp lady, he thought. "Condoms. I'm wondering if he's sexually active. Having them doesn't necessarily mean he is." He exhaled dispiritedly. "Unfortunately, not having them doesn't mean he isn't, either."

"You don't want him to repeat his mother's transgressions," Sheila offered.

The observation rattled him. "You think I was wrong in the way I dealt with the situation with her, don't you?"

Sheila shook her head. "I wasn't there, Adam. I don't know. I'm certainly not going to pass judgment."

"The truth is, I screwed it up royally. If I hadn't, Kerry wouldn't hate me, and she wouldn't have stolen the single *possession* that's ever mattered to me—this ranch." He got up from the table and carried his mug to the sink. It was still hot; he poured it out anyway. "I failed Kerry, but by God, I'll do better with Brian. Maybe then she'll understand I never meant to hurt her. I'll give her back a son she can be proud of, even if she can never be proud of me."

He'd said too much, revealed a part of his soul he never meant for anyone to see. Sheila looked at him with compassion in her eyes. Or was it pity? He put his empty mug on the counter and walked out of the room.

CHAPTER EIGHT

"ARE YOU COMING with us to the rodeo?" Davy asked Sheila at dinner that evening.

Michael, Clare, their son and three girls were there. Even Gideon and Julie showed up to lend Brian moral support and a sense of family. The teenager was morose, displayed no signs of gratitude and didn't even respond to his younger uncle's teasing banter. Coming to the table late because he had to wash the truck twice might have contributed to his low morale, as well.

"Rodeo?" Sheila asked.

Adam brought his attention back to the woman sitting halfway down the table on his left. Tonight they'd sleep separately, alone. Again. He wouldn't make love to her in the middle of the night or wake up with her warm body spooned against his. Tomorrow morning he'd fly her back to Houston, to what he pictured as the very humdrum life of a management consultant. Was she looking forward to it? She claimed to enjoy her work, to find it challenging and fulfilling. All he knew was that his house wouldn't feel the same without her in it. Even if she did sleep in a different room, in a different bed.

"The Coyote Springs Stock Show and Rodeo is in two weeks," Michael explained.

"We've entered several of our horses," Gideon added. "You ought to join us."

"Please do." Clare passed the bowl of mashed potatoes to her husband. "If you've never been to one, you're in for a treat."

For a fleeting moment, Sheila had a faraway look on her face. "It's been years since I was at a rodeo," she admitted.

"It runs the twenty-second through the twenty-sixth," Adam informed her. He'd planned on inviting her himself later that evening. "Why don't you join us. Our racing horses didn't particularly impress you. Maybe our cutting stock will."

"I was impressed, Adam," she insisted.

"Good," he commented around a bite of roll. "Then let me impress you again."

A telling smile passed between Gideon and his sister.

"I have other work to do, too, Adam," she reminded him. "My desk will be buried under paperwork."

He took a perverse satisfaction in the note of regret he heard in her statement. He'd seen the way she'd taken to country life. She'd told him all about growing up on her father's ranch, about how she'd loved the land, the hard work, the sense of belonging. She'd talked about her father, but she'd been revealing herself, too. Losing their ranch had broken her heart every bit as much as it had broken her father's.

Adam couldn't give back her lost heritage, but maybe he could give her something to replace it. The past was history. The future lay before them, a future, he realized, he wanted them to share.

He grinned wryly. "You've got two whole weeks to attend to all that stuff." And her final report will have been submitted. "Besides, I am your most important project, aren't I?"

Smiling at him, she answered, ''Well, my biggest, anyway.''

He chuckled. He enjoyed word games with her. ''Big. Important. As far as Texans were concerned, it amounts to the same thing.''

She scanned the people sitting around the table. ''Are any of you competing?''

''Not me,'' Michael replied neutrally. ''Not this year.''

''Stu was the rider,'' Clare contributed, referring to her late brother-in-law. ''How that kid could ride!''

Adam's buoyant mood plummeted at the mention of his youngest son. Twenty-one when he died, a grown-up with an almost childlike zest for life. He'd always be a kid now.

Adam scooped up some of Elva's squash casserole with his fork but didn't bring it to his mouth.

''An absolute natural on a horse,'' Clare told Sheila. ''When he was mounted, you couldn't tell where the animal left off and the man began.''

''He took first place in cutting three years in a row,'' Julie pointed out.

''That's because the horse did all the work,'' Gideon jeered good-naturedly, but the huskiness in his voice made the quip fall flat. Suddenly everyone seemed uncomfortable.

Sheila nudged Davy. ''Would you pass the okra, please. So who's riding this year?'' she inquired of the group at large.

Davy struggled with the serving bowl that was as close to Sheila as it was to him. ''Emilio says he's going to try bull riding this year.''

Clare managed a chortle. ''The poor bull.''

Emilio weighed at least three hundred pounds.

Knives and forks resumed their syncopated cadence as they cut into crusty chicken-fried steaks.

"It'll take a ball and tackle to get him on board," Michael agreed. "I don't remember that in the rule book."

"Actually," Adam told Sheila with a grateful grin, "Gideon's riding three of our best cutting horses, and Julie's entered in the barrel races."

Sheila's face brightened. She looked around the table. Finally settling on Adam, she asked, "What are those dates?"

"IT SEEMS you're in a pickle no matter which way you approach the problem," Mildred Pounder said as she poured tea from a delicately flowered pot into matching cups.

"Precisely." Sheila sat at the kitchen table in her aunt's patio home in a pleasant retirement community. "If I let the conclusions of my preliminary report stand, I'm doing Adam a disservice. If I amend my report rather than simply flesh it out as is expected, I come across as weak and ambivalent."

Mildred mulled the situation over for a minute while she placed butter cookies on a small plate and set it between them. "Are there errors in your initial assessment?"

Sheila shook her head. "The facts are correct."

"Has new information come to light, then?" the older woman asked. "Maybe something Adam or the bank left out, something you weren't aware of?"

Sheila blew across the top of her uplifted cup. "I'd love to say yes, but the factual aspects of the report are accurate. What I'm taking another look at is my interpretation of them."

"Why?" Mildred peered at her with keen brown eyes. "Because you disagree with the conclusions you drew, or because you don't like the consequences of those conclusions?"

Mildred had a knack for putting things in a nutshell.

"I wish I knew," Sheila replied despondently. "From a short-term economic point of view, I'm sure my recommendations are valid. They'll improve the immediate profitability of the operation."

"Which is what the bank wants," her aunt reminded her, "what you were hired to do."

"Yes, but in the long term, Adam is right. They'll alter the essential character of the ranch."

"Is that in the best interest of the bank?"

Sheila sighed. "That's a matter of opinion. From the people perspective, I don't think so. From the purely corporate view..." She shrugged.

"I guess the question then is which is more important—people or the institutions they form."

"How can you separate them?" Sheila asked in frustration.

Her aunt tilted her head philosophically. "Damned if I know."

The admission brought a smile to Sheila's lips.

"I gather your involvement with Adam has gone past the realm of platonic admiration," Mildred commented.

Sheila's head shot up. "Am I that obvious?"

"Only to me." She patted her niece's hand. "There's a certain glow in your eyes when you mention his name. If you didn't care about him, I don't think you would be having this problem."

"So it's him and not the situation that's driving me to rethink this," Sheila concluded.

"That doesn't mean your rethinking it is wrong. It's not just Adam First you care about. It's trying to save a rancher from losing control. Like your father did."

"Adam isn't my father," Sheila said sharply.

Mildred grinned. "No. But he is a rancher who's in danger of losing what's left of his ranch."

"I wish Bill were here," Sheila blurted out. "He'd know how I should handle this."

"If he were here, you wouldn't have the problem."

Sheila chuckled. "You're right, of course. Funny that I should think of asking my husband how to deal with my lover."

Mildred didn't respond, but her expression didn't show disapproval, only an acknowledgment of the irony. "Would it be possible for you to let Jonas work this problem? He might be a little more objective."

"I considered that—just dumping the whole thing in his lap. But under the circumstances, he doesn't have the time—or, I'm afraid, the energy—to put into this. If we were to get a continuing contract with Homestead, he'd be the logical one to head the project, but I couldn't possibly ask him to be away from Catherine for weeks on end."

"No. Of course not," Mildred conceded. "Is he aware of your dilemma?"

"I haven't discussed it with him. He's got enough on his plate without worrying about this."

"What will you do?" Mildred finally asked.

"I don't know."

IT WAS THE END OF MARCH. The wind blew at near gale-force intensity, scattering trash from uncovered containers, lifting untethered hats off heads and bringing tears to squinting eyes. Fortunately, the competitions were inside a covered arena.

The Coyote Springs Stock Show and Rodeo was on the circuit leading to the big competition in Fort Worth the following month. It had it all: barrel racing, cutting-horse competitions and a rodeo, complete with bull and bronco riding. There was even a carnival along the river. Schools and businesses closed down on the day of the rodeo parade, when horses, wagons, floats and marching bands wended their way through the center of the city. A contingent of modern-day "Buffalo Soldiers" from Fort Concho in San Angelo, the black cavalry troops who had protected this frontier territory for nearly two decades after the Civil War, passed proudly in review, wearing dark-blue, nineteenth-century wool army uniforms. Since rodeo day was the one day of the year when the clear blue skies of West Texas inevitably failed, they might have been the only participants dressed comfortably. The bare-legged cheerleaders and baton twirlers certainly weren't.

Still, there were friendly smiles all around, from spectators and ticket takers at the fairgrounds to the mariachis in restaurants who sang and strummed songs ranging from the traditional "La Cucaracha" to the latest rock hit.

Adam had offered to fly to Houston to pick up Sheila on Tuesday, but she had a business meeting scheduled in Austin Monday and chose to stay overnight and drive from there.

For Sheila, walking into the ranch headquarters, being greeted familiarly by the housekeeper, going up to her regular guest room, was like coming home. A strange contentment, made uncomfortable by awareness that she had no right to feel happy in this place with these people. With this man, who met her with a kiss on the cheek that promised more.

Misgivings were quickly forgotten, however, when she and Adam strolled the show grounds Wednesday afternoon.

He touched her arm and with a smile directed her attention to a laughing child being swung between a young man and woman.

"Oh, isn't she darling!" Sheila exclaimed at the face paint on the little girl, who resembled a precocious kitten with whiskers and freckles.

Adam held her hand as they wandered among stands of handcrafted silver-and-turquoise jewelry. His tall frame beside her, the affection in his voice as they discussed individual pieces and the warmth of his fingers on her skin when he clasped a necklace she'd particularly admired behind her neck conspired to make her feel like a woman being courted, a woman desired and cherished.

At last they went inside. The conflicting aromas of cotton candy, ranch animals, corn and chili dogs and crispy fried pork rinds, called *chicirones,* assailed their nostrils. Adam found his son and daughter-in-law seated with their children in their regular box near the center of the sandy arena.

"Where's Brian?" Adam asked.

"Went with Gideon, Lupe and her kids," Michael responded absentmindedly. "He seems to have taken a sudden interest in cutting horses."

"Oh?" Adam chuckled. "What's her name?"

Michael shrugged with a grin. "Haven't got a clue."

"Or maybe it's just a better option than putting up with me," Adam muttered to Sheila.

She tightened her fingers around his and gave him a

reassuring smile. "Don't let it bother you, Grampa. The boy needs a big brother right now, too."

He snickered. "Probably a lot more than a preachy old grandfather."

"Gideon fills the role very well. You can be proud of him."

Mildly embarrassed by the compliment, Adam craned his neck to see who was "on deck" for the next ride.

The announcer's voice squawked over the public-address system, identifying riders, their mounts and the names of the ranches they represented. Julie was entered in barrel racing.

The horn sounded, and Julie's brown-and-white paint bolted out of the gate and charged into the arena, where three fifty-five-gallon oil drums had been set in a triangle. Bosco charged toward the barrel on the right, circled it from the right, crossed diagonally to the one on the left, careered around it from the left, then dashed to the third and circled it from the left, as well.

Julie was bent forward on the galloping horse, her legs urging the eager animal on, her butt suspended above the saddle. The competitors completed the cloverleaf pattern at breakneck speed, then charged once more through the gate. The horn blew again as they tripped the electronic timer. The entire ride had taken less than twenty seconds.

"Whew!" Sheila slumped against the back of the seat. "Just watching is exhausting."

"But exciting, too," Adam commented as he winked at her.

Grinning, she agreed, "Yes, exciting, too."

She turned her head, catching his profile. He was checking things out at the in-gate, but she knew he was aware of her watching him. "Exciting being here with you," she murmured.

He swiveled his head toward her, a smile just short of a leer playing on his lips. He fumbled to wrap her fingers in his. Leaning toward her so his words didn't carry beyond her ear, he whispered, "The feeling is mutual."

There was a conspiratorial awareness radiating between them as they observed the rest of the competitions.

"Anybody thirsty?" Adam asked when they took a break between events.

"Me," the girls chorused as one.

Sheila went with him to carry back orders that had grown from soft drinks to include potato chips, popcorn, a bean burrito and one hot dog with mustard.

"People won't want dinner tonight," Adam commented.

Sheila clucked. "They might if they get a chance to brush their teeth after they throw up."

He laughed. "Ugh. Nasty thought." With one hand pressed to the small of her back, he ushered her through the noisy crowd.

She became momentarily serious as they approached the concession stand. "They are putting away an awful lot of junk food, Adam."

"What are you talking about? Hot dogs and burritos are honored institutions. Besides, one day a year won't hurt them. Even if they do throw up."

Since it was intermission, everyone at the event went for refreshments at the same time, so it was a while before they finally resumed their seats. The hot dog had cooled by then, but Michael didn't seem to mind. He consumed it in three healthy—or unhealthy—bites.

"Cutting's about to start," Clare told them.

Gideon was the first rider up, the pacesetter.

A couple dozen head of cattle occupied the arena, now cleared of barrels. The young stock, loosely gathered in a rough circle, milled around at one end of the wide enclosure. The chute at the far end opened and a cowboy wearing jeans, a striped blue-and-green long-sleeved shirt and black cowboy hat walked his horse out. His leather-shrouded stirrups hung long, the reins slack. Gideon, tall and slender, nudged the mount calmly forward.

Pewter moved among the cattle. They split into two factions, then re-formed into a single unit. At the other end of the arena, three horsemen waited, prepared to crowd them into a compact group. Wandering around in no apparent hurry, Gideon and his cutting horse isolated three cows. As the heifers rushed to rejoin the others, the horse stepped in front of one.

Then began the choreography. As the lone cow darted to one side, Pewter pranced, obstructing her path. She changed course. The horse shifted on his hindquarters and dropped his forelegs in the animal's path. The cow bolted once more for freedom; the horse pivoted and cut her off. Frantic now, the cow made a mad leap in the other direction and was foiled yet again by the dancing horse. Thrust and parry, the duel went on. The cow would charge; the horse would block. Every strike for freedom was met with a counterblow. Finally, defeated, the cow hung her head and turned away from her prancing tormentor.

Gideon culled a second heifer and repeated the process. He was working a third when the whistle blew. Check and mate. Gideon garnered eighty-six points.

"It always amazes me," Sheila commented to

Adam, who seemed unwilling to let go of her hand. "The horses are so graceful. It's like watching a ballet. How much of it is horse and how much rider?"

"Probably seventy-five twenty-five."

"How do you ever train a horse to do that?"

"They know it instinctively," Adam explained. "Like pointers pointing. Good training capitalizes on it, draws it out. A good rider guides the horse, but basically gives it its head."

"I still marvel at it."

Adam rubbed his thumb across the back of her knuckles. "Me, too."

They watched for over two hours as cowboys let their cutting horses have their heads to do what they did best. Points were noted and announced, the team of horse and rider garnering the most being declared the winner. First horses won every class in which they competed.

"Awesome," Brian was admiring the marble-and-shiny-brass trophy Gideon had earned, when Adam and Sheila joined them in the barn after the last round.

"You're not too old to learn," his uncle told him.

Brian's eyes widened at the unexpected comment. Adam smothered a chuckle. Like all teenagers, Brian apparently had never considered the possibility that he might be too old to do something. In fact, rodeo competitors usually started practicing at half his age.

"You think?" he asked, sounding both doubtful and hopeful at the same time.

"I think." Gideon laughed and pulled a punch to his shoulder. "We'll start next weekend."

"Cool."

While Gideon enlisted his willing nephew in gathering his gear and checking the horses' feet, Adam and Sheila turned back toward the arena.

"Brian's mellowed," Sheila commented as they walked past stalls of tired horses, some of them munching contentedly at cribs of hay and grain, others dozing on their feet. The smells were warm, pleasant and familiar.

Adam nodded. "He'll be all right. I can't remember being sixteen exactly. At least, I don't recall it being so tough. Kids have too many choices these days and not enough rules to help make them."

They gathered their belongings and started moving out of the box. Adam looked around. "Where's Michael?"

"He went to get the car," Clare explained. "He thought if we left right away we might beat the crowd."

It was four o'clock. There were other events but none that First people were participating in.

Adam turned to the broad exit and observed a number of cars inching through the parking lot. "I suspect he's already too late."

Beth Ann bounced along with Sheila and Adam, each of them holding one of her hands. They laughed in their grandparent roles as they swung the child between them. Kristin and Sally were with their mother a few steps ahead as they all made their way down the wide aisle to the main entrance of the indoor arena. The excitement of the day still bubbled in them as they chattered about horses and bulls and riders. Julie, Gideon and Brian were already in the parking lot, talking animatedly about something, when they reached it. Michael had not yet appeared with the minibus.

Sally looked up at her grandfather. "Gramps, can I learn how to ride broncos?"

Brian scoffed. "Girls don't ride buckin' horses."

Gideon poked his shoulder. "Hey, they can try anything they want to. I know some pretty good lady bronc riders."

Sally ignored the exchange. She gazed at her grandfather. "Can I?"

Sheila could see he was torn. He wanted so much to please his granddaughter, but the decision was not his to make.

"That's up to your mom and dad, honey. Let's wait and see."

Michael pulled up in the van. Sally repeated her question after they climbed in. Her parents pointed out the dangers, but they didn't say no. Sally seemed content for the time being. Sheila admired the girl's wisdom in not pushing too hard.

Adam, sitting in the front seat, peered out the window at the slate-gray sky. "We might be in for a gully-washer. Let's go home."

There were two days a year that Coyote Springs could lay claim to genuine traffic jams. One was on the Fourth of July, when most of the town crawled along Prairie Dog Lane on its journey back from the lake after the gargantuan fireworks display there. The other was to and from the city arena on rodeo day.

It took Michael nearly twenty minutes to get out of the parking lot. Every so often, huge raindrops would splat against the windshield.

"Hmm. Looks like a twelve-inch rainfall," he commented wryly as he finally turned right onto the two-lane road that would take them west. "Twelve inches between each drop."

A quarter mile farther and they were on the highway headed south to the ranch. Michael accelerated to cruising speed. A sharp gust of wind caught him broadside and practically pushed him into the lane of oncoming traffic. He corrected competently and leaned forward to examine the ever-darkening sky. "I have a feeling this'll get worse before it gets better."

"Must be the tropical storm that was brewing in the Gulf," Clare commented. "The weather bureau said it might move inland. We can certainly use the rain."

"I don't begrudge West Texas its much-needed precipitation," Sheila declared, trying to sound casual about it. "I just wish it didn't have to come all at once."

She wasn't the only one gazing out the windows now. All the cars and trucks on the road had their headlights on. Slate gray had metamorphosed to black marble, except the variegated streaks weren't stationary. They twisted and tightened into ominous fists that hurled jagged bolts of lightning to the ground ahead of them.

Michael slowed and negotiated cautiously onto a side road. In a mile or so, the pavement ended. Rain, now mixed with pea-sized hail, pounded the windshield in blasting sheets that limited visibility dangerously. Chalky white caliche made excellent roadbed substrata and compacted into a hard, stable surface when dry. Wet, however, it became slick goo.

Sheila had confidence in Michael's driving ability, and certainly no one else in the vehicle manifested concern with the savagery of the storm, but she couldn't keep herself from asking, "Shouldn't we stop and wait this out?"

Adam, still studying the cloud formation through the

windshield, commented, "This might last awhile, and we'll be safer and more comfortable at home." He turned, a ready smile on his face, but it froze when he saw the paleness of her skin, the anxiety in her eyes.

"Besides," Michael added, "we've only got a few miles to go."

A streak of lightning flashed off to their left. Sheila jumped. Thunder cracked a split second later.

"Are you all right?" Adam asked with concern.

She pasted on a smile. "Ooh, that was close."

Sally, sitting next to Sheila, pressed herself into her side. Strangely, the child's sudden anxiety lessened her own.

She stroked Sally's back. "You know, when I was a little girl and we had thunderstorms, my mother always told me it was the angels moving furniture."

Gideon snorted. "I think one of them just dropped the piano."

Everyone laughed, and Sheila felt a little more of the tension ebb away. She was with...she wanted to say family...with friends. With Adam. Safe, in spite of the howling wind, the driving rain, the flash and boom of the storm.

It seemed to take forever before they turned in at the gate. The land looked bleak, eerie, a gothic moor drenched in silver and purply black. The high-profile van rocked like a horse-drawn coach as it whined its way up the steep slope to the dark house silhouetted against an even darker sky at the top of the mesa.

The rain hadn't let up. In the short distance between the vehicle and back door of the house they all got thoroughly wet. Elva met them with fluffy towels to dry their heads.

Amid the stomping feet in the mudroom, Adam asked his housekeeper if everything was all right.

"Lights flickered a few times."

He wasn't surprised. They were on public utilities. Interrupted service wasn't unusual in heavy storms.

"I'll check the auxiliary generator," Michael volunteered. "Fire ants crawled into the relay switch last time this happened."

He threw a slicker over his already damp clothes and disappeared out into the shadows.

Adam's cell phone warbled. He moved into a corner to answer it.

Clare and Julie removed the girls' wet outer garments and took the children upstairs to change.

Michael shot back inside, slamming the door behind him. Water streamed from his hooded rain gear and pooled on the tile floor at his feet.

Adam clicked the phone shut. "Dusty Creek's already over its banks. Charlie's worried about the levee above the stables holding. We'll have to move the horses."

"In this rain?" Clare asked. "Won't your trailers get bogged down in the mud?"

"Not if we keep them up on the paved road and bring the horses to them." Adam turned to Brian. "Come on, son. We'll need your help, too."

The boy's face lit up. "Cool. What do you want me to do?"

Within minutes the three men and a boy were all wearing yellow slickers. Sheila went up to Adam and kissed him. "Be careful out there."

Unmindful of the others watching him, he ran a finger down her cheek. "Are you going to be all right here?"

She heard concern in his voice, but she could also see excitement in his eyes. He and his boys were going out to work, to confront the tempest, challenge Mother Nature and defeat her.

"Of course," Sheila assured him, pressing back the fear she knew was unreasonable. "We'll be fine."

He bent down and gave her a peck on the cheek. "See you when I see you."

CHAPTER NINE

SHEILA WATCHED Adam dash out the back door behind the others. They wouldn't be returning for hours, and when they did, they'd be covered in mud, soaked to the bone, probably shivering. Displaying a cut or scrape or two, they'd also be as happy and boisterous as children with new Christmas toys. They'd tease one another about falls in muck, congratulate themselves on their feats of daring-do and narrow misses with disaster, and maybe even award themselves celebratory shots of whiskey—to cut through the cold.

She wouldn't begrudge them. They'd work hard over the next few hours in miserable and dangerous conditions. A kick from a stumbling horse could break a man's leg. A slipping trailer could crush him.

Worrying about what might happen was foolhardy, she told herself. Besides, there was plenty to keep her mind off what was going on outside...and memories of what had once happened. While Clare put Beth Ann to bed and coaxed the other children into pajamas, she, Elva and Julie filled water jugs, checked flashlights for batteries and got out candles in case the power failed and the auxiliary generator didn't kick in.

Lightning strobed as Clare entered the kitchen, washing the room in a blue-white glare. "Can you believe it? Those girls say they're hungry."

Thunder rumbled, then cracked so sharply it shook the house.

Sheila, already tense, dropped the plastic water jugs she was carrying from the pantry to the sink. They made a boinking sound as they skittered across the tile floor. Sheila folded her arms over her chest and went stock-still.

Julie picked up the one that had bounced closest to her. "Aren't you glad they aren't glass?" she teased, apparently unaware of the depth of Sheila's reaction.

But Clare hadn't missed it. She came up beside the older woman. "You okay?"

Sheila let her shoulders sag and gave out a nervous chuckle. "Fine. Just caught me off guard. I'm fine," she repeated. Before Clare could inquire further, Sheila bent and retrieved the other three water jugs. "That's ten gallons, Elva," she called out, trying desperately to sound matter-of-fact. "Do you think that'll tide us over?"

The housekeeper agreed, then asked Clare, the tallest of the four of them, to get down the kerosene lamps she kept stored in one of the overhead cabinets in the laundry room.

The steaks Adam had seasoned that morning and returned to the refrigerator to marinate stayed there. The girls wanted macaroni and cheese. Clare insisted they drink milk with it. The adults opted for hot tea and sandwiches. When the girls showed signs of being scared at the storm's violence, Sheila persuaded them all to sing silly songs.

In two hours everything changed. The wind died down. The rain stopped. The sky cleared, and the men came back. As expected, they were wet, muddy and talkative, but mostly tired.

"Moving them over to the high corral wouldn't have been a problem if that old cottonwood hadn't fallen," Gideon said as he stripped off his poncho.

"Thanks," Adam said. "All of you." He turned to Brian. "You were a great help out there, son. We couldn't have done it without you."

The teenager shrugged nonchalantly, but the pure pride in his modesty spoke volumes about earning self-esteem.

"Go change. The lot of you," Elva ordered. "There're sandwiches, and I can heat up some soup, too."

"Thanks," Michael said, "but I'll just grab a sandwich to eat on the way."

"You're leaving?" Sheila asked.

"I have work in the morning and the girls have school. It'll be easier to go home tonight and get a good night's sleep than spend tomorrow playing catch-up."

"I'm hitting the road, too," Gideon seconded.

"Me, three," Julie chimed in. "Early classes."

"Dad," Michael said, "why don't you let Brian come home with us tonight. The truck he's driving is so light ended, it'll probably get bogged down in mud in the morning. I'll drive him and the girls to the bus in my four-by."

"I can do it," Adam objected.

"You'll be busy with cleanup around here. It's no trouble. I have to drop my kids off anyway."

Adam dared not glance at Sheila. Even if she didn't realize what Michael was up to, he did.

"Take the truck keys with you," he instructed his grandson. "I'll have someone park the Ford at the gate for after school, or one of us will pick you up."

While Michael carried sleeping Beth Ann to the van,

Adam helped Clare gather the other children and their belongings. A few minutes later, when everyone had left, Elva announced she was putting the last load of washed towels in the drier and then would be going to her room. All at once, Adam and Sheila found themselves alone in the big country kitchen.

"Go change into something warm and dry," Sheila urged him. "I'll have soup and sandwiches ready when you return."

"Thanks for all your help," he said as he inched closer.

She screwed up her face in mock annoyance. "I hate to tell you this, Mr. First, but your twenty-four-hour deodorant is in its twenty-fifth hour."

"Don't hold back, Ms. Malone." He balanced her chin on the tip of a finger and touched his lips to hers. "Tell me what you really think."

She laughed. "You stink. Now, go on before you come down with pneumonia."

He moved toward the door and turned around. "I'll be back."

She awarded him a mischievous grin. "I'm counting on it."

The shower should have been a cold one, Adam told himself as he dressed in worn-out jeans and a soft chambray shirt that was tattered at the cuffs and thin at the elbows. No socks, just an old pair of sandals he slipped easily into—and out of. His mind wasn't occupied with the clothes he was putting on but the ones he was fantasizing about taking off.

He descended the staircase and stopped at the door to the kitchen. Sheila was at the stove, stirring soup in a pot. Its tomato-vegetable tang and the aroma of warm bread filled the room with the smells of home, of nostalgia and contentment. Gazing at her slender back, at the rounded line of her hips in faded jeans, incited other thoughts, other emotions, senses that were already on edge, on alert.

"That feels better," he said as he stepped through the doorway.

She spun around like a coiled spring suddenly let loose. The spoon clattered to the floor. Her fist flew to her heart. He could practically see it pounding. Her mouth formed an O before her face relaxed in relief. *What thoughts did I interrupt,* he was tempted to ask.

"Careful." He picked up the spoon. "You didn't burn yourself, did you?"

She shook her head. "I'm all right."

"You seem jittery." His eyes stayed on hers as he deposited the spoon in the sink.

"You startled me," she replied defensively, and took a deep breath. "That's all."

Was it? He studied her more closely. The storm outside had been over for a couple of hours. That wasn't what had her jittery now, at least not solely. When her lashes lifted, he gazed into the blue depths beneath them. There was a different kind of tempest brewing inside her. "Sorry," he said, smiling. "Didn't mean to."

"You must be starved," she insisted. Her cheeks were pink, as though she had been the one out in the wind and rain. "You worked for hours without any dinner."

"Comes with the territory." He watched her tear off a sheet of paper towel from the roll by the sink. She knelt at his feet and swiped the wet spot where the spoon had fallen. Her movements were clumsy, lacking her usual smooth grace. He bent, supported her elbows and helped her up. "The soup smells good."

"I didn't know what kind of sandwich you wanted," she babbled on nervously, gesturing toward the place setting at the table. "I'm heating some rolls in the oven for you." She dropped the soiled towel in the garbage container on her way to the refrigerator, opened the door and peered inside. "There's roast beef, turkey and some tuna salad Elva made for lunch. And steak, of course, if you want to light the grill. Or I can broil one for you. Just tell me what you'd like—"

I'd like you, he almost said.

She stopped abruptly when he reached around her from behind and gathered her at the waist. The warmth of her body, the inviting softness of her breasts brushing his forearms, sent flashes of heat radiating through him.

"You don't have to wait on me," he whispered, and drew in the delicate scent of her hair. Tension lurked just below the surface of his grasp. Not fear, he realized, but anticipation.

Grinning, he spun her around to face him. The shy little-girl expression he glimpsed surprised him and aroused incredible protectiveness. He stroked her cheek. "The storm's over, Sheila." The one outside, at least.

Her eyes watered; she bit her lip, then impulsively coiled her arms around him and pressed her cheek to his chest. Nothing she could have done had the power to make him feel more like a man than this wordless appeal for shelter and security. He drank in her feminine scent and massaged her back, stimulated by her warm closeness, the tremor rippling through her.

"You're safe now," he murmured.

"I know," came her muffled reply. "Just hold me a minute, Adam."

He tightened his embrace. "My pleasure."

They stood alone in the kitchen, arms intertwined, rocking to the unheard rhythms of their heartbeats.

The timer on the stove dinged. She released him and pulled away.

"Why didn't you ever tell me you were afraid of storms?" he asked as she turned back to the open refrigerator door and closed it.

"Who told you?" She wandered to the in-wall oven and selected a hot pad from one of the hooks beside it.

He leaned casually against the neighboring counter, observing her. "No one. I saw it in the van when we were driving home. I didn't want to leave you, but—"

"I was perfectly safe here." Sheila used the pad to remove two kaiser rolls from the oven. She placed them in a shallow napkin-lined wicker basket on the counter nearby.

"I know." He closed the oven door and switched off the dial. "That's the only reason I was able to go. I wanted to stay here and hold you."

The tenderness she saw in his eyes melted the last frosty layers of fear and helplessness. His warmth filled her and made her feel safe.

Sheila delivered the bread to the table in the middle of the room. "It's silly for me to be so afraid of storms," she confessed.

"Or wise." He took his place at the table. "Storms can be dangerous. It's smart to respect them."

She ladled steaming soup into a deep crockery bowl and brought it to the table for him, then sat in the chair opposite him.

"Aren't you eating?" he asked.

She shook her head. "I had something earlier. I'm not really hungry. Go on before it gets cold. I'll keep you company."

He stirred the soup, watching the steam swirl and dissipate. "You said your ranch was hit by a tornado back in '60. Is that why storms bother you?" he asked over the spoon poised above the rim of his bowl.

She nodded, picked up one of the rolls, broke off a piece and took a small bite. "My younger brother and I were running to the house from the main road, where the school bus had dropped us off. It was a dark and stormy day." She chuckled weakly, the humor not reaching her eyes. "It had started to rain." She lowered her head, concentrating on the bread her fingers were tearing into tiny crumbs. "We were making for the storm cellar behind the house when a gust of wind lifted Neil off the ground. I grabbed his foot and for a minute I thought I was going to be carried away with him. The next thing I knew, Neil slammed against the side of the house. He fell on top of me. I couldn't breathe. Suddenly, my father was there. I don't know where he came from. He picked up Neil, asked me if I could walk, then practically dragged me down into the cellar. The twister didn't last long. I wasn't hurt, but Neil was still unconscious. My mother was frantic."

Adam leaned forward in his chair and covered her fluttering hands. "Was he all right?" he asked softly.

"My parents took him in to the hospital in Wichita Falls right away. By then he was awake, but groggy. He never did regain memory of the event. I guess that's pretty common with concussion—you lose the minutes leading up to the trauma."

"But he did recover?"

She gave him a weak smile. "He's alive and well and living with his wife and six kids in Cincinnati."

"Obviously, it affected his brain if he left Texas."

Sheila snickered, this time with genuine humor. "I've told him the same thing."

"Considering the alternatives, he was damn lucky." Adam slurped a spoonful of soup.

She slid back her chair. "I've destroyed half of one of your rolls, and you still haven't told me what kind of sandwich you want."

"This and—" he grinned at her "—what's left of the bread will be fine."

"Do you want more?" She rose and reached for his nearly empty bowl. "There's plenty."

He seized her wrist and captured her eyes with his. "No more soup. No sandwich. No steak." His voice softened with each phrase.

He stood up, laced his fingers with hers and moved around the corner of the table. He liked what he glimpsed in her eyes now, a hint of uncertainty, of wariness, but definitely not fear. Desire. He slipped his other arm behind her waist and pulled her against him. Without another word, he lowered his mouth to hers, skimmed his lips across hers, then captured them with a desperation she quickly matched.

The kiss was long and hard and consuming. When they broke off, she remained cuddled against his chest.

"Brian isn't here tonight," Adam whispered.

Her soft chuckle vibrated through him. "I know," she murmured. She gazed up at him, a silly grin on her face. "But we're not ready yet."

He arched back. "We're not?"

"Nope." She shook her head. "I'll wash. You dry."

He laughed and planted an affectionate kiss in the middle of her forehead. "Slave driver."

It took them less than ten minutes to clean up the kitchen. They kept smiling at each other the whole time, awareness simmering in their glances. Finally, he bracketed her shoulders, guided her to the doorway and switched off the kitchen light.

FRIDAY MORNING it was raining, not heavily but steadily. Adam had already finished one cup of coffee and was polishing off the last of his hash browns by the time Sheila came downstairs. She'd hastily put on last evening's clothes and gone back to her room to shower and dress. She wondered if Elva could see the glow in her as she filled a mug with steaming coffee and sat opposite Adam. Probably. It must be hard to miss, but the older woman gave no indication of awareness.

"With this much rain all the washes and creeks are going to be running and there'll be flooding in the lower pastures," he said. "I'll check out conditions in the bird. Chances are we'll have to move some of the cattle to higher ground."

"Is there anything I can do?" Sheila asked.

"Would you mind manning the telephone and radio? Charlie and the others will be calling in from time to time with progress reports. If you could help coordinate their activities..."

"Be glad to." It pleased her to be useful.

Adam spread prickly-pear-cactus jelly on his biscuit. "If Brian still wants to help when he gets home from school this afternoon, give me a call on the radio. I'll come by and pick him up."

"He seems to be taking to ranching," Sheila said

after her first sip of black coffee. "Why, all of a sudden, do you suppose?"

Adam shrugged. "Maybe he just needed encouragement. Kerry's never shown a lick's interest in the place. Her mother was a town girl. I used to tease Helen that there must have been a bunch of Yankee city slickers in her background and that Kerry inherited all her genes from her." He took a last bite of buttermilk biscuit. "Now that my daughter's got all the money she needs, I wouldn't be surprised to see her take off for a big city somewhere."

This was the first time Sheila had heard him mention Kerry's newfound wealth. Had last night's lovemaking also prompted memories of the woman he'd shared most of his adult life with, just as it had prompted her to think of Bill? Was it with a sense of sadness or relief that he envisioned his elder daughter leaving Coyote Springs?

He surprised Sheila again. Rising from his chair he came over and kissed her on the cheek, the way a husband would say good-bye to his wife on his way to work. "I'll keep in contact on the radio," he assured her, put on his hat and went out through the mudroom.

A LITTLE AFTER TWO Sheila received a call from Homestead Bank and Trust.

"They told me at your office I might find you at the First ranch," Nedra Cummings said.

Sheila had an uncomfortable gnawing in the pit of her stomach. Being tracked down here by the vice president for investments didn't bode well. "I'm planning to return to Houston Sunday."

"Good timing, then," Cummings commented. "The board has scheduled a meeting to go over your report and establish guidelines for managing the Number One Ranch.''

"Is Adam…Mr. First going to be present?''

"This is bank business.''

"It's his ranch," Sheila argued before she thought. She should have phrased it differently, less confrontationally.

"It's *our* ranch," Cummings corrected her pointedly. "Adam First is a minority stockholder.''

"Yes, I know that, but he's managed this ranch for more than twenty years. No one knows it better than he does. Don't you think it would be beneficial to include him in the discussions?''

"You might be right," the bank's vice president acknowledged after a brief pause. "Very well, we'll invite him to attend and give us his input." Then she added ominously, "As long as he understands that the decisions are ours, not his. He can advise us, but we don't have to take his advice.''

Sheila wasn't encouraged by the tone, but she had no control of the situation. "When is the meeting?''

"Tuesday, two o'clock in the staff conference room.''

"We'll be there.''

THE RAIN QUIT around noon, but that didn't stop the flooding. Creeks and lower washes would be running for days. Within two weeks the surface of the land would again be cracking from lack of moisture. At least the water table would have been raised.

It was almost four by the time Adam returned to the headquarters. He'd checked all the low spots, worked out a priority plan with Charlie to move several herds of cattle over the next two days. It would be slow and dangerous on the spongy, water-slicked land. They'd probably lose a few head, either from drowning or the cattle breaking legs fighting their way up slippery slopes. The alternative of entire herds of animals standing knee-deep in water and slowly starving to death was far worse.

Michael's girls greeted him as he came through the back door. Clare had brought them there directly from school, since they'd planned on staying the weekend.

"Where's Brian? Is he ready to go?"

"Go where, Grampa?" Sally asked.

"To help move cattle."

Sheila came out of the radio room. "I haven't seen him, Adam. I think I heard him drive up a little while ago, but he didn't come inside."

"Take me," Sally begged. "I can help. Are we going to fly in your helicopter?"

"Not this time, Sweet Pea. Do you know where your cousin is?"

Sally sulked. "He took Davy in his truck." Apparently, she hadn't been invited to go with them either. "Brian said they were going out mudding."

"Mudding?" Adam repeated with alarm.

Slipping and sliding in the thick, sticky goo with off-road vehicles was a favorite sport of teenagers after a heavy rain. Except that Brian had a pickup, not a balloon-tired off-road buggy with crash bars, and he'd only been driving a few months. From what Adam had observed, the boy, like most kids, who thought of themselves as immortal, had a lead foot and more nerve than brains or skill behind the wheel.

Sheila caught the concern in Adam's eye and turned to the eight-year-old. "Did he say where, Sally?"

The girl shrugged. "He wouldn't tell me. Davy

didn't even want to go,'' she whined, ''but Brian wouldn't take me. He said girls didn't go mudding.''

''I'll find him.'' Adam removed his hat, wiped the sweatband with a red bandanna and put it back on. ''He couldn't have gone very far.''

Ten minutes later, he was again airborne. He hadn't been watching specifically for the truck when he flew in from the south, but he was sure he would have noticed it if it had been within sight. He headed northwest. There was a wide sloping pasture on the other side of a rise. That was the most logical place for the kid to head.

Over the ridgeline, Adam saw ruts crisscrossing the soggy pasture. Judging from the thick curls of mud, it was a wonder the light-ended vehicle hadn't become hopelessly mired. Having to walk out of there would have served the kids right. They'd resemble abominable mudmen by the time they reached the house. The image almost brightened Adam's grim mood.

Then, up ahead, he spied the circular earthen tank at the bottom of the hill. The water was at the point of overflowing, the land at its base shiny with puddles. Along the precarious rim, Brian was fishtailing the old Ford.

''Damn fool,'' Adam muttered. Brian was in for more unhappiness when he had the Ford taken away for the next two weeks. He or Elva would have to drive him to the main road for the school bus every morning and pick him up every afternoon.

Adam hung suspended in place, maintaining his distance, observing the scene. His grandsons must have heard the *whop-whop* of the helicopter, but Adam didn't want to encroach too suddenly and panic the juvenile driver. He began a slow circle to the bottom of the draw, his eyes continually drawn to the sloshing truck below him.

He clicked on the radio. "Sheila, I've found them. They're at Inner Tube Tank. It's on the map, northwest of the house."

"I've got it."

"I'll signal them to return home. It'll probably take them twenty minutes or so, provided they don't get bogged down. I'll keep you posted."

As he was talking to Sheila, he'd been keeping close tabs on the old truck. The grass at the top of the embankment had been churned under, so that the rim resembled a train yard of interlocking rails. Brian was obviously losing traction in the slick silt. Adam couldn't decide if the driver was deliberately playing with the situation or couldn't get himself out of it.

Suddenly, the rear end of the Ford began sliding down the outside slope of the levee. Mud fanned out in liquid brown sheets from the back wheels as Brian struggled to recover. Did the kid know to turn the wheel in the direction of the skid, not away from it?

Adam watched, his stomach muscles clenched, wishing he were able to grab the wheel out of the hands of the driver and yank his grandchildren to safety. The truck was on enough of an angle now that if Brian caught an edge the wrong way, he'd probably tip it over. Did they have their seat belts buckled?

Abruptly the pickup caught traction and shot forward, not along the edge of the water but straight toward it.

Adam's blood ran cold. "Sweet Jesus," he murmured.

He stared, dry mouthed, as the old rusty vehicle plunged nose-first into the muddy tank.

CHAPTER TEN

THE DRIVER'S-SIDE DOOR wedged narrowly open against the pressure of the enveloping water. Adam's chest pounded violently as the truck sank rapidly below its surface. His heart lurched when Brian's head broke through. It stopped when he realized only the older boy had gotten out.

Brian whipped his long dark hair away from his face, rotated frantically and scanned the surface of the pond. His cousin was nowhere in sight.

Dread consumed Adam and threatened to paralyze his will. Reflexes had him automatically adjusting the controls of the helicopter. He maneuvered the chopper to the base of the tank, possessed with the impossible wish that he could roll back the clock ten minutes, do something to make this not be happening. Logic kept slamming into him. *There is no going back. What's done is done. The past cannot be reclaimed.*

Brian spun once more in search of the ten-year-old, puffed out his cheeks and dived below the surface. Adam prayed the sixteen-year-old's impulse could save his younger cousin.

Adam managed to settle the chopper onto the soggy ground below the tank. Unable to see what was happening above him, he scurried out from under the swirling rotor blades. Muscles hard with tension, he clawed his way forward and climbed the slick embankment. His boots and jeans became instantly caked with red mud, its weight a further encumbrance. Grunting sounds cascaded down from above him like hailstones, agonized cries and vocal prayers laced with tears.

He reached the crest and saw Brian crouched over Davy. Relief at the sight of his second grandson was swept away when he realized the boy wasn't moving. Brian was mumbling semicoherently about "him still having his seat belt on." He was pushing on Davy's chest in what Adam recognized as a poor simulation of CPR. For all Brian's good intentions, his actions were useless.

Adam bolted to the side of the older boy and pushed him away. Forcing himself to calm down enough to feel a pulse, he laid two fingers on the side of Davy's neck. The artery throbbed. Thank God.

Adam tilted the boy's head back, making the jaw sag. He put his mouth to Davy's and filled his grandson's lungs with air, then placed the heels of his hands on the boy's sternum and applied thrusts. Bubbles issued from Davy's mouth. Adam did it again—and again got only bubbles. The fourth time the youngster started coughing violently. Adam turned the boy's head on its side so he wouldn't aspirate his own vomit.

"Sweet Jesus," Adam whispered, this time not in supplication but thanksgiving. He gathered the child in his arms. "You're going to be okay. You're going to be fine," he repeated over and over, not certain whom he was trying to reassure.

Scalding Brian with a glance, he saw a mask of agony. "Let's go," he ordered.

Adam carried Davy to the helicopter. Brian followed. Adam made sure both passengers were securely buckled in, started the engine, then got on the radio. He notified the hospital in Coyote Springs that he was bringing in a near-drowning victim and called home base and informed Sheila concisely of what had happened.

"Call Michael and Clare and have them meet us at the hospital. All of us will need changes of clothes… and see if you can get hold of Kerry."

The discipline of flying calmed Adam somewhat, but he repeatedly checked back at Davy. The boy seemed alert. His older cousin kept his eyes downcast. Later, Adam decided, would be soon enough to discuss this with him.

They were met at the helipad by a medical team who, to Davy's chagrin, wanted him to stretch out on a gurney.

"I'm okay. I don't need to lie down. I can walk."

Adam was encouraged by the boy's stamina and feistiness. "Don't argue," he mildly admonished him. "Do as you're told."

"But—" the boy began to protest.

"How about this?" asked another man in green scrubs, who was gripping the handles of a wheelchair.

"I wish we had someone to race." Davy now seemed to think it was a lark.

The medic laughed. "Maybe another time." Once the boy was seated, he was pushed at a near run through the electronically operated sliding doors.

Inside the hospital, Adam stood by while a doctor listened to Davy's heart and lungs, poked and prodded for other injuries. The boy kept babbling about his awesome adventure.

All the time, Brian lurked in the corner, wet, alone, watching, saying nothing.

Half an hour later, Michael and Clare burst into the emergency room. Sheila was with them. The doctor greeted them with a calm, encouraging smile.

"Your son is fine," he reassured them. "His lungs are clear. His other vitals are good. I'm prescribing some antibiotics, though, to make sure he doesn't develop an infection from that nasty water. If he shows any signs of respiratory discomfort, bring him back in. Otherwise just continue the antibiotics until they're gone. He's quite a trooper." He ruffled the boy's head. "You can wear that snazzy pink gown home if you want, compliments of Coyote Springs General Hospital."

"No way," Davy protested. "Mom, did you bring me clothes?"

"Were you able to get hold of Kerry?" Adam asked Sheila.

"I rang her home and cell phone numbers but didn't get any answer. I left a message on her machine to contact Michael. I thought—"

Adam nodded stoically. "You were right. She'll call him. She won't call me."

Sheila was caught between contradictory impulses. Adam's appearance was comical. The brown sludge transformed him into a gingerbread man dressed as a scarecrow, and he was leaving little particles of mud with every step he took. Despite his upbeat attitude, though, the expression in his eyes was one of pain.

"Are you okay?" She had an urge to wrap her arms around him, but aside from the fact that she would herself be covered in mud if she did, she sensed he needed to regain his internal equilibrium first.

"I'm fine," he answered.

She held out an oversized tote. "Elva threw together a clean set of clothes for you."

"Thanks." Taking the bag, he retired to a nearby rest room.

Sheila wanted to go to Brian to talk to him, but at that moment a nurse beckoned him behind a curtain to get a quick examination.

Adam reappeared a few minutes later, clean but still looking gray.

"What exactly happened?" she asked him.

"Yeah, Dad, what went on out there?" Michael had come up beside him. Clare was still talking to the doctor.

Adam explained about Brian dragging his cousin with him to go mudding, then plunging off the side of the tank into the water.

Michael's large hands tightened into knuckle-white fists. "I ought to take the little bastard outside and beat the—"

Adam clamped his son's wrist. "Don't ever call him that," he said with low-volume intensity. He released his hold. "An hour ago I felt the same way. What he did was asinine and irresponsible." He glanced over at the teenager, who was emerging from behind the curtain. The sixteen-year-old moved to a bench against the wall, where he sat down away from the others, head lowered. "But I suspect he's hurting inside a lot more than even your fists could hurt him. He'll be all right. Basically, he's a good kid."

"Good?" Michael's jaw dropped, his blue eyes hard as steel. "He's been nothing but trouble, Dad. He wrecked his new car, vandalized the school, got hauled into court. He's embarrassed the family, and now he damn near killed my son, and you're telling me the spoiled brat's a good kid?''

"You weren't there, Michael. I was."

"Dad," Michael pleaded. "Davy almost drowned."

"Don't tell me what happened, damn it," Adam snapped, then lowered his voice as heads turned. "When Brian popped to the surface of the tank, the first thing he did was look for Davy. As soon as he realized the boy was still in the truck, he dived back down after him. He was underwater so long I was afraid he'd gotten stuck and that I wouldn't see either of them alive again."

Sheila instinctively grasped Adam's arm. His muscles were rigid.

"Brian dragged your son out by himself, Michael. Without any help from me. He was scared, not for himself but for Davy."

"He should never have gotten them into that mess to begin with," Michael insisted, but the violence was spent from his words.

"I agree. Riding the rim of the tank was a stupid, reckless thing to do. Of course, you and I have never done anything stupid or reckless, so we can judge—"

"Dad—" Frustration sounded now in Michael's words.

"When the chips were down, Brian did the right thing. I'm not happy with him, but I'm damn proud of him."

Michael gaped at his father. "You're not serious."

"Brian got your son in trouble, but he also saved his life."

The boy's father shook his head in disbelief of what he was hearing.

"Michael, I could never have gotten to Davy in time

by myself. If Brian hadn't gone down after him..." He
let the phrase hang.

"Well, you'll have to pardon me if I don't kiss him
on the cheek and pat him on the back." Turning on
his heel, Michael went over to his wife and boy.

Adam grimaced at his retreating son.

"Don't you think you ought to tell Brian what you
just told Michael?" Sheila asked. "The boy's pretty
upset."

"He should be," Adam responded.

"But you said—"

"I know what I said. I also know Brian almost
caused the death of his ten-year-old cousin today."

"Adam, the kid's in hell. He could use a word of
encouragement about now."

"No." Adam's eyes were as hard as Michael's had
been a minute before, and Sheila realized he wasn't
nearly as reconciled to the situation as he'd sounded,
that anger and dread were still very close to the surface.
"Not now. Let him stew in his own juices for a while.
If I spoke to him at the moment I'd probably say some
of the things his uncle is thinking right now."

"I don't understand," Sheila protested. "A minute
ago you said—"

"That in the end he did what was right? He did, but
this isn't the time to tell him he's a hero. It's the wrong
message at the wrong—"

"He's hurting, Adam," she repeated. "He's a boy
who made a mistake and almost drowned himself. He's
confused and needs—"

Adam's characteristic upraised hand stopped her in
mid-sentence. "He needs what, Sheila? To be told everything's all right, that it was just an accident? That
it could have happened to anyone? Let me tell you

something. I'm glad he's hurting. He deserves to hurt. He did something today that was foolish and irresponsible. My grandson's not stupid. He's smart enough to work his way through what he did today, and figure out what he can do to make amends. As for being a boy…it's time he became a man.''

Adam had admitted he wasn't very good at seeing gray areas. It certainly seemed true in this case. If he had treated Kerry with the same aloof self-righteousness when she'd approached him for help, no wonder he'd lost her affection. It didn't justify or mitigate what she'd done to the entire family, but it did at least explain her mind-set in doing it.

''Are you coming back with us?'' Clare asked Sheila when the family was about to leave.

''I'll return with Adam.''

Clare nodded. ''All right. I'll see you tomorrow. We're driving directly home.''

Adam hooked a thumb in a hitchhiking motion at the figure sitting motionless against the wall. ''Come on, Brian.'' It was more an order than an invitation. ''Let's go.''

The boy stood, blank eyed, and proceeded sluggishly toward the door behind his grandfather.

Sheila followed. She was inclined to massage Brian's shoulder in a gesture of reassurance but wasn't sure how he would react. Would a kind word or sympathetic smile soothe, or would it only humiliate him and make him more angry?

''Clean clothes help,'' she said as they climbed into the chopper, ''but I bet you'll be glad to get a shower.''

He said nothing as he buckled up. She sat beside him and motioned for him to put on the earphones, which also offered protection against the high-frequency whine of the engines. They would allow conversation, but she didn't expect any on the short flight back to the Number One.

Indeed, the ten-minute trip passed in silence. Only when they were in the house did Adam speak to his grandson. ''Go shower and get the rest of that mud off you.'' He looked at the old Regulator on the living-room wall. ''Dinner is in half an hour. Don't be late.''

Sheila wanted to suggest to Adam that he soften his approach. His hostility was apt to further alienate his grandson, but like putting her arms around him earlier, she recognized this wasn't the time or place to question or challenge him. With a heavy heart, she watched Brian climb the stairs to his room.

In the kitchen she found Elva preparing fried catfish, though earlier in the day she remembered the cook mentioning tuna casserole for dinner. Sheila suspected the batter-encrusted fish was one of the men's favorites.

''Can I help?'' she asked.

''I am running a little behind,'' Elva admitted. ''If you could set the table—''

''Done.'' Sheila was grateful for the opportunity to keep busy. Today's near tragedy had her stomach aching.

The catfish was crisp and tender, the mashed potatoes fluffy, the mustard greens vinegary. In spite of Elva's culinary success, however, supper was a disaster. No one, it seemed, had an appetite. Sheila ate more than anyone else, but even she didn't eat everything she'd put on her plate.

She was also the only person at the table who tried to make conversation. When she failed to get even non-verbal responses to her questions, she refused to be daunted and went on to recount stories about her travels and the silly incidents that had earned laughter on other occasions.

Pushing back his barely eaten apple pie à la mode, Adam rose from his seat and addressed his grandson. "Tomorrow I want you to get with Charlie and pull the truck out of the tank. You'll clean it and overhaul it. Maybe your uncle Michael will advise you, but I want you to do the work. You will also reseed the pasture you managed to tear up today. I'll add the cost of engine parts and seed to your debt."

Brian looked up at him with hurt, red-rimmed eyes.

"Davy can help you with the reseeding," Adam added.

"I'll do it myself."

"Davy *will* help you." Adam's tone was dictatorial. "Do you understand me?"

"Yes, sir." The words were tense, defiant, yet strangely humble.

Adam picked up his coffee cup and left the room.

Brian sat motionless for some time, then he stood up. Remembering the rules, he clumsily gathered his dishes and milk glass and carried them to the kitchen.

Sheila heaved a sigh of frustration. The struggle between the generations gave every indication of being every bit as changeless as the prairie in the darkness outside the window. Adam said he intended to do better with Brian than he'd done with the boy's mother. The prospect at the moment certainly didn't appear bright.

"Everything was delicious, Elva. I'm sorry we didn't do it justice," she said a few minutes later when she placed her own dishes on the counter beside the sink. The cook shrugged grateful acknowledgment of the compliment and began scraping plates.

"Where's Brian?"

"Went outside," Elva muttered. "Said he was going to chop firewood." She deposited the dishes into the soapy water. She had a perfectly good dishwasher but rarely used it. "There's a woodpile out behind the garage, but I've never known that one to show any interest in tending to chores before."

"I suspect he just needs time by himself."

"Hrumpf." Apparently, Elva wasn't in a particularly forgiving mood, either.

Sheila found Adam in his office, staring at papers on his desk. "No word from Kerry?"

He shook his head. "Michael stopped by her place. She's not home."

Adam seemed to retreat into himself. What was he thinking? Sheila wondered.

"I received a call today from Nedra Cummings," she said. "There's a board meeting Tuesday at two to discuss my report. You're invited."

Adam glanced up at her with annoyed indifference. "Fine," he mumbled, and went back to his papers.

"It's been an eventful day," Sheila noted. "I think I'll read for a bit and turn in early."

"I'm sorry I'm not very good company this evening. I know you don't agree with the way I'm handling this. I screwed up with Kerry and now you think I'm doing it again with Brian."

She settled into the chair at the end of the desk. "You're pretty good at reading minds, Adam, but this time you're wrong. For one thing I wasn't here. For another I don't know Kerry. I've seen her twice, neither time under very good circumstances. I have no right to judge what went on between the two of you then or now."

He smiled thinly. "Are you saying you approve of the way I'm handling Brian?"

"Your way is definitely different from how I would deal with it, but I'm me and you're you. My responses are those of an outside woman, not of a man or a loving grandfather. You said Brian has to grow up. Of course he does. I'm just not sure making him a pariah is the way to do it."

"I'm not making him a pariah, Sheila. He's doing that to himself. Until he acknowledges he did wrong and apologizes to the only people who have the right and power to forgive him, namely Davy and his parents, he is and will remain an outsider."

"Does he know that's what you expect of him?"

"It's not what I expect." His tone rode the edge of exasperation. "It's what he has to do whether I'm here or not." He eased off. "I told you this afternoon, Brian's not stupid. I have every confidence he'll figure it out for himself."

"He's too confused right now to figure anything out, Adam, and you're not helping him."

The muscles around Adam's mouth tightened. "I am helping him, Sheila. I'm affording him the opportunity to think for himself. It may take him a while, but eventually he'll reach the correct conclusion, and he'll also have the satisfaction of knowing it was his decision to do the right thing. If he wants help, he can always ask for it."

"Will you give it to him when he does?" she challenged him. "Or will you turn your back on him again?"

The papers in his hand made a rattling noise. Carefully he laid the papers flat and splayed his fingers on both sides of them. "I have never turned my back on any one of my children or grandchildren," he replied in clipped tones, his eyes blazing, "and I never will."

"I'm sorry," she hadn't meant to hurt but to appeal. "I had no right to say that. I know you love your family, Adam. It's just that…" She paused. "Do you mind if I talk to him?"

"About good and evil, right and wrong? No objection at all."

IT WAS LATE by the time Brian returned to the house. The distant, even rhythm of the ax at work had gone on for hours, the crack and split monotonous in the black silence of the star-filled night. His stride faltered when he saw Sheila sitting at the kitchen table, a cup of tea at her fingertips.

"You chopped a lot of wood," she remarked casually.

Was it tension that straightened his shoulders, making them appear broader than she remembered? Perhaps it was the physical labor that had given them new bulk. Whatever the cause, Sheila perceived, in his set and carriage, more of the strength of a man than the softness of a boy.

He walked over to the sink, slapped heavy work gloves on the counter and began washing his hands. She heard him suck in his breath. Blisters, no doubt, but he didn't voice a complaint.

"You must be thirsty after all that work. Why don't you get a soda and join me."

He turned to face her, his hands rolling a dish towel delicately to absorb the moisture. "Why?" Then he as quickly capitulated. "Oh, all right."

"It's been a tough day, hasn't it?" she asked as he popped the top on a can of Pepsi and slid into the seat next to her. It was easier that way to avoid eye contact, she realized. She smiled sympathetically, trying to put him at ease. "I think they call it a character-building day."

He took a long slug of his drink.

"I know this is none of my affair, Brian, and if you want me to mind my own business, just tell me. But sometimes it helps to talk about things that bother us, and strangers are often easier to talk to than the people we know."

"I screwed up. All right? Is that what you want me to say?" Beneath the armor of belligerence she detected a measure of self-loathing.

"Is that why you're admitting it, because it's what you think people want to hear?"

His shoulders sagged. "Mudding is fun, and I thought Davy would enjoy it, but he was scared the whole time."

"And the more scared he became, the more you taunted him," Sheila ventured.

Brian pinched his lips together. To acknowledge that she was right was hard. "Yeah, it was stupid," he conceded despondently. "I probably wouldn't have gone on the top of the tank if he hadn't been screaming so much."

Sheila decided to push a little harder. "Or you might have gone to the rim to see if you could make him scream more."

He looked up and for the first time smiled. "Yeah, maybe." Embarrassed by the sudden admission, he grew somber again.

"Do you enjoy scaring people, making them afraid?"

"I'm not a sadist, if that's what you mean. But sometimes, yeah, it's fun to tease people."

"Except today you miscalculated."

He hung his head. "I...he... Jeez, I didn't mean for it to happen that way."

"Nobody supposes you did."

Brian's head shot up. "He does," he snarled.

She didn't have to ask who *he* was.

"As far as he's concerned, I'm not even worth yelling at."

"Do you think you would be here if that's what your grandfather believed?" She reached over and was relieved when the teenager didn't pull away from her touch. "He's angry with you, Brian, and I suspect you agree he has a right to be." The boy contemplated his soda can. "He's also proud of you."

Brian's eyes went wide. "Give me a break." He started to get up, but she tightened her hold on his hand.

"Just hear me out. Please." She could see in his eyes the cry for help and the man-pride that wouldn't let him ask for it.

He studied her warily and after a moment's pause reclaimed his seat. Refusing to meet her eyes, he picked up his soda can and began twirling it between his fingers.

"You saved your cousin's life today and risked your own. That was very courageous."

"It wasn't courage," he protested.

Even now she could see the terror crouching behind his slumped posture.

"Courage is doing what is morally right even though you're scared. That's what you did."

She glimpsed a silent battle between his wish that

what she said might be true and his shame for what he'd done.

"He still would have died if Gramps hadn't known how to do CPR."

"Didn't you learn that in school?"

He shied away. "Yeah, but I guess I didn't pay much attention."

She let the moment linger. "Do you think your grandfather's punishment is unfair?"

Brian raised his head. "Why won't he at least talk to me?"

"Maybe it's up to you to start the conversation by saying you're sorry to the people you hurt. Have you thought about that?"

"All he cares about is his precious ranch and his name."

Somehow the words weren't those of a sixteen-year-old male. Was this what Kerry had taught her son?

"This ranch is important to him, Brian. It's been his life's work, and his name is part of it. But the most precious thing in your grandfather's life is his family."

Brian scrunched up his face in adolescent disdain, but Sheila could see he was thinking.

"You have a wonderful family, Brian. Unless you plan to separate yourself from them for the rest of your life, you're going to have to face them."

He jumped to his feet, nearly toppling his chair. "In a couple of months Mom and me will be out of here." He was about to turn away, when Sheila spoke.

"No matter where you go, Brian, you'll still be taking your conscience with you. No matter how hard you try, you can't get away from yourself. Doing the right thing isn't always easy. It wasn't easy for you to dive back into that muddy pond today, but you did it. Facing your cousin, your aunt and uncle—and your grandfather—won't be easy, either, but you can do it.''

Puffing out his chest and holding his breath, Brian slammed down his empty soda can and stomped from the room.

CHAPTER ELEVEN

THE NEXT DAY Sheila accompanied Adam and Brian to the equipment barn to meet with the ranch foreman.

"How far down is the truck?" Charlie asked. In his early forties, he had the beginnings of a beer belly, but his upper arms were the size of other people's thighs.

"I'd say a couple of feet to the roof of the cab," Adam estimated. He received a confirming nod from Brian.

"Shouldn't be too difficult then," Charlie noted, "provided it hasn't rolled forward. That tank must be twelve feet deep in the mid—"

They were interrupted by the sound of a vehicle skidding around the end of the huge tin building. It was more like a shiny steel skeleton than a car, with fat tires and bug-eye headlights. A canvas top covered the sporty two-seater. Kerry released the wide shoulder harness and jumped out. Her long hair trailed behind her cowboy hat in a sleek black ponytail. She ignored everyone's greeting and ran to her son.

"Honey, are you all right?" she asked, encircling Brian in a smothering embrace.

"I'm okay." Suddenly embarrassed by her hugging him in front of people, he struggled out of his mother's grip. "I'm fine."

Charlie withdrew to a tractor parked a short distance away and fiddled with something to make himself inconspicuous. Sheila took a step backward into the shadow of the barn but remained close enough to hear what was going on.

Seemingly unaware of how ill at ease she was making her son, Kerry rambled on, "Your uncle Mike stopped by this morning and told me what happened yesterday." She ran nervous hands from his shoulders down to his wrists while her eyes explored his torso and legs. "You didn't break anything?"

"No, Mom," he assured her in an annoyed tone.

"You didn't get sick?"

"Jeez, I got wet. Okay?"

Impulsively, she tugged one of his ears and examined it. "How about your ears. Did the doctor check them?" He squirmed away, his face now glowing red. "You always used to get earaches when you went swimming in the tank."

He tsked impatiently. "That was when I was a little kid, Mom."

"So your ears don't bother you?"

Brian backed away from her. "Mom, I told you, I'm all right," he snapped, beginning to chafe under her scrutiny.

"Where were you last night?" Adam asked his daughter. "Sheila called and left a message on your answering machine. Michael stopped by your house—"

She wheeled around at him and stuck her nose up. "I was out with some friends."

"Must have been till pretty late. I kept phoning you until way after midnight—"

She stood her ground defiantly. "What time I got home is none of your damn business."

Adam considered her for a long minute. "You were

out drinking, weren't you? I can still smell it on your breath."

Brian sprang to his mother's defense. "Leave her alone."

"It's all right, sweetheart," Kerry assured her son with a grateful glance. Whirling back at her father, she snarled, "This would never have happened if you hadn't taken my precious baby away from me."

"Oh, jeez," Brian muttered, and hung his head, mortified.

"This is all your fault," Kerry continued ranting at her father. "You may think I'm an unfit mother, but my son didn't get practically killed until he came to work for you."

Brian's head shot up. "Mom," he implored, "I don't think you understand. It really wasn't Gramps's fault."

She gazed at him with teary eyes. "Oh, honey, you don't have to defend him. I'm going to talk to the judge. When he finds out what happened—"

Brian's eyes grew wide. "Uh, Mom, I'm not sure that would be a good idea. I mean—"

His mother didn't seem to hear, or didn't want to listen. "The judge will send you back to me. Everything will be all right. You'll see."

"Mom listen," Brian pleaded. "You can't do that."

Kerry's eyebrows furrowed. "You want to come home, don't you?"

"Sure I do." He looked at his grandfather. "But if you tell the judge what happened, he might cancel…revoke my probation and put me in jail. Please, Mom, let me stay here."

Her face froze, then, as the truth of what her son said sank in, contorted into something ugly. She stood directly in front of her father. "This must make you very happy. You've turned my own son against me," she yelled. "You never let me have anything, and now you're taking him, too. Payback time, Pops?" She narrowed her eyes. "I hate you for this. I'll always hate you."

"Sweetheart—" Adam implored, but it was too late. She strode over to her contraption, jumped in and tore away from the group.

Sheila emerged from the shadows and moved up to Adam's side. "I don't think she should be driving."

He whipped around, grateful for someone to vent his anger at. "And how do you suggest I stop her?"

Sheila bit her lip. "Will she go directly home?"

"I can only hope so." He took a deep, unsteady breath. "I'll check in a few minutes. If she's not there, I'll take the chopper and look for her."

Sheila glanced over to where Brian, arms folded, was leaning on the front bumper of his grandfather's pickup. Adam followed her gaze.

"I think it's time I have that conversation with him."

She nodded. "Go on. I'm sure Charlie will drive me back to the house."

He kissed her quickly on the cheek and walked over to the boy, who had his head bent and was examining the band on his wristwatch. Adam squeezed his shoulder.

"Get in, son," he said mildly. "Let's go for a ride."

"What about the truck—"

"It'll keep." Adam circled the front of the vehicle, climbed in and waited for his grandson to close the door on his side. They both buckled up.

Adam drove around the side of the equipment barn and took the road toward Kerry's house.

"Are you taking me back to her?" There was surprise and confusion in the question.

"No. I just want to spin by the house and make sure she got home safely."

They traveled in silence over the damp caliche road. Finally, they arrived at the entrance to the driveway leading to the two-story house. The sports vehicle was parked haphazardly near the front door.

"She didn't really mean it," Brian said, "about hating you."

It wasn't what Adam had expected to hear. "I hope not, son, but she's mighty upset with me and has been for a long, long time."

He put the pickup in gear and proceeded to a stand of live oak trees that marked a spot where a small creek widened into a pond, then continued on to join other streams that eventually formed the Coyote River. He parked the truck. They got out and walked under the dark shade of the giant five-hundred-year-old trees. Because of the recent rain, the earth under their feet was spongy and fresh smelling.

"I've made some terrible mistakes with your mother, Brian."

"You mean about Dad. Mom says you hated him and that if you hadn't forced him to leave he'd still be alive."

"Maybe he would and maybe he wouldn't. Your father had some problems that probably would have caught up with him sooner or later. I didn't send him away to hurt you but to protect you and your mother."

Adam wondered how much of his father's violence Brian remembered. Hopefully none of it, but he suspected there was some awareness, if only subconsciously. Did the boy miss having a father around? Probably.

"I'm as convinced as ever that I did the right thing, son," Adam said. "But sometimes doing right isn't enough."

Brian bent over and pulled at a long blade of ryegrass. "What do you mean?"

"How we do things can sometimes be as important as what we do." It had taken Adam years to understand this. "I completely mishandled the situation with your mother. She was young—not much older than you—confused and scared. You have to remember her mother had died only a year before and she felt all alone. I didn't help her when she needed me most, Brian. In fact, I made matters worse."

They leaned against a flat boulder under the dense foliage of an overhanging limb.

"If you could do it over again," Brian asked quietly, "would you still make her marry my father?"

Adam's angry words to Kerry echoed in his memory: *"No grandson of mine is going to be a bastard."* Had his proclamation been to spare this grandchild humiliation, or himself? Legitimacy was important when he was growing up. Nowadays no one seemed to care. It was a tough question, one Adam had pondered for years. He still didn't know what the answer was. Maybe if he'd been a better parent, his daughter wouldn't have had sex with Rafe Durgan to begin with.

"I think I would try to persuade them to marry," Adam said, hoping he was being truthful and that it would console his troubled grandson. "Then I would do everything I could to help them be good parents. It still might not have worked out—"

"Mom says he was no good," Brian blurted out, "that he was a loser."

Another surprise. It wasn't what she'd told her father. To hear her, Rafe Durgan was the true love of her life. Adam suspected the truth lay somewhere in between. He'd seen the look in Kerry's eyes sometimes when she gazed at Rafe. Call it love, attraction, infatuation—it didn't matter. She'd felt something for the scoundrel.

"There's good in everybody, Brian," Adam said. "Never forget that. Your dad was strong and a good worker when he put his mind to it, but he lacked discipline. Maybe if he'd had a better home life himself and stayed in school—"

"Mom says his father was in jail and his mother was a whore."

Adam heard the anger and shame in the cavalier statement. Might it not have been better not to know who his father was than to live with the knowledge that his paternal grandparents were social outcasts?

"I'm afraid that's true, too, son." Then Adam realized why the teenager had mentioned it. "They had their choices and you have yours. Who and what they were has nothing to do with what you make of yourself. We're responsible for our own lives, our own decisions." Adam wasn't sure if the message was getting through, though he could almost feel the young man mulling over his words.

"The way I treated your mother was my decision, my choice—and my mistake." He mused for a moment about what might have been. His little girl had grown up to be a beautiful woman. Could she have become the country singer she'd once dreamed of? Neither of them would ever know now.

"She always was contrary," he continued. "It used to make me laugh when she was small, how she would go out of her way to do the opposite of what we wanted her to. She thought she was being so clever and independent. She didn't realize it made her just as predictable if she'd been obedient. Her mother understood how to guide her. Maybe if she had lived...I never learned the knack of tricking her into doing—"

"What was she like?" Brian asked abruptly. "Grandma First."

Adam felt a sudden lump in his throat. No one had ever called her that, Grandma First. Helen hadn't lived long enough to be a grandmother. She would have loved it.

"She was kind and loving and patient. She was strong, too. You always knew where you stood with her."

"Like Sheila?"

Adam's eyebrows rose and warmth came to his face. He didn't meet his grandson's eyes, afraid of what his own might give away. "Yes, sort of like Sheila. I think they would have liked each other very much."

Before he realized it, a sigh of longing slipped between his lips. Brian glanced over at him. Time to get back to the point of this conversation.

"Your mother's contrariness turned into irresponsibility, Brian," Adam continued a little too forcefully. "Her penchant for independence hasn't brought her happiness."

"She gets mad sometimes and I don't know why."

"At you?"

"When I do stuff that's really stupid, but then she starts blaming herself, like it was her fault and not mine."

Adam realized her behavior was typical of alcoholics. Unfortunately, the guilt was also transmitted to their offspring.

Brian shredded the blade of grass he'd been toying with. Adam perceived a sadness about him, as if he wanted to say more but didn't know how or was afraid to let it out.

"About yesterday, Gramps. I didn't mean for anyone to get hurt." There was a knot of humility in his words, a hint of unshed tears in his voice.

Adam's chest tightened. He reached over and clasped the teenager's shoulder.

"I know that, son," he said softly. "I never meant to imply you did."

"I just thought…"

"It would be fun," Adam finished for him sympathetically.

Brian nodded and sniffled, embarrassed by this sudden show of emotion.

Adam gently massaged the thin, angular shoulder. "Now you know that having fun can have unpleasant consequences."

Brian lowered his head, apparently not willing to trust his voice to speak.

"Then you've learned a valuable lesson."

Adam dropped his hand and they remained side by side against the coarse rock for several minutes. The sound of wildlife—birds fluttering through the trees, squirrels chattering and jumping from limb to limb, the faint murmur of the shallow brook—brought a gradual release of tension. When the time seemed right, Adam pushed away from the boulder.

"I guess we better get going if we want to accomplish anything today."

Brian straightened up.

"You still have to repair the truck," Adam said lightheartedly, "and reseed the pasture, you know."

"I will," Brian replied matter-of-factly.

Adam was both proud and relieved that his grandson wasn't sulking, that he was taking responsibility for his actions and not expecting someone to clean up his mess.

"What about Mom?" the boy asked more seriously.

Adam stopped brushing off the back of his jeans. "You realize she has a drinking problem." Brian merely hung his head—as if it were his fault. "I thought...hoped she'd gotten past the booze years ago. Another of my miscalculations." They walked slowly back toward the truck. "How long has she been hitting the bottle this time?"

"Since right after Uncle Stu died."

Adam shook his head in self-contempt. He should have realized Kerry would need help coping with her brother's death. Stu was the baby of the family. As the elder daughter, it had fallen on her to be a sort of surrogate mother after Helen died.

"We'll get your mother help, son. I promise." They were within a few yards of the pickup. Adam turned to his grandson. "It won't be easy. I hope you understand that. She doesn't think she needs help, so she'll fight us. It could get pretty ugly. Think you're strong enough to stand up to her hostility?"

There was a brief pause. "She's my mom, Gramps. I've got to."

Impulsively, Adam put his arms around his grandson and hugged him. He was surprised and then relieved when the young man returned the embrace.

"Yes, son, you do. We both do." He smiled and felt a kind of elation he hadn't experienced in a very long time. "Now, what do you say we go back and see what we can do about getting that rusty old truck out of the drink?"

ADAM AND SHEILA SPENT most of the weekend discussing the final report she'd submitted before her arrival at the ranch. Adam didn't like it, but he admitted he could live with her revised recommendations. She'd dropped the issue of the ranch hands paying rent and changed her recommendation on selling the racehorses to monitoring the market very closely. Those had been his two biggest concerns. Grudgingly, he conceded that her strategy of going along with changes now in order to gain the bank's confidence and cultivate a reputation for being flexible was a realistic one.

"Choose your battles, eh?" he scoffed mildly.

"Exactly. Hold your fire for the big issues."

"Makes sense to me." He leaned over and kissed her fleetingly, teasingly. "I think we'll need more personal preparations, private drills to ensure we get it right."

Grinning, she said, "You think you can sweet-talk your way through my defenses?"

"I plan on using more than words."

Her eyes crinkled at the corners into a seductive smile. "I do admire a man of action."

He brought his lips back to hers and drew her into another kiss. "Unfortunately, it won't be tonight."

Brian's room was next to Sheila's. For the present, they would have to be content with kisses stolen in the office.

TUESDAY AT TEN MINUTES to two Adam parked a rental car in the lot next to the Homestead Bank and Trust. They'd flown in that morning and had lunch at a sandwich shop. After one of Elva's breakfasts neither of them was very hungry, and they both agreed they didn't want to go into what could be a very boring meeting ready for a siesta.

"I still think cloud seeding is important."

"We've been over this, Adam. There's no way to prove it works." She gathered up her purse, stepped out of the car, slammed the door and checked her reflection in the side window.

He joined her at the foot of the vehicle and wanted to put his arm around her waist. Discretion forbade it, however, and he had to be satisfied with walking casually beside her to the main entrance of the thirty-story building. He opened the glass door into the lobby and followed her inside.

Sheila pressed the elevator button and stared at their reflection in the polished brass doors. An eerie sight, the two of them standing side by side, slightly distorted, like a latent image seen through the ages of time.

"Pick your fights. I know," he said. "I hope you're right."

The boardroom of the Homestead Bank and Trust was about what he'd expected. Formal and stuffy. Nedra Cummings stood at the head of the long conference table. No more than five feet tall, small-boned and gristly, she wore a V-neck black suit, but even the high collar of her white blouse didn't hide the crepe wrinkles of her neck. Her bejeweled fingers were splayed determinedly on the shiny surface in front of her.

"Thank you for coming, Mr. First," she walked over and offered her hand.

Adam had taken a dislike to the woman the first time they met, years ago. His rare subsequent encounters with her, while never explicitly hostile, had not persuaded him to change his mind. He suspected she wasn't particularly fond of him, either, but they kept their manners in place.

"You may sit there." With the sweep of her hand, she indicated a chair on her left at the far end of the table. "Ms. Malone, if you would sit here, please." Next to her on the right. It made the opportunity for eye contact between him and Sheila almost impossible. Adam had no doubt that was the intent.

"We have several issues from Ms. Malone's report to discuss," Nedra began after all the introductions were completed. Altogether there were ten people in attendance. Adam had met most of them at one time or another, though there were a few new faces. "One, cloud seeding. Two, racehorse breeding. Three, the amenities in vehicles. The fourth and last one pertains to whether ranch hands should pay fair market value for the quarters they're currently being furnished free of charge."

"Nedra...Ms. Cummings." Sheila shifted in her seat. "In my final report, I dropped the issue of racehorse breeding and rent—"

"I'm well aware of that, Ms. Malone, but the issues still have to be discussed. The fact that you revised your original recommendations doesn't remove them from consideration."

Even from the far end of the table Adam could see Sheila's shocked expression. The others quickly looked self-consciously away.

The old witch scanned their dour faces. "Shall we proceed?"

Nods and mutters encouraged her.

"First is the matter of cloud seeding. Last year, the Number One expended more than a quarter million dollars to seed clouds for rain. The results do not appear to have been very satisfactory." She riffled through the papers stacked neatly in front of her and pulled out a single sheet. "According to the meteorological reports I've gathered, the average rainfall in that part of West Texas is less than twenty inches a year." She returned the paper to the pile. "Last year the region received twelve."

"That's why it's called a drouth," Adam muttered loud enough for the man next to him to overhear. The guy didn't look at him, but he did smirk.

"The year before that," Adam spoke up, "we received ten inches."

"While spending over $250,000 on cloud seeding," she reminded him.

"Clearly," Adam concluded calmly, "the cost was worth the investment."

"For two inches of rain?" a man, probably in his late fifties, questioned. "Doesn't sound very economical."

"Perhaps you don't realize how much two inches of rain is," Adam observed. "It's more than 54,000 gals per acre. How much do you think it would cost to truck in that much water? Then multiply it by half a million acres. I'd say $250,000 wouldn't even begin to cover it."

"It's all hocus-pocus," the young man opposite him spoke up. "How do you know the cloud seeding was what caused the rain?"

Several others voiced similar objections. Adam watched Sheila tap her finger on the edge of the table as they listened to the arguments she and Adam had anticipated. Maybe it was just as well they couldn't make easy eye contact. They'd be grinning at each other like lovers after sex.

"I think it's safe to say we're at an impasse here," Adam finally conceded. "You can't prove seeding doesn't cause rain, and I can't prove it does, though there is significant evidence pointing to its effectiveness. Certainly we can let the current contract lapse, if you want, but I would suggest you study the technique further and be willing to reconsider it later when drouth conditions worsen."

"When? You mean if," the woman across from Sheila stated.

"Based on past experience," Adam commented, "we can expect two or three more years of below-average rainfall ahead of us."

Impatient now with the dickering, Nedra called for a vote. They unanimously agreed to discontinue cloud seeding.

Adam shot Sheila a glance down the table and received a cautious but approving crook of an eyebrow in reply.

"Next, racehorse breeding," Nedra announced.

Adam was prepared to argue that even in off years, when profits were low or nonexistent, the reputation of the Number One was largely linked to the overall quality of First equine stock and bloodlines. He soon realized, however, that he didn't have to say anything. Several of the board members were avid horse lovers and racing enthusiasts, who argued his points for him.

The motion to discontinue breeding racehorses was rejected. Nedra alone had voted for it.

"Sound systems, specifically compact disc players in ranch vehicles," she intoned, obviously not happy with her defeat.

"Are you suggesting we take CDs out of the vehicles we currently own?" asked a man Adam recognized from the accounting department. "It'd be a waste of effort. As used equipment they wouldn't bring more than pennies on the dollar."

"If you'd read the package I sent you," Nedra informed him none too gently, "you'd know we're talking about future buys."

"Oh, well, that certainly makes sense."

"You might save a few bucks," Adam admitted, "but I wonder if it's worth it. We get very good terms on fleet purchases, considerably less than list price. If you check the invoices, you'll see we receive these amenities at no additional charge. They're thrown in to sweeten the deal, one of the advantages of large acquisitions."

"There's no such thing as a free lunch, Mr. First," Nedra informed him. "The cost of those luxuries is simply recouped by the seller in higher prices somewhere else."

"You may be right, Ms. Cummings. Nevertheless, since they're currently carried as freebies, I don't think you'll see dealers dropping their prices. They'll simply make more profit." He saw several nods.

By a narrow margin sound systems were allowed to stay.

"Finally, we come to the last issue," Nedra announced. "House rental."

From her almost gleeful tone and the way she rubbed

her hands together, Adam realized that this was the battle Nedra Cummings had chosen to fight. He'd thought it would be to his advantage when she had made this the last item to be discussed, that his reasonableness and flexibility on the preceding issues would earn him points for the big campaign. Now he began to wonder if she hadn't outmaneuvered him and made him look weak.

CHAPTER TWELVE

"As Ms. MALONE pointed out in her preliminary report," Nedra declared, "there are twenty-five working families living on the Number One. All of them occupy their quarters on the ranch free of charge. Based on the size and quality of construction, Ms. Malone estimates those houses have an average fair market lease value of $750 a month. Combined with maintenance and other expenses currently being borne by the ranch, which home owners or renters are normally expected to absorb themselves, this perquisite amounts to over a quarter of a million dollars in revenue that we're giving up every year."

Adam could feel his blood pressure rising. The arrogance of the old woman was enough to do that, but even if her words had been said with gentle, grandmotherly concern, he would have been incensed. Jaws tightening, he took a deep breath and was about to explode, when Sheila dropped her pen on the folder before her, straightened her back and spoke up.

"Ms. Cummings," she said in obvious surprise and alarm, "I showed mitigation for that perk in my amended report, and I withdrew the recommendation."

Nedra nodded almost sympathetically. "You offered Mr. First's justification for his practices, Ms. Malone. That doesn't change the fact that more than $250,000 a year in potential revenue is not being realized." She addressed the other board members at the table. "I recommend we perform a formal survey of the properties involved, assess their true market value and charge the residents monthly rent. I believe the least painful way for the workers and most efficient method for us would be through salary withholding."

Several people commented in one form or another that to get a job with house and vehicles included must be nice. Sheila tried to dissuade them with the arguments Adam had used to change her mind. The ranch hands were underpaid, considering the hours they put in, and that having them living on the land was to the ranch's advantage. After several minutes, however, it became clear she wasn't making any headway against the determined woman at the head of the table.

Unable to stomach the situation any more, Adam rose from his chair. He was disappointed that the soft carpet muffled the sound. A harsh scraping noise would have served his purpose and his mood better.

"What you are suggesting, Ms. Cummings, is outrageous."

Everybody's head turned to him.

"Mr. First," Nedra intoned with condescending patience, "you'll have a chance to speak when I tell you—"

"No," he boomed. "You'll listen to me now." He started walking up to the head of the table. "Sit down."

The old woman stared at him in utter dismay. She wasn't used to people questioning her authority. "Mr. First, you have no right—"

"To treat you with the contempt you've shown me and the people who work on the Number One? The hell I don't." He stood over her, dwarfing her, knowing his size alone could intimidate. "You want to stay on your feet? Go ahead. Just keep out of my way."

For the first time the woman showed genuine fear. It pleased Adam, and for a moment it made him want to laugh. What did she think he was going to do, pummel her? Even in his worst fury he would never strike a woman. As far as he was concerned, any man who did wasn't a man. The image of Kerry, bruised and beaten by her husband, flashed before his mind. He'd been relieved when he'd later heard Rafe Durgan was dead.

As Nedra Cummings looked up, he stared her in the eye. "I've got a lot to say, so you might as well get comfortable," he informed her almost politely. She pinched up her mouth and sat very stiffly in the oversized leather chair.

He glanced for a fleeting moment at Sheila. Her shock and disapproval of his actions were clearly written on her face. This was a big mistake, her eyes communicated. But the die was cast. His patience had reached its limits. Right and wrong wasn't a subject for compromise. He hoped she understood that.

He turned back to the assembly and stared at each one individually before speaking in a strong, unyielding tone. "How many of you own your homes outright?"

No one raised a hand, but he saw a few timorous nods.

"How many of you live or have lived in homes your parents or perhaps grandparents bought or built?"

This time he saw two people smile, almost nostalgically.

"They earned those homes, paid for them through industriousness and hard work. So how would you feel if someone came along now and told you that you had to pay rent if you wanted to live there? You'd probably raise holy hell. And you should. Because it wouldn't be right.''

He paused and studied each of them. They weren't all hostile, but most of them were probably intimidated by the coldhearted crone who'd called them together. He decided the best way to keep their sympathy was by attacking the real villain. ''Well, that's exactly what this woman—'' he waved scornfully at Nedra ''—is proposing.''

She started to say something, but swallowed her words at his glowering glance.

Another woman asked, ''Are you saying, Mr. First, that the parents and grandparents of these workers actually paid to build those houses?''

''That's exactly what I'm saying.''

Nedra finally found her voice. ''There are no records to indicate—''

Adam didn't give her a chance to continue. ''Those families have lived on that land for over a hundred years, some of them for much longer. They built everything on that ranch, every fence, every barn, every corral and shed. So who do you think built the houses they live in? Just because they were never given titles to them doesn't mean those houses aren't their homes. To tell them now they have to pay rent for them is detestable and immoral. They've already paid for them with hard work, loyalty and dedication. Their parents and grandparents are buried on that land—'' then he added more softly ''—and some of their children. To order them now to cross your palms with silver for the privilege of being close to the land they love and the heritage they've built is monstrous.''

"This isn't your decision," Nedra reminded him, her voice etched with anger.

"No, it's not," he agreed sadly, and smothered a curse at the turn of events that had brought him here. He continued to roam the faces at the long table. "It's your decision. I suggest you think about it very carefully, because you can't afford to make the wrong one."

"Is that a threat, Mr. First?" Nedra asked, wide-eyed with both defiance and disbelief.

Adam peered down at her. She was practically shaking with rage and for a moment he was afraid she might actually be having a fit or a heart attack, but he couldn't leave without making himself perfectly clear. In a low, simmering tone he answered, "It's a promise, Ms. Cummings."

He held up a finger and shook it at the people seated before him. "Here's the deal. You ask for one penny in rent from the workers on the Number One Ranch and I will slap you with an injunction to prevent you from ever collecting." He gripped the edge of the table and leaned menacingly forward. "Then I will personally bankroll lawsuits against this institution and each one of you personally for blackmail, fraud, embezzlement, criminal conspiracy, racketeering and any other criminal and civil charge I and my lawyers can dream up. The Homestead Bank and Trust won't get a red cent in rent, and by the time I'm finished with you, ladies and gentlemen, you'll all be on the welfare rolls."

Nedra rose to her feet. "If you don't leave immediately, I'll call security."

"No need," Adam replied. "I'm leaving."

He turned sharply, strode across the room and

walked out, leaving the door open behind him and the people at the table dead silent.

"I suggest we adjourn to give these matters some thought," an older gentleman halfway down the right side of the table said after a long minute. Nedra insisted the meeting go on, but the man who proposed adjournment ignored her, pushed back his chair and casually gathered the papers in front of him. Others followed suit. Nedra stammered and blustered, then fell back into her seat.

Sheila, too, got up. "If you'll excuse me…"

Nedra tightened her wrinkled lips and gave a dismissive flick of her wrist.

Her heartbeat pounding in her ears, Sheila hurriedly collected her papers and bolted out of the conference room. She caught up with Adam at the bank of elevators. He stood, head up, unmoving, staring at the closed doors.

"Well, congratulations, Adam. You sure told them off." She was seething and had every right to be. "Losing your temper, insulting and then threatening the board…now, that was a brilliant strategy."

"Your sarcasm doesn't help," he mumbled. "So why don't you just be quiet."

She drew back, sucked in her cheeks and expanded her chest in a wave of fury and an unparalleled urge to haul off and slap him. She was saved from the indignity by the double ding of a down elevator and the doors sliding open.

He stepped to the side, faced her and stretched his arm across the gateway. The mortification she glanced in his eyes as he allowed her to precede him slaked a little of the fire. There were several people in the car, so they descended in silence.

He rode next to her, his hands at his sides, inches from hers, but the chasm between them might have been miles. The door opened; he waited for her to exit. Together they marched across the marble-floored lobby.

The sky had darkened since their arrival, hope-filled cloudless blue yielding to ashen overcast. The wind whipped at Sheila's linen skirt and ruffled the lapels of Adam's western-cut suit.

He acted the perfect gentleman, opening her car door and watching to ensure she was comfortably seated before closing it with a gentle click. Wordlessly he climbed in behind the wheel, inserted the key, started the engine and backed out of the parking space. He could have been a novice in drivers' ed, the way he looked both ways before pulling out into traffic. Normally an aggressive driver, he showed no inclination now to cut and weave to exceed the speed limit.

Sheila recognized the symptoms—a man battling with cold fury.

Well, that was something they shared.

"We both know what your little performance back there cost you," she said, not raising her voice, but putting a bite in her words. "Do you have any idea what it cost me?"

He kept his hands on the steering wheel, his eyes trained on the road.

"Well, since you were so polite to ask, I'll tell you. It cost me any further business with Homestead Bank and Trust, and before this episode is over, it might cost me other clients."

He negotiated a turn onto the interstate and melded smoothly into traffic. "Why? Why would it cost you anything?"

"I changed a report for you, Adam."

"You corrected a report that was in error."

Was there no way of getting through to him? "In your opinion, but that's not how they'll see it. In their eyes, I'm indecisive. Incompetent by ambivalence."

"I'm sure they'll understand you were just doing your job."

"Damn it, Adam, don't try playing the martyr on me, as if you were the only victim in this mess."

"Victim?" He lifted an eyebrow. "I'm not a victim."

"Don't give me that crap. I know what you're thinking. If I hadn't raised the subject..."

"Somebody else would have," he said so calmly, so reasonably, she wanted to scream.

"I'm the one who needs to apologize," he continued, "for talking you into changing your report. I should have known with an institution like Homestead Bank and Trust truth, justice and the American way are meaningless concepts. Sorry you came out looking like a bleeding heart."

"Why, you..." she sputtered, "insufferable, patronizing..."

"That, too."

If air could be purple, it would have been. She'd worked long and hard to build her business. She'd spent hours agonizing over her report on the Number One. And now, all she'd gotten for it was a ruined reputation and a paternal pat on the head for giving it a nice try.

Her car was at the ranch. Should she abandon it? Hire someone to pick it up and drive it back to Houston for her? That would be the sensible thing to do, but it was also the coward's way out.

They arrived at the airport. She waited nervously fingering her purse, while he turned in the rental car. She was even more infuriated when she realized she wasn't just angry and hurt but heartsick. *Hold me,* she wanted to beg him when he came back. When he did rejoin her, though, he didn't show any such inclination.

"What will you do now?" she asked when he escorted her to the hangar.

"Exactly what I said. If they go through with that old bat's plan to bill the vaqueros for their quarters, I'll haul their asses into court individually and collectively." He opened the door for her into the flight operations section. "My kids are grown and have lives of their own. They don't need my money, so I can afford to spend my last dime, if that's what it takes, to protect my workers." He looked at her. "And I will."

Now that she had calmed down a little she wanted to keep the conversation going, but Adam's checking flying conditions and filing his flight plan took precedence. Once they were in the Cessna and airborne the mood again chilled. Quiet time was probably what they both needed, she consoled herself. At the ranch, they'd be able to sit down quietly and explore the situation over a cup of coffee or perhaps a relaxing glass of wine in his office.

She didn't doubt that he fully intended to tie the bank up in litigation, though she wondered if, after his brazen threat, the bank's executives would even go forward with Nedra Cummings's proposal. Given a choice between putting their own assets on the line and standing up to the "battle-ax," they might actually find their backbones.

Whether Adam would fight for "his" people, however, hadn't been the point of her question when she asked him what he planned to do. It was patently obvious Adam First would not now be kept on as general manager of the Number One. How would he handle "retirement"? Would he make life miserable for whoever was appointed to the job?

They landed a few minutes after five o'clock. The sky was clear in West Texas. Rain clouds would have been more welcome and would certainly have suited her mood better than this idyllically deep cloudless blue.

Elva was waiting for them when they came in the back door. "In time for supper. Good. I wasn't sure if you would be."

"Sorry," Adam growled. "I should have called to let you know when we'd be in."

"Gramps, the wiring harness for the truck came in this afternoon," Brian announced enthusiastically. He was standing in the doorway from the living room. Adam said they'd had a good talk, though he'd declined to go into detail.

"Uncle Mike asked if I could stay over at his house tonight so we can work on it," Brian added.

Michael had had the drowned truck hauled to his place, where he had a fully equipped shop. There weren't many things mechanical Adam's eldest son couldn't fix. Uncle and nephew seemed to be getting along easily now that Brian had apologized to him, Clare and Davy. It reinforced Sheila's perception that, while Michael obviously shared his father's quick temper, he didn't hold on to it very long. He must have inherited that virtue from his mother. Adam clearly believed in harboring grudges, and so apparently did Kerry.

"Tomorrow's a school day," Adam reminded him, using the timeworn objection for late nights.

"Aunt Clare said she can drop me off for the bus on her way to work." For the first time, Brian seemed to recognize his grandfather's ugly mood. "I'd really like to get started on rewiring the truck tonight, if it's all right, Gramps."

"Oh, before I forget," Elva interrupted, addressing Adam. "Charlie called. He said you need to check the heifers first thing in the morning to see if there are any in the lot you wanted to keep. He's sending them off to market tomorrow."

"Thanks. I tell you what," he said to his grandson, "give me a minute to change clothes and I'll drop you off at your uncle Mike's. I might as well check over the stock tonight. I have other things to do in the morning."

"Cool. Thanks, Gramps."

Adam glanced at Sheila in a way that had her breath coming short, her pulse jumping. Was he thinking about their sharing a bed tonight since Brian wouldn't be in the house?

"What about supper?" Elva asked him. "I fixed meat loaf."

"Aunt Clare said if I was going to spend the night, I can eat over there, too," Brian announced.

"Humpf," Elva snorted. "It'll be ready in half an hour."

"I don't want to wait," Adam said. "Feed Sheila. We didn't have much of a lunch. I'll grab something with Charlie and the boys later." He placed his hand on Elva's plump shoulder. "Tomorrow I'll take a couple of your meat loaf sandwiches, though."

"On rye bread with mustard and pimento," she

huffed, then smiled. "Your mother must have washed your mouth out with soap one time too many."

He laughed. "There's no disputing taste, Elva," he commented as he left the room.

"I'll go pack," Sheila said as she listened to Adam's booted feet taking the stairs two at a time.

"You're leaving, too?" Elva frowned with disappointment.

Until that moment, she hadn't realized she'd made the decision, but what was the point in hanging around? Adam obviously wasn't interested in her company and she had a great deal of professional repair work to do back in Houston. She wasn't particularly fond of night driving, but if she left now, she could be home by midnight, which would allow her an early start in the morning.

"I returned because my car's here."

"Please don't go." Brian pleaded.

"I..."

"He's ticked about something," Brian noted. "I can tell." He grinned. "But he'll get over it. Hang around. He needs you."

It was an appeal that took her completely by surprise. Brian was wrong, though. His grandfather didn't need her. Not anymore. So why was her resolve weakening? The answer was shockingly simple. She needed him.

"You shouldn't be driving tonight anyway," Elva told her.

"Yeah, you look real tired," Brian added, leaning against the counter by the refrigerator.

Sheila sputtered. "Don't hold back, Brian. Don't sugarcoat it. Okay," she admitted with a chuckle, "so

I'm a mess." She at least had the satisfaction of seeing him blush.

"Driving tired is dangerous," the housekeeper observed. "Stay tonight and see how you feel in the morning. Things always look better after a good night's sleep. Besides, someone's got to eat my meatloaf before it becomes leftovers."

Sheila gave her a quick hug around the shoulders. "Now, that's an offer I can't refuse."

Adam reappeared in the doorway a moment later, still buttoning the cuffs of a work shirt. Feet planted apart, he gazed at Sheila under bunched eyebrows, his lips slightly parted. He appeared about to say something but hesitated. The moment was lost when Brian slammed the refrigerator door and popped the top of a soft drink. "Ready?" he asked his grandson. Without a backward glance, he was out the door.

"Thanks," Brian whispered, and followed.

Stung by Adam's coldness, Sheila sank weakly onto a kitchen chair. How long would he be gone? It shouldn't take more than an hour to cull out a few heifers. That would give him a little extra time to calm down in familiar surroundings and put things in perspective. Of course, he and Charlie and whoever was with him would talk, exchange a few jokes, maybe drink a couple of beers. Would he tell his ranch hands what might be in store for them?

Sheila ate alone, reliving the events of the day with every bite of meat loaf, which she was sure must be delicious. How could she have gotten herself into this predicament? She knew when she met Adam First he would be difficult to work with. What she hadn't anticipated was becoming emotionally involved with him.

Had she let affection cloud her judgment, compromise her professionalism?

After supper she went to Adam's office and flipped through livestock and ranching magazines. She looked up periodically, expecting…hoping to see him standing in the doorway, tall, straight and proud, yet with a playful smile on his face. She imagined him beckoning her into his arms and begging her forgiveness for his temperamental moods. Then he'd kiss her and hurry her upstairs. They'd make gentle love tonight, slowly drawing each other to intense peaks of pleasure neither of them had experienced before. They'd sleep entwined, wake and make mad passionate love again.

Elva stopped in at ten o'clock to say good-night. Eleven rolled around, then eleven-thirty. There was no point in staying here. Adam knew where her room was.

She mounted the stairs, her ears alert for the rattle of Adam's diesel chugging up the narrow mesa road. Only gentle night sounds wafted in through the open window, crickets and a hoot owl, and the lonely bay of a coyote calling for a mate. She left her door ajar, allowing the light of her bedside lamp to spill out into the hallway let him know she was there, waiting.

"I'll read," she muttered as she slipped into a silk nightgown. But even her favorite suspense author couldn't hold her attention or keep her eyelids from sagging.

Abruptly, she jolted awake. A vehicle was pulling into the gravel driveway. It stopped under her window. Adam was home. The bedside clock said a quarter past midnight.

She rubbed the sleep from her eyes, compulsively ran fingers through her hair to make sure it was reasonably in place. She spread her hands across the floral duvet, smoothing it out needlessly, and picked up the hardback that had fallen open on her lap. Her heart was beating faster, almost painfully. In anticipation. Adam was coming. Would he still be mad at her or would his anger be spent? They both needed to give and receive solace, she thought as she shifted nervously against the satin-covered pillows.

Through the screened window she could hear the back door open and close. A minute later his steps were on the stairs, in the hall. Her pulse raced. She ran her tongue across dry lips, and waited, her heart singing. She couldn't keep the smile from her face.

The footsteps receded and she heard a door close at the other end of the hall. He'd gone to his room. To change? To freshen up? She waited. Silence. Her heart ached.

At last she shut her eyes against the pain that gnawed where joy had thrummed. Brushing away the tears that suddenly coursed down her cheeks, Sheila reached over, turned out the light and cried into her pillow.

ADAM STRIPPED OFF his clothes, crammed them into the hamper in the bathroom and crawled between the cotton sheets of his bed. He wouldn't think about the woman down the hall. But even if he could have switched off his mind, he couldn't ignore his body. It hadn't forgotten what it was like to touch and be touched by her. He turned on his side, but the throbbing loneliness wouldn't let him rest.

He'd seen the expression of hope in her glance when she realized Brian wouldn't be in the house tonight. He'd stirred at the thought of making love to her. He'd run from the temptation. Even now, he couldn't face her, couldn't bear to see the disappointment in her eyes.

He'd blown it today with his outburst, let his temper overrule his intelligence. He'd given the bank no alternative but to dismiss him as general manager of the Number One. Sheila had jeopardized her professional reputation to save him, and he'd squandered her gift.

Yet he certainly wasn't going to apologize for defending people he'd known all his life, friends who'd always been honest, hardworking and loyal. What kind of man would he be to abandon them so he could go on running a ranch for somebody else—for a cold, faceless, heartless institution?

He lay awake, wishing he'd accepted Charlie's casual offer of beer or liquor. Maybe if he were drunk he could forget all the things that had gone wrong in the past year: the death of a son, the betrayal of a daughter, the loss of a heritage.

He'd lost something else, too—the respect of a woman he'd grown fond of. Fond of, hell. A woman he'd fallen in love with. After Helen died, he'd given up hope of finding anyone to share his life, not because his marriage had been unhappy but because it had been so good.

Sheila made him feel alive in a way he'd almost forgotten—young and virile and full of hope. He hadn't missed the light in her window as he drove up tonight, a signal. She wanted him; he wanted her. Why couldn't they simply enjoy each other? But it was more than want, he acknowledged as stared at the ceiling. He needed Sheila Malone.

He climbed out of bed, threw a robe over his naked body and stepped out of his room. He was halfway down the hall before he realized her light was out. Another message? A romantic call to steal into her bed in the darkness softened only by the three-quarter moon outside? Without making a sound, he moved to her door. A muffled sound stopped him. Had she said something?

His heart sank. She wasn't speaking—she was snoring. Not loudly, just a delicate, ladylike hitch in her breathing.

He tiptoed back to his room, quietly closed the door and slid once more into his empty bed.

CHAPTER THIRTEEN

IT WAS AFTER nine o'clock when Sheila came downstairs and walked into the kitchen.

"Good morning, sleepyhead," Elva greeted her.

Sheila had dozed on and off until after four, when she'd finally slipped into the deep sleep of emotional exhaustion. She couldn't remember the last time she'd gotten up this late. The day felt already half over.

"I guess I was more tired than I realized."

"Coffee?" Elva asked.

Sheila sat at the table in the breakfast nook. "Absolutely. Is Adam still here?"

Elva carried a large mug and a pot of steaming coffee to the table. "He left over an hour ago." She poured. "I offered to wake you, but he said not to disturb you."

"Where'd he go?" Sheila asked before she realized it was none of her business.

"Over to Michael's. A water main broke at the school complex and everybody's being sent home. Clare called to ask if I could watch the kids until she or Michael got home, but I have a dentist's appointment in town. Mr. First is picking them up at their house and bringing them over here." She returned the carafe to the coffeemaker. "I have some waffle batter left—"

"No, thanks. Just some toast. I still have to pack."

Elva spun around. "You're leaving after all? I thought...last night...you'd be staying for the week."

Sheila wondered if the housekeeper suspected them of having slept together. Elva's coy grin suggested she did.

Brian's plea and his words "He needs you" had given her hope the evening before, but the darkness of night and the cold light of day told her she was no longer wanted...or needed.

"Unfortunately, I have a business to run," she said with more heat that she intended. "I've already been away too long."

Elva peered at her skeptically but didn't comment.

Thunder rumbled overhead.

"Rain?" Sheila asked hopefully. She'd noticed the sky was overcast, but in her haste to get downstairs, she hadn't bothered to look out the window.

"Maybe. There's another storm system moving up from the Gulf. You'll probably run into it on your trip home."

Great. She didn't relish driving in heavy rain any more than she did driving at night. It would make a good excuse to stay, but she didn't want to linger, not under the circumstances. Adam's distance last night had confirmed the unhappy realization that what they might have had was gone.

He hadn't come right out and blamed her for what had happened. In fact, he'd said just the opposite, excused her with the rationalization that if she hadn't raised the rental issue in her preliminary report, someone else would have. But he didn't believe it, and in all honesty, neither did she.

She'd done enough harm. It was time to break contact, end their affair. Adam would never forgive her for being the instrument of his final humiliation. She had to acknowledge her own anger, as well. His temper tantrum had killed her chances of a long-term business relationship with Homestead. Her priority now had to be Malone Economic Consulting and Services.

With both hands, she brought the coffee mug to her lips. Glancing up, she realized Elva was studying her. It took a moment to remember what they had been talking about—rain on the way home.

"Bad weather is all the more reason to get on the road as soon as possible," Sheila muttered.

She ate her toast laconically and drank another cup of coffee, her mind wandering to the parallels between Adam and her father. They were both hardworking, both bullheaded. In the end Jim Pounder's inflexibility had destroyed him. She wouldn't hang around to see Adam consumed the same way.

Elva reappeared wearing a conservative dark dress, stylish pumps and carrying a black purse. "I must go or I'll be late," she said.

They hugged and told each other to take care. Sheila watched her leave, then washed up her mug, plate and silverware, left them in the drain board to dry and went upstairs to pack. Twenty minutes later she slid behind the wheel of her Lincoln Town Car.

The sky was a dark churning gray now. Erratic raindrops were kicking up dust. Did this mean the drought was over? These storms, so often encouraging, just as frequently failed to keep their promises. Another parallel with life, but she chose not to explore it. She did keep her eye in the rearview mirror, however, to see if anyone—Adam—was following her. She used the security code he'd given her to open the gate, then meticulously made sure it closed solidly behind her.

She'd driven several miles on the caliche road leading to the paved highway, when the rain began to lash her windshield. She stomped on the accelerator and tried hard to suppress the shimmer of panic that was beginning to clench her stomach as her nerves went into overdrive. It was just rain, she told herself. The hands gripping the steering wheel were suddenly cold and clammy. She nearly drew blood as she clamped her lips between her teeth. The car began to rock, buffeted by the growing force of the wind.

Her ability to think seemed paralyzed. All that remained was the instinct to flee. Then she remembered Adam and the children. He was picking them up at Michael's house. Would they be safe? Would he be able to cope with four frightened children by himself? Her eyes misted up, but she couldn't tell whether it was from her own panic or fear for the welfare of the people she'd left behind. Or her loneliness for Adam.

A blast of wind slammed into the side of the car, nearly pushing her off the road.

"I'll be safer at the headquarters than on the open road," she said out loud. And in her heart she murmured, *I'll be safe with Adam.*

Willing vainly for her heart to stop its vicious thumping, she remembered what she'd told Brian about courage—that it is doing what you have to do in spite of fear. Fighting panic, she turned back.

Warm rain transformed itself into a cool downpour and quickly filled the bar ditches along the side of the road. The wind gathered strength and buffeted Sheila's high-profile car from side to side. If she ran into a ditch, she'd be stuck, prey to every rock and stick tumbling down the man-made rapids. Her nerves quivered, and apprehension settled like a dull leaden spike in her belly.

She reached the gate without mishap, only to find a tree limb lashed across the front of the call box. Forced to get out of the car to enter the security code, she was completely drenched by the torrential downpour in a matter of seconds. A long, sharp mesquite thorn pierced her skin when she reached through the writhing branches to the keypad. The pelting rain washed the blood away with alarming efficiency.

Cautiously, she fed in the code, no longer certain she correctly remembered the sequence of numbers. The motor whirred, the gate clicked open. Thoroughly soaked, bloody and muddy now, she climbed behind the wheel.

Nature seemed infuriated by her success and retaliated with a vengeance. The wind howled across the prairie like a woman in pain. Crackling and snarling in a fit of temper, it threw all manner of objects at her: limbs of trees, sheets of corrugated metal that must have come from sheds and buildings miles away, gardening tools and farm equipment.

Lightning blinded her a mere second before the crack of its report. Biting her lips, Sheila glanced in the rearview mirror in time to see a towering cedar sway like an upended beer bottle and crash across the road behind her. She was cut off now. There was no going back, only ahead—to find Adam and the children.

Lightning streaked in jagged veins across the gunmetal sky, outlining the dark house perched on the edge of the mesa, a haunted castle from some gothic tale. The growl and rumble of thunder a moment later had her bones rattling. She was shaking violently from the wet cold as well as her old terror.

She turned onto the narrow road that would take her to the top of the butte. Fighting the urge to ram her foot down harder on the gas pedal, she locked the transmission in low gear. The engine whined as it fought the pull of gravity on the slick chalky slope.

A rock the size of a basketball came tumbling down the middle of the rutted lane and crashed against the right edge of her windshield before continuing on its merry way. The point of impact instantly cobwebbed into a milky mush of twinkling glass crystals. She was effectively blind on the right side now.

Breathing raggedly, her chest pounding, she motored slowly forward—myopic, unbalanced, unsure of the world around her. No nightmare had ever been so cruel...or terrifying. Her rear wheels spun on the unstable surface. The car weaved capriciously across the road like a drunken cowboy, bringing her to the edge of the precipice and back again.

Windshield wipers slapped ineffectively to clear her vision. She could see only the dark demon sky and its jagged strobes of lightning. She pressed on. Her jaw aching, she fought to keep her teeth from chattering.

The roiling clouds swirled in vicious knots of black, purple and sickly green. Hail joined the rain and drum-rolled the roof and hood of the car with ear-splitting intensity.

At last she reached the crest and the land opened up. But it offered no salvation. Raised high above the plain, the tabletop was all the more vulnerable to Mother Nature's fury. Her mighty wind tore across it with gale force. The trees and shrubs that had made this aerie a green thumb defying the gray-brown world around it had been shorn and shredded. Even the litter had been tidily removed. The house was poxed, the windows shattered. A sprawling mulberry leaned against one corner of the gabled roof, a frightened, hoop-skirted child clinging to its mother.

The car rocked, and Sheila wondered if she was about to sail away. A flying carpet, American-style. She almost giggled.

Where were Adam and the children?

She spied his truck where a flower bed had once been. Had he parked it there in haste, or had the storm placed it whimsically? She studied the house. Something was very wrong, something beyond broken windows, torn shutters and missing shingles. Craning over the steering wheel, she stared up.

The building was lopsided. The imposing two-story brick-and-stucco structure, seemingly so permanent and immovable, had been shifted by the tempest, slipped from its pier-and-beam foundation.

The storm cellar. It was underground, the safest place. Access was through the mudroom. She looked toward the breezeway that separated the house from the garage. There was no breezeway. The three-car garage had been rammed against the back door.

The blood drained from Sheila's face. Tears gathered in her eyes. If Adam and the children were in the cellar, they, at least, were protected. Please God.

But she'd been counting on that concrete shelter for refuge. A terrible mistake. She'd come to the most dangerous place possible in a storm—high ground.

There was no possibility of reaching the cellar now, no way to get off the mesa. The inner room of a building, preferably a windowless bathroom, was the safest spot in a storm, but the house itself was unstable and in danger of breaking up. Staying in the car was not an option. A wind that could tear a building from its moorings would have no mercy on a boxy container that weighed only a couple of tons. She had to abandon it. But where to go?

Awareness of the nearness of death drained her of the last shred of energy and strangely brought a kind of peace. She pictured her children, Derek and Melanie, and her two granddaughters. She'd never see them again. How sad, she mused, but it was an intellectual awareness. Emotion seemed to have forsaken her. Despair left her numb to pain or loss.

Only the thought of Adam racked her heart. She loved him and now it was too late. No, she decided, she wouldn't mourn what hadn't been, what couldn't be. Their union had been too late, too short, and the promise in their touches hadn't been fulfilled. Maybe that was best. Sometimes completion brought disappointment because there was no more. Yet she couldn't imagine reaching an end of exploring pleasure, of finding joy and happiness with Adam First.

A flash of light, the crack of another tree splintering and the metallic taste of raw fear in her mouth brought her to her senses. Maybe she would die. *We all die,* she reminded herself, but she wouldn't be taken without a fight.

She searched the area, desperate for a refuge. She needed a low spot. The few she saw were filled with water and debris.

Beyond a ragged hedge, not far from the cockeyed garage, was the long, low wall of Elva's garden. Concrete bonded stone, two feet thick, not more than three feet high. If she could lie up against it…in the angle between the rock and the ground.

She tried to open her car door, but the blast of the wind was pushing too hard against it. Even if she did get out, she wondered if she would last more than a couple of seconds before she was picked up and tossed away like a rag doll. Where would Adam find her body? On some stretch of prairie miles from here?

She slid over to the passenger door. It wouldn't budge. The rock that had shattered her windshield must have bent the door frame. She climbed over the back of the seat and grabbed the handle of the rear door. It not only opened but was instantly ripped from her grasp.

Every muscle tense, she sank onto the floor of the vehicle, then to the cold sodden earth. The car rocked and skittered toward her. Crouching as low as she could make herself, she crept around the trunk of the sedan and snaked forward on her belly. Behind her the luxury car continued to hop across the once neatly landscaped garden. Then the wind picked it up like a tin toy and flung it out of sight.

That was when she heard it, the eerie sound of a speeding freight train rushing toward her.

Tornado!

Her heart slammed painfully against her chest. For a brief moment, she dared look up. The head of the funnel was overhead, whirling, writhing. Laughing at her.

The outer fringes of the twister were tossing chunks of debris like so much confetti. She was within a few yards of the wall now. Adrenaline gave her an impossible burst of energy. Then she saw him. Adam bent over a child.

Fear and hope had her bolting to his side. He was unconscious, his head cut and bleeding. His youngest granddaughter was pinned under his bulk. Questions, shock, indecision nearly paralyzed Sheila. Was the four-year-old injured? How badly was Adam hurt? Could she safely move either of them? How? Where were the others? Focus. She had to focus.

Beth Ann appeared to be frightened rather than in pain. Sheila pulled the unwilling little girl free and scampered with her to the low wall. Eliciting a promise to stay put was unnecessary. The child was too panic-stricken to wander. Rushing back to Adam, Sheila puzzled over how she could possibly move him. If he had a head or spine injury movement might kill him. Leaving him out in the open almost definitely would. Pulling, pushing and rolling him, she maneuvered him to the narrow gorge by the wall.

The screeching funnel was behind her. Its velocity and strength made it impossible to determine more. She spread herself over the two prone figures, palms covering her ears against the noise and felt the finger of death touch her back. Cowering away from it, she prayed.

The noise receded, then suddenly stopped. Sheila began to breathe. She looked over her shoulder. The house was gone. Disappeared. So was the garage.

She lifted her head. They were three people, prostrate on an open plain. Alone.

Beth Ann, sobbing now, tugged at her sleeve. Sheila turned and beheld the muddy face of Adam First. He smiled wanly and slipped back into unconsciousness.

KERRY COULD HEAR the wind screaming at her, objects beating against the side of the house. She loved the wild freedom of storms, the raw strength and cunning violence of them. The thrill of danger, of living on the edge excited her. It always had. Rafe had been like that, a free spirit, strong and sometimes violent. No, she decided, it wasn't the violence she enjoyed, but the threat of it that got her blood heating and racing and throbbing.

She'd delayed as long as possible rolling down the European shutters her father had insisted on installing on the windows and doors when he'd built the house for her and Rafe. They were supposed to make her safe, but all they brought was a feeling of being confined, restricted and suffocated. They didn't keep the storm out; they kept her locked in.

The table lamps flickered. The thought of darkness scared her far more than the noise. She scurried to the wet bar and poured a jigger of whiskey to calm her nerves.

Sitting on a corner of the couch, she nursed her drink. Had the auxiliary power kicked in? Was that why the lights had blinked? Maybe she should go into the storm cellar under the house. It was hooked into the aux power, too, but had battery-operated emergency lighting, as well. She wouldn't be in the dark.

A booming thud overhead shook the whole house, making her jump, her heart pound. She could easily imagine a tree, a rock, even a car, crashing onto the roof.

She began to tremble. It was silly to be afraid. Daddy had built this house right. He'd made sure she'd be safe in it. So what if a few windows got broken or the roof damaged; she wouldn't be hurt.

The lights went off again, this time for nearly a minute. What the hell was the matter with that damn generator? It was supposed to prevent this.

She sat motionless in the inky blackness, afraid to

move, unable even to lift the glass to her lips to slake her suddenly dry mouth.

The electricity flashed back, and she exhaled so thoroughly her whole body went limp with relief. But how long would the lights stay on? Draining the glass and dropping it onto the carpet, she bolted to the door behind the staircase, yanked it open and switched on the lights below.

"Everything's going to be all right," she muttered as she descended the iron stairs. She pulled the weighted trapdoor down over her head, then gripped the banister to negotiate the last few steps.

The low-ceiling room was big enough, about the size of a two-car garage. There were a couple of foldout couches for sleeping, a few books to while away the time and enough food to last a week or more.

"I'm as snug as a bug in a rug." She giggled.

She was also isolated and alone, and somehow that was more frightening than the storm above.

Why the devil was she still living on this godforsaken ranch, anyway? She belonged in a city. Not a burg like Coyote Springs. A big city. Chicago or New York. Except it got cold in those places. California was the place to be. San Francisco? A lot of rain and fog there. How about Los Angeles or San Diego? She'd have to check them out. Hell, she had enough dough to live in all those places, if she wanted. Just for grins, she'd check out Dallas, too. There was something inviting, intriguing about Big D. Maybe because she liked cowboys.

She turned on the radio and tuned it to the emergency alert station. Instead of constantly repeating the same damn obvious thing, that there was one bitch of a storm blowing, that a tornado had been sighted, why didn't they put on some music? She needed a good, solid rock beat to calm her nerves.

Then she heard what she didn't want to hear, that the twister was ripping right across the northeastern corner of the Number One.

"Oh, God," she cried. "Brian!"

She'd caught the news on the radio an hour before, when she was dressing to go into town to meet a friend for lunch. The bulletin had interrupted one of her favorite country-and-western groups to say the schools had been closed because of a water main break and the kids were all being sent home. Home. This was Brian's home. This was where he should be. With her. Not living with that son of a—

She shivered in the slightly damp coolness of her cave and wished she'd remembered to bring a drink with her. When this was over she'd install a bar here and make sure it was kept well stocked.

Brian was out there…somewhere. With her father, damn him. He'd sent Rafe away from her. Now he'd taken her son. Then Rafe was killed. She pulled at her hair with unsteady fingers. She wouldn't draw the next parallel. Not Brian, not her baby.

Had he reached the ranch in time? At least the headquarters had a tornado shelter. A good one. Nothing short of an earthquake would touch it, and even then…

Damn it. Was he all right? Safe? Uninjured? She definitely should have brought a bottle with her. If anything happened to her sweet baby, she'd kill her father this time, not just take the goddamn ranch away from him.

After what seemed an eternity alone, her thoughts going round and round in her head, the weather bureau finally gave the all clear.

Kerry slid back the dead bolt, threw open the heavy steel door and crawled out of the cellar. The lights were on in the living room. Commercial power or auxiliary? It didn't make much difference. She marched directly to the wet bar. The ice in the freezer hadn't even begun to melt. She put several cubes in a clean old-fashioned glass and splashed a couple of fingers of quality bourbon over them. Nothing was quite like that first sip. Nectar. She savored the crisp sensation of it warming its way down her throat, then strode back to the hall-way, to the electronic panel that controlled the shutters. Pushing a button to raise them, she breathed a sigh of relief when daylight streamed in.

Maybe the school bus had been caught up in the twister. The mere thought had Kerry's blood running cold. She gulped her drink and refilled the glass, not even bothering to add more ice. Who needed ice, any-way? She wanted to feel the fire surge through her.

Or maybe the bus hadn't left Coyote Springs to be-gin with. Yes, that's probably what happened. They hadn't been able to get the drivers right away, so the buses hadn't left town. Brian would be safe.

She had to be sure. Refilling her glass, with extra ice this time, she picked up the phone on the end of the bar. Dead. Well, of course, silly, the lines are down. She looked around the cluttered room. She'd better get after that new maid; the woman wasn't doing a very good job of picking up. Now, where had she put the cell phone? She rifled under newspapers and maga-zines. It had to be here somewhere. Oh, there it was, between the cushions on the couch.

Punching buttons with one hand, she used the other to take another slug of her drink. Her nerves were a-jangle. Damn storms anyhow.

No answer at the headquarters. That was all right; she didn't want to talk to the old man anyway.

Maybe Brian was at Michael's house. No response at his place, either. Was the damn phone even working? Obviously, there was only one way to find out what the hell was going on. She'd take the new off-road vehicle she'd bought last week.

CHAPTER FOURTEEN

ADAM LAY MOTIONLESS. Sheila checked his pulse. It seemed strong and steady. The bleeding had stopped. Was that a good sign or bad? His right foot was angled funny, too.

She stood up. The scene around her was one of total devastation, yet the air smelled fresh and clean as a forest after a spring shower. There was water enough, in pools and puddles, coating everything with a sheen. A gentle, caressing breeze soughed its way across the open plain.

A dozen thoughts battled for attention. Foremost was the question of how to get help. Where were the others? In the storm cellar? Could she reach them?

"Grampa, wake up. Wake up, Grampa," the four-year-old begged as she jostled Adam's shoulder.

Sheila gently pulled the child away. "He's going to be all right, honey. He just needs to sleep for a few minutes."

For how long? Didn't the longer he was unconscious mean the worse the concussion? She folded the sniffling child in a tight embrace to soothe her and spied the cell phone hooked on Adam's belt. She grabbed the instrument, hit the "on" button and dialed 911.

The dispatcher's unexcited voice calmed her enough to respond to his questions. Sheila also remembered to tell him about the other members of the family who were missing: two girls, aged six and eight, a boy ten, and maybe a sixteen-year-old if Brian was with them.

While she waited for the medevac, she rocked Beth Ann in her arms, and stared at the collapsed figure on the ground beside her.

No, she decided. She couldn't leave this man. Even with all his flaws, she loved him. Their relationship might turn out to be as tempestuous as the storms that terrified her, but she couldn't abandon him. Whether he kept or lost the ranch wasn't as important as being by his side and sharing their love.

But first, dear God, he had to survive.

THE SCENT OF RUBBING alcohol and disinfectant wafted from the glare-filled corridor into the dimly lit lounge. Sheila felt too weak to stand and too nervous to remain sitting. The torment of waiting for word on Adam's condition would have been unbearable if his family hadn't been there, supporting her and one another. Michael and Clare were already at the hospital when she arrived in the second medevac helicopter with Davy and the two older girls. Adam and Beth Ann had been on the first. The child, dirty but uninjured, clung to her mother's neck. Elva had also arrived, her jaw still tingling from her recent dental work.

"Is he all right?" Sheila blurted out when she saw a man in green scrubs enter the room. She jumped to her feet and joined the others moving toward the doctor.

"He has a broken leg and an egg-sized knot on the back of his head, but he's going to be fine," Dr. Dullighan assured everyone. "They're putting a cast on his leg now."

When Sheila staggered with relief, Gideon wrapped

his arm around her. He and Julie had blown in together a minute earlier. Only Kerry was unaccounted for. Michael had tried calling her, but the telephone lines were down, and she hadn't answered her cell phone. He'd located Brian, though. His bus hadn't left the school when the tornado warning was issued, and school officials had kept everyone there until things got sorted out.

"He'll need physical therapy when the cast comes off, but I don't expect any significant loss of function."

People started asking questions at once, forcing the doctor to raise his hands in surrender.

"Everyone calm down," Michael called out above the din. "Davy, take your sisters out to the snack bar and get something to drink."

The boy protested. He wanted to stay.

"Dave," his father said, using his son's "grown-up" name, "you'll help the most if you do what I ask." He reached into his pocket and gave the boy a fistful of change. "If that's not enough—"

Gideon extracted more coins from his jeans and passed them to his nephew. Partially mollified, the kids traipsed off down the hall.

Dr. Dullighan smiled appreciatively and motioned the adults to the corner of the room. They sat down along the walls, Sheila in the middle. The physician pulled up an empty chair and faced them.

"There is one thing," he began. "The blow to his head—"

Sheila covered her mouth with her hands as alarm shivered through her. "You think the concussion is serious, then?"

Julie, sitting next to her, stroked her back.

"Probably not," the doctor said confidently. "He

doesn't seem to have any problem remembering the event leading up to his being hit on the head, and he's had no difficulty recognizing people or getting names straight. Nevertheless, that's a pretty big goose egg on his head. I don't want to alarm you, but there's always a chance of a delayed reaction, of a blood clot forming. I would like to keep him here for a few days...to make sure—"

"Of course," Michael agreed, letting out a huff of relief and reaching an arm around his wife's shoulders. "If it's a question of money, Doctor, of insurance paying...we'll make up whatever isn't covered."

The man in the white coat waved the comment away. "I'd appreciate it, though, if you could convince your father that it's in his best interest to stay here."

"You mean he doesn't want to?" Sheila asked incredulously, though it took hardly a moment's reflection to realize she shouldn't be surprised. Adam wasn't one to accept help—even when he needed it.

"Not only doesn't he want to," the doctor responded with a wry chuckle, "he refuses to."

Michael laughed. "Totally in character, Doctor. Dad's fine."

Clare rubbed her husband's arm and smiled in happy agreement. "We'll browbeat him into staying another day or two, Doctor. Will that be long enough?"

Dullighan smiled pleasantly. "Great."

Sheila moaned a prayer. She'd lost one man in her life. She couldn't lose another. "When can we see him?"

The doctor glanced at his watch. "Come on. The cast should be set by now."

ADAM'S HEAD pounded like one of his racehorses at full gallop and his leg felt as if someone had parked a bulldozer on it. The sawbones didn't want to give him medication that would knock him out—not that he would have accepted it. A headache and bunged shin-bone were mild compared with all the other things that had transpired in the past twenty-four hours.

He looked up at the sound of the door whooshing open and reflexively shielded his eyes against the stabbing bright light flooding in from the hallway.

His family invaded like foot soldiers armed with cheery expressions and upbeat greetings. Sheila led them, her face haggard, concerned. Beneath the forced smile, he saw she was on the verge of tears. How much he wanted to soothe away those care lines and see her laugh again. She'd saved his life. Too bad he had nothing to offer in return.

Opening his arms, she lurched forward to slip between them. Her cheek was warm and sweet and soft. He bracketed her face and kissed her on the lips. Just a taste, not nearly enough.

Beth Ann was sleeping soundly against her mother's shoulder.

"She okay?" he asked.

Clare's lips quivered as she caressed the little girl's back. "You saved her life, Adam."

"Not me," he said, focusing on the woman holding his hands. "Sheila's the one you should thank—" his eyes locked onto hers "—that I thank." The love he saw there blocked out the hammering in his head and the throbbing in his leg.

Clare offered a tearful smile to Sheila. "Both of you." Her voice was husky. "I don't know how to thank you. Words aren't enough. They'll never be enough."

Sheila smiled crookedly and swallowed her own tears. This bond of family had been missing in her life. They were all so blessed by the closeness they shared. Adam might think of himself as a failure with Kerry, but he'd been a wonderful success with his other children. They were truly caring and generous with their affections.

The youngsters rejoined them and Sally started jabbering about their time in the storm cellar and how Davy had made them sing songs so they wouldn't get scared.

Adam gave his grandson a thumbs-up sign. "Good thinking. That was exactly the right thing to do," he congratulated him.

The boy shrugged nonchalantly, but his pride in the compliment was unmistakable. "That's what Sheila did."

The back of the bed was raised, but Adam winced when he tried to straighten himself up. Sheila rearranged the pillow behind his head.

"Where's Kerry? Is she all right?"

"Phone lines are down, so we haven't been able to get hold of her," Michael told him, "and you know how careless she is with her cell phone. I talked to the pilot of a rescue helicopter that flew over the house. He saw some roof damage, but otherwise everything seemed to be untouched. I'm sure she's fine."

"And Brian?" Adam asked.

"He never left the school campus. He's on his way over now."

Adam sighed heavily. "How'd the rest of the ranch fare? Was anyone hurt?"

"I checked around. Lonnie Dominquez lost his new

carport,'' Michael told him, ''and the Ramirezes have a tree down in their backyard, but no one was hurt.''

Adam nodded on a deep breath. ''That's the important thing. We can always replace a carport and plant a new tree.''

''Lost some cattle and sheep, too. Charlie will get back to me with the numbers.''

Adam nodded again.

''I didn't get there for the beginning of the movie,'' Sheila said lightly. ''Tell us what happened, what you remember.''

He gave her a quick smiling wink. ''I'd just gotten Davy, the girls and their dog, Bullet, up to the house when the sky turned that ugly black and blue. Having witnessed a twister or two before, I recognized the signs and knew we were in for it.''

All the time he kept wondering where she was, whether she'd gotten to Coyote Springs safely. He should have been with her, protecting her. Instead, he'd driven her away—into a tornado. The harm he imagined she'd done to him didn't compare with his abandoning her.

''I knew we'd be totally safe in the storm cellar. As soon as I opened the truck door, though, Bullet ran off.''

''He's always been afraid of storms,'' Clare noted.

''Anyway,'' Adam continued, ''I rushed the kids inside the house and hurried them downstairs, except Beth Ann took a right turn in the mudroom and made a beeline for the bathroom. I figured half a minute wouldn't make any difference. I should have known better.''

Clare shook her head. ''You had your hands full.''

''No excuse,'' Adam countered. ''I went into the

pantry, grabbed a couple of extra flashlights, and came back to find the bathroom door empty and the back door both wide-open, and I realized Beth Ann had gone outside.''

He pictured the little girl being picked up and tossed helplessly. If anything had happened to her, he would never have been able to live with himself.

"I found her hanging on to the garden wall, calling Bullet. I scooped her up and told her the dog was hiding somewhere safe and we had to get inside.''

"Oh, dear,'' Clare lamented. "I never even thought of old Bullet. I wonder what happened to him.''

"He's all right, Mom,'' Davy answered. "He was waiting for us when we came out of the cellar. I wanted to bring him with us, but the man in the helicopter said there wasn't room.''

"I'm sure he'll be fine,'' Gideon assured him. "Bullet's obviously a pretty smart old mutt.''

"You were saying,'' Sheila prompted Adam.

"I'd turned back to the house with Beth Ann cradled in my arms, when a two-by-four slammed against my right shin. I heard a crack, whether it was the wood or my bone, I don't know, but I went down like a ton of bricks.''

"You must have been in horrible pain,'' Clare said.

"If I was, it didn't register,'' he replied. It sounded very brave, but he'd been too terrified to feel physical pain. "I was worried about Beth Ann and the others.''

Sheila squeezed her eyes shut and massaged his forearm.

"Beth Ann was terrified, of course. There was no way I could send her to the cellar by herself, so I covered her as best I could. I remember glancing back and seeing the house tilt.'' He smiled. ''Ridiculous. A house that size.''

''Do you remember getting hit on the head?'' Julie asked.

''No,'' he admitted, ''but I do remember waking up by the garden wall and seeing Sheila hovering over me.'' He gazed at her. ''You were there, weren't you? I didn't imagine it?''

She tightened one hand on his arm and with the other brushed away a tear. ''You didn't imagine it.''

''How did you get me to the wall? That's not where I went down.''

''I think it's called the superhuman strength of pure terror,'' she said with a tight grin.

''Seems to me I remember your hair being mussed up.''

She snorted. ''I resembled a drowned rat, you mean.'' She hadn't recognized herself when she'd finally seen her reflection in the helicopter window on the flight in. Hair hanging down like the Medusa's snakes, her clothes sopping and mud caked.

He smiled at her. ''You don't look like one now.''

That soft chuckle he loved came out. ''Thanks to Clare. God bless her, even with everything else going on, she thought to bring me clean clothes.''

''So where are mine?'' Adam asked.

Michael raised a hand. ''Whoa, not so fast.''

''Adam, you've got a broken leg and a concussion,'' Sheila told him. ''You need to stay here for a while longer.''

He figured they'd gang up on him. ''They've done all they can for the leg. No sense taking up a bed somebody else can use. As for my head, I have a headache, not a concussion. I just showed you I remember exactly what happened—"

"Sorry, Dad," Michael said. "You'll have to stay here another day or two, whether you want to or not."

"The hell—" Adam caught himself on the last word in front of the children. "Why is that?"

"Because you don't have any place to live," Sheila told him. "The headquarters is gone."

"Gone?" His eyes went wide. "You mean damaged."

"She means gone, Dad," Michael said emphatically. "It's a jumble of pickup sticks at the foot of the mesa."

Adam scowled under knitted eyebrows. It seemed inconceivable that a building that size could be tossed off the end of the butte.

"You'll stay with us until you get a new house built," Clare told him. "We'll turn the den into your bedroom and the game room next to it into a living room and office for you. You'll have plenty of privacy and your own bathroom."

Adam pondered the faces around him. All the people he loved were here. Except for Kerry. What would become of her? he wondered sadly, then mentally shook himself to focus on the immediate situation.

His chances of ever running the Number One again were gone, thanks to Sheila's original report and his own damn temper. "There won't be a new house."

Everyone stared at him with mouths hanging open. The expressions almost made him laugh.

"I'll take you up on your generous offer," he continued, "until I can get myself resettled. Maybe in Dallas or Austin." Or Houston, he thought. "But I'm finished with the Number One."

"You don't mean that," Michael objected.

"You love the Number One," Clare reminded him.

"You're exhausted—" Julia added.

"This isn't the best time to be making a decision," Gideon pointed out.

Adam waved them all to silence, then turned to Sheila, who hadn't said a word. "Convey a message to the Homestead Bank and Trust of Houston, Texas, for me, Mrs. Malone. Tell them they can take their job and shove it."

The room was filled with stunned silence.

Finally, Sheila broke it. "Why don't y'all get something to drink and see if there's any news on Kerry. I'll meet you downstairs in a few minutes."

"Good idea." Gideon extended his arms in a gathering motion. "Brian ought to be getting here soon, too."

Each of them in turn came up, kissed or rested a hand on Adam, wished him a good-night, then shuffled out of the room. The last to leave was Clare. She placed a comforting hand on Sheila's. "Take your time," she whispered.

Sheila waited until the door was closed and the sound of feet in the corridor had receded. When she turned to the man in the bed, her face was tight, her pulse high.

"Why are you doing this?" she demanded. "Who are you trying to punish? Yourself? Your family? Me?"

He shifted in the bed. "What are you talking about?" he snarled without making eye contact. "I'm not trying to punish anyone."

She studied the lines of his face, the deep creases gouged by age and adversity. "Aren't you? I wouldn't have thought you were into self-mutilation, but you seem to be—cutting yourself off from the people who love you and the place that is a part of you. Leaving it is stupid, Adam, and senseless.''

He came close to grinning, as if this were all another of their word games. ''So you think I'm stupid?''

Her stoic expression didn't change. ''Yes.''

The shock on his face told her he'd expected her to retreat into some benign statement that he was smart enough but was being foolish. As if being a fool were better than being an idiot.

''You're also a coward.''

This time his eyes went wide and his jaw dropped. If she were a man and he was standing on his feet he would undoubtedly have planted his fist squarely on her nose.

His chest heaved. Coldly he rearranged the neat fold of sheet across his midsection. ''I think you'd better leave,'' he said in a tone that was low and rough.

''Not until I've had my say.'' She attempted to concentrate on the muffled sounds of people in the hallway while she struggled to collect her thoughts, to ignore the pain in his eyes, the hurt pride, the fury generated by her insult.

''You're running away, Adam. You're acting like a spoiled child, picking up your marbles and going home because the game isn't turning out the way you want it to.''

He glowered with rage. ''You said I have no home left.''

Word games. She wasn't going to stand for it.

''Just shut up for once and listen,'' she snapped.

He glared tight-lipped; she glared back. When he closed his eyes and raised his hand to his head she realized he wasn't just angry but in physical pain. It gave her pause, but even the guilt of imposing more discomfort wouldn't make her back down. There couldn't be any accommodating this time. He opened his eyes, inhaled deeply and, placing his hands calmly in his lap, leaned back. "Say your piece," he said resignedly.

It annoyed her that suddenly she was there on his sufferance. Nevertheless she wouldn't let petty irritations distract her.

"When I first came here," she began in a tone as neutral as she could make it, "you asked me what my qualifications were for passing judgment on you. I enumerated my academic and professional background, which didn't impress you—"

He started to object, but she waved him to silence.

"Later I let you in on my personal experiences."

Her legs felt rubbery and she wanted to sit, but she was too jittery to stay in one spot, so she paced. Her stomach ached, from hunger and nervous tension.

"I watched my father go through a similar crisis in his life, and I saw him fail. He was a good man, Adam, and I loved him. I still cherish his memory. But goodness wasn't enough. I thought he was smart, too. He didn't have the schooling you've had. He never went to college, but to me he could do anything, and after all, isn't that what smart means—being able to do things? I found out, though, there was one thing he couldn't do. He couldn't bend." She paused, not for emphasis, but because her emotions were rising. "And so he died."

She wrapped her arms across her middle, trying unsuccessfully to ward off the icy chill of regret that seemed to surround her. "I came here to Coyote Springs, to the Number One Ranch, hoping I could help you succeed where my father failed, that in some mysterious way, I could help overcome the forces that had destroyed him.''

Her heart was pounding now, in slow, heavy beats that drummed in her ears and made her feel vulnerable.

"I'm not your father, Sheila," Adam said softly.

She looked over at him, at the man she'd slept with, made love to. To the man who had, in an all-too-brief moment in time, filled her with hope and joy. And false happiness. She knew now she'd had her eyes closed. Maybe she'd been a coward, too.

"No, you're not, Adam, and I never pretended you were," she replied quietly. "What I felt for him was the love and adoration of a little girl for a wonderful daddy. What I've felt for you has been the response of an adult woman for a strong man. A man who's love I could share. Whose strength I could respect. Whose wisdom I could depend on, learn from and revere."

Tears were dangerously close to the surface. She forced them back.

"Sheila…"

"But I was wrong, Adam." She turned away from his bed as the first tear fell. "I was wrong," she muttered, opened the door and walked out of the room.

BONE-WEARY and emotionally drained, Sheila gratefully accepted Michael and Clare's invitation to stay at their home on the Number One. She would have preferred the privacy of remaining in town, but even with Michael's help, getting a hotel room without credit cards, driver's license or checkbook would have been a hassle. Besides, she had no clothes except the borrowed ones she was wearing, and she would have been left without transportation.

She could have attributed the tears that continued to blur her vision to exhaustion, but it was much more. Her children were off in the world making lives of their own—without her. These people had become her family. The realization was bittersweet. The man she'd come to love was lying in a bed, shattered physically and emotionally. He'd credited her with saving his life and blamed her for ruining it.

"I have so much to do tomorrow," Sheila muttered as they pulled out of the hospital parking lot. The kids in the seat behind her were quiet. She leaned back against the headrest and closed her eyes.

What was to become of Adam now that the Number One was no longer his, even to run? What about their relationship? She'd opened Pandora's box. Even together they'd never be able to stuff all the pieces back inside again.

The road to hell is paved with good intentions. She'd come to Coyote Springs with the best of them—to save a family-owned ranch. She'd done her work hellishly well—to the point of falling into Nedra Cummings's trap of seeing dollars instead of people.

Adam's stiff-necked self-righteousness aggravated her. The same stubbornness in her father had puzzled her, too. They were both intelligent men. Why couldn't they understand...

The lulling rhythm of city lights segued into continuous darkness behind her eyelids. Of course her father had been smart enough to understand that change might save the ranch. His unwillingness to bend could be attributed to inflexibility...or maybe all the time she'd been missing the obvious. Jim Pounder had been a rancher, not a farmer. He knew nothing about planting and harvesting because he had no interest in them.

Turning his land into neat rows of corn or cotton would have been as foreign to him as drawing up plans for a nuclear power plant.

She'd always thought losing the ranch was what had shattered him; now she was beginning to understand it wasn't just the land that had been vital to him. He could have kept it if he'd adapted. It was losing the only way of life he knew and valued that had broken his heart. Adam had lost his way of life, too...

Sheila jerked when Clare gently jostled her awake. "We're home."

Home. In the semiconscious stupor before her vision cleared, she pictured Adam standing by the fireplace. Adam lying beside her in bed, surrounded by moonlight; the murmur of contented breathing. She struggled to focus. Clare smiled sympathetically and beckoned her out of the vehicle.

"What about Kerry?" Sheila asked, remembering they were supposed to check on her.

"We stopped by her place. She wasn't there, but her car was. Michael and Brian stayed to search the area."

Sheila followed her hostess through the garage into a large country kitchen. "You think she might be hurt?"

Clare shook her head uncertainly. "The house sustained some roof damage, but that's all. No broken windows. Her purse was on the kitchen counter."

Together the two women helped the younger girls dress for bed. Longing for her own grandchildren washed through Sheila as she tucked them in.

Sheila trailed Clare to the master bedroom. "It doesn't look good, does it?" she took up the subject again as if there'd been no interruption.

"We're not going to think the worst yet." Clare removed a nightgown and underwear from her dresser, passed them to Sheila, then entered the walk-in closet, where she selected a change of clothes for the next day. "Kerry's a free spirit, but she isn't stupid. The lights were on in the cellar, which means she probably went there during the storm."

The possibility that Kerry might have been killed, that Adam would lose another child and that the tension between father and daughter would never be resolved pressed around Sheila's heart. "I want to help in any way I can."

"Then get a good night's sleep. There'll be plenty to do tomorrow, I promise."

Sheila would have crawled directly into the double bed in the guest room, but she needed to remove the sweat and grime that clung to her body. The warm shower refreshed without invigorating. She dried herself, changed into the donated nightclothes and slipped between the pastel-blue cotton sheets. Her arm reached out for Adam, her skin still tingling from the water's gentle spray, but of course he wasn't there. She fell asleep with his name on her lips.

CHAPTER FIFTEEN

BY THE TIME she awoke the next morning, donned the robe and slippers Clare lent her and padded down to the kitchen, it was nearly eight o'clock. Elva lowered the gas on the hash browns she was preparing in an iron skillet, topped off her coffee cup and joined Clare and Sheila at the breakfast bar.

"Any word on Kerry?" Sheila asked.

Clare shook her head despondently. "Michael and Brian stayed at the house all night, waiting for her. Michael took the helicopter about an hour ago to widen the search. He thinks she might be shacked up with someone in town."

Sheila bit her lip and was tempted to say she hoped so. At least she'd still be alive.

Elva returned to the stove and tended the potatoes, then whisked half a dozen eggs in a stainless-steel bowl.

"The three of us are going shopping this morning," Clare decreed as she set plates on the wide bar separating the kitchen proper from the family eating area.

"It's just me and my old Taurus now," Elva said fatalistically.

"We'll start with clothes."

Sheila nodded. Clothes were a small part of it. She still had to notify insurance and credit card companies, ask her bank to overnight-express new checks to her, obtain a replacement driver's license, buy, lease or rent a new car...

Michael trudged through the door from the garage. The dark circles under his eyes attested to his all-night vigil. "We found her." The good news didn't seem to please him.

A ball of fear settled in Sheila's stomach. "Is...is she all right?"

Michael strode to the coffeemaker, drew off a cup of the dark hot liquid, turned and leaned against the counter. He poised the steaming cup halfway to his lips. "Yes and no."

Sheila could feel Clare's impatience matching her own. "So what happened, Michael?"

He gulped coffee and moved over to the end stool at the bar. "She went out in her off-road vehicle yesterday after the storm—"

"I take back what I said about her not being stupid," Clare muttered.

"Go on," Sheila prompted.

"Apparently, she was going up to the headquarters to make sure Brian was all right...and she ended up in a ditch."

"Was she hurt?" Elva asked with genuine concern.

Michael shook his head. "She's pretty badly bruised. I flew her to the hospital."

"Did your dad know she was in the E.R.?"

"I stopped in and saw him. He's not exactly chipper."

Sheila tried to imagine what Adam must be going through. He'd lost a son in a car accident, almost lost two grandsons at the tank and a granddaughter in a tornado, and now his wayward daughter was injured in another vehicle mishap. "I need to visit him," she said. She should be by his side.

"We'll drop by after shopping," Clare suggested.

Sheila didn't want to wait. He wouldn't forgive her for the things she'd said the night before, but she had to see him one last time before she got on with the rest of her life—without him.

"That'll work out fine," Michael agreed. "Brian wanted to stay with his mother at the hospital, but she was a mess emotionally as well as physically. There was nothing he could accomplish by hanging around. I convinced him to go to school, then come back after his last class. You can meet him there and bring him home with you."

"What's the prognosis, Michael?" Sheila asked.

He stroked his chin. "She had a few cuts that needed stitching…"

"I don't think that's what Sheila meant, dear," Clare said softly.

He slouched on the stool. "I know, but I can't answer the bigger question. She was sober when we found her, but that was because she'd lain in that gully all night without a bottle. I'm sure she was drunk when she ran off the road." He sipped his coffee. "Dad's pretty upset. I asked the staff to keep him away from her for the time being." He looked at Sheila. "I'm hoping you'll talk him out of making matters worse. He'll listen to you."

She lifted her cup. "There's no reason he should."

"I can think of a very good one," Clare said softly. "He loves you."

She'd always thought love conquered all, that it was enough to get two people through any crisis. She didn't believe it anymore. It wasn't enough, not in this case.

Love was supposed to heal, not hurt; yet all she'd accomplished was to alienate the very man she wanted to spend the rest of her life with.

"I'll try," she said, "but don't expect much."

Clare gave her a wan but encouraging smile and a quick hug.

"By the way, we found your car," Michael told Sheila. "About three miles from the mesa. It's sitting on all four fully inflated tires in the middle of a pasture, as if a giant had plopped it down there. It looks like it's been through a tornado, of course, but—" He broke off and returned to the garage and retrieved a canvas sack. After placing it on the end of the counter, he withdrew her black leather purse and held it out to her.

Dumbfounded, Sheila stared in disbelief. She opened the clasp. Everything was inside. Her wallet and checkbook, house keys—she hadn't even thought about those. Inhaling deeply, she kissed Michael on the cheek. One complication, at least, had been eliminated.

"It's not even scratched," Elva noted as she brushed her fingertips over the soft leather.

"How it managed to stay in the car with a door blown off is beyond me," Michael commented, "but it was sitting on the front seat as if you'd just placed it there." He grinned.

In spite of lingering fatigue, Sheila enjoyed her shopping trip with Clare and Elva. Sheila needed only to replace the clothes she'd brought from home; Elva needed a whole new wardrobe.

"The Number One is paying for everything," Clare assured the housekeeper when she gasped at the price tags on the dressy outfits Clare was sorting through in one of the better women's clothing stores. It took a few fittings before Elva finally fell into the spirit of things, then the three women went at it with a vengeance.

All the time, Sheila kept thinking about Adam lying in his hospital room. It was impossible to imagine him living in an apartment in Dallas or any other place for that matter. He was a rancher, and without a ranch to live on and be part of, he would die. It sounded melodramatic, but she had seen it happen to her father, watched the anger fade and a kind of fatalism replace it. What she remembered most was the haunted look in his eyes. He'd failed and he could never recover from that humiliation. The heart attack had been for him a blessed relief.

She couldn't let that happen to Adam.

ADAM ALWAYS GOT backaches when he was forced to sleep on his back, and with the damn cast on his leg, that was his only option. So now, in addition to his head and leg throbbing, his sacroiliac was killing him, as well. To make matters worse, a nurse had come in every couple of hours during the night and asked stupid questions to make sure he didn't have a concussion. So now his head, leg and back hurt, and he'd had a miserable night's rest. Not that he'd really slept, not after what Sheila had said.

She'd been right, of course—about some things. He wouldn't be running the Number One anymore, and that was his own damn fault. But leave it? Maybe he should rebuild the headquarters, but his heart wasn't in it. The house had been big and impressive and he'd spent most of his life there; it surprised him that he felt no compelling nostalgia for it.

The ache in his heart wasn't for a house, but for the person he wanted to share it with. He'd blown any chance of that now. He'd lost her respect, and without that there could be no love.

Did he blame her for the crisis at the bank? Yes. If she hadn't brought up the issue of the vaqueros' paying rent, it would never have become an issue. Oh, eventually someone might have stumbled onto the fact that they were furnished free housing, but by then it would have been a moot point. Practices long established tended to remain in force. If she'd written her report in positive terms, they might have continued cloud seeding, too. Hell, she'd almost lost him his horses.

He didn't discount his own culpability in the fiasco at the bank, but had his temper really made any difference? They were going to do what they were going to do. At least they knew plainly that he wouldn't collude in the destruction of his family's heritage.

You're a coward. The words still twisted like a blade in his gut. Was he? Was he running away as she'd claimed?

He'd never been a quitter.

He wouldn't be one now.

He adjusted the contour of the bed. It helped some. A little later, he'd change it again. "This is one miserable excuse for exercise," he grumbled to the sterile room.

She'd accused him of ruining her professional reputation, too, maybe even driving her out of business. Well, he could darn well do something about that.

He waited until a decent morning hour, then dialed Hawkins Heavy Equipment. Caleb wasn't in yet, and his secretary refused to disclose his private home number to a voice on the telephone.

"Would you please contact him and ask him to call

me back?'' He gave her his room extension. "It's urgent.''

It was nearly half an hour before the phone rang.

"What the hell are you doing in a hospital, little feller?" the huge man's voice boomed over the line. "Very unhealthy place. I advise you to leave as soon as possible.''

Adam snorted. "I'll keep that in mind." He paused a moment. "Cal I need to ask a favor of you.''

"Shoot.''

Adam smiled and began to feel the first traces of hope. His friend didn't ask what it was, or hedge that he'd try. Caleb Hawkins was the kind of man who still sealed a contract with a handshake and kept his word.

"I hear you've bought a new company.''

"Part of my plot to take over the world.''

Adam laughed in spite of himself. Twenty minutes later he hung up.

He'd asked Cal to hire Malone Consulting and Services to evaluate his newest acquisition, and he'd offered to reimburse him for the expense. Adam couldn't draw on the financial resources of the Number One anymore, but he wasn't personally destitute. The ranch had never been about money. Homestead didn't understand that, but he'd expected Sheila to. Or maybe she had and he just wasn't listening.

The business tycoon had refused his offer. He was getting ready to contact her anyway, he insisted. Adam wasn't sure it was true, but it could have been, and he was hardly in a position to argue the point. Besides, this way he'd be able to deny any collusion in Sheila's getting the high-figure contract—if she ever questioned him.

He rested back and closed his eyes. Her business was safe, at least. Now, what about the rest of the chaos he'd created?

Michael's visit a few minutes later deepened the depression he'd been slipping into. Kerry was down in the emergency room. His child was hurt, and they wouldn't let him see her.

Who'd told them to keep him away? Michael or Kerry? Maybe both. It didn't make any difference. He was her father. He had to help his child. But how? She wouldn't listen to him, and he had no right to order her to do anything. He'd have to find a way. He wouldn't give up on his daughter, either.

"Hello, Gramps."

Adam looked up to see Brian walk through the doorway. His brown hair was tousled by the wind, his hazel eyes troubled. Maybe he'd been slow to mature, but he was growing up fast now.

"Hi yourself. Have you been to see your mom?"

Brian merely shook his head. "Uncle Mike says she was drunk when she went out after the storm."

"We don't know that for sure, son."

"She was," Brian said, certainty overlaid with shame and humiliation. "I know she was." He hung his head as if it were his fault.

"Remember when we talked?" Adam asked. "We agreed to do whatever it takes to help her, even if she didn't want the help?"

The boy nodded.

"I think it's time to talk her into going away for a while—to a drug and alcohol rehabilitation center."

Brian's head shot up. "You mean like Betty Ford's?"

Adam grabbed the trapeze suspended over his head and shifted his weight in a futile attempt to ease the pain in his back. "She needs professional help, son, more than you and I or the rest of the family can give her."

"Then you'll send her there, won't you?" There was hope in his eyes.

Adam shook his head sadly. "It's not up to me, son. She has to go of her own free will. Nobody can make her, and even if we could, it probably wouldn't do any good. She has to want help, which means she has to recognize and acknowledge she has a problem."

The hope dimmed. "Maybe Uncle Mike—"

"Right now I'm not sure she'll listen to him, either."

Brian fell silent for several moments before what his grandfather was saying clicked. "You want *me* to tell her?" His eyes went wide. "No, I can't." He backed away from Adam's bedside. "I won't. You can't make me."

Adam understood the urge to withdraw from what would undoubtedly be a very ugly confrontation.

"Have Uncle Gideon talk to her." Panic had Brian's voice rising. "Or Aunt Julie."

Softly Adam said, "I think you're the only one she'll listen to now, son. You're the most important person in the world to her."

The two men faced each other, generations apart, united by the common bond of family. Finally, looking down, Brian shuffled his feet, and Adam saw the decision was made. He hoped someday Kerry would be as proud of her son as he was now.

"I'll try," the boy responded none too happily.

ADAM WAS SITTING in a wheelchair, his plaster-encased leg projecting forward like a battering ram, when Sheila and the others arrived.

"Is Brian not here from school yet?" Sheila asked. Their eyes darted, met and darted again, both of them guarded, gauging, unsure.

"He's visiting his mother."

"How is she?"

"According to the nurses, in a foul mood."

Dr. Dullighan tapped on the door and walked in. "How are you doing, Mr. First?"

"Just peachy keen, Doc." If the surgeon recognized the sarcasm in his patient's reply, he didn't respond to it. "When am I getting out of this place?"

"How about tomorrow?"

Sheila saw Adam's face light up and her heart sank. Her last stop in their shopping trip had been to rent a car. It was time for her to go home, too. She'd leave in the morning after Adam was discharged. It wouldn't be the parting she'd envisioned, but then nothing had worked out the way she'd planned, the way she'd hoped.

After the doctor left, she realized she'd heard almost nothing of what he'd said. All she knew was that Adam was going back to the Number One—at least temporarily—and she was returning to Houston.

Brian joined them.

"How did it go?" Adam asked quietly.

"Okay," he said without enthusiasm. "She's agreed to go to Betty Ford's...but..." Brian flexed his fingers as he looked at his grandfather. "She insisted on one condition."

"What's that?"

Brian hesitated, obviously uncomfortable with the

message he had to deliver. "She said you have to promise never to see her again."

Tears welled as Sheila turned to the man in the chair. The only sound was of dinner trays being distributed out in the hallway.

Adam's face froze; he stared straight ahead, then he lowered his eyes and tightened his lips. "If that's what she wants."

"She'll come around, Adam. She'll change her mind," Sheila tried to assure him.

He nodded but didn't say a word.

THE NEXT MORNING, while Clare and Elva supervised the installation of new furniture in the den and game room, Michael and Sheila prepared to pick up Adam in the helicopter.

"I promised you a tour of the damage," Michael reminded her. "We've got some time. Still want to see it?"

"Very much."

The tornado had cut a swath a quarter of a mile wide and six miles long across the northeast corner of the huge spread. Fortunately, most of the land was pasture, but several outbuildings had been destroyed, a few dozen animals injured or killed and two homes damaged.

The scene at the bottom of the butte was incredible. The ranch headquarters had tumbled onto its side and collapsed under its own weight, leaving a jumbled pile of wood, brick and shingle, furniture and glass.

"As soon as we get the homes of the two vaqueros repaired, we'll start clearing this," Michael explained over the intercom. "I'm going to have them take it nice and slow so we can sort through the debris. I don't expect to salvage much, but maybe we can find family photo albums, things like that.''

"I hope you do,'' Sheila replied. It was another example of the family's strong sense of history and continuity. She gazed out at the mess. "What about the home place? How did it fare?''

He swung the chopper to the south, making Sheila's stomach lurch. "Let's go see.''

Instead of flying over the site, Michael landed where Adam had on her first visit. There were no ranch hands barbecuing beef brisket, lamb and goat. No trucks scattered haphazardly about. No welcoming committee to greet them. Together she and Adam's son walked the short distance to the derelict ranch house. It had escaped unscathed. The rolling hills around it had apparently protected it from the worst of the winds.

"I guess your great-granddaddy knew what he was doing when he built here,'' Sheila commented as they strolled the path she'd walked with Adam on the day of the picnic.

As she surveyed the peaceful scene, an idea struck her. She studied the tree-shaded building. "My job when I came here was to assess the management of the ranch, not its value...'' She trailed off.

"It's value?'' He regarded her under hooded brows. "I can see the wheels turning in your head, Sheila. What're you thinking?''

"I'm not sure yet...exactly.'' She paused. "How about current files, numbers of livestock, various assets. Do you have them?''

"I keep the books, remember? Dad transfers his day-to-day files to my computer every week. What I have at home is current as of last weekend, and I can reconstruct the transactions we've made since then. We'll have to anyway.''

"Do you mind if I examine your records?''

"No problem. But will you at least give me a hint of what you have in mind?''

"Yes.'' She combed her fingers through her mussed-up hair. "Because I'm going to need your advice, as well.''

"HOW IS ADAM taking his retirement?'' Mildred asked.

Sheila pulled into the huge parking lot. Insurance had paid off on the Town Car, but not enough for her to buy another one. This compact was more modest in size and more economical to run.

"According to Michael, reasonably well.'' She killed the engine and gathered her purse. "I'd hoped the bank might offer the general manager position to Mike, but of course they didn't. Nedra hired a guy from Montana. E. J. Hoffman, who has a proven track record running large spreads.''

Mildred got out and closed the door on her side, then waited for the click that indicated it was locked, before stepping away from the vehicle. "How does Adam get along with him?''

"Apparently, pretty well. He comes to Adam regularly for opinions and advice.''

"Smart move.'' Mildred linked her arm with Sheila's as they walked toward the main entrance to the mall. "Have you talked to Adam?''

"A few times,'' Sheila commented offhandedly as she opened the wide glass door to JC Penney's. They were among the first ones there, so the place was still relatively empty.

Mildred fingered a blue cotton blouse with delicate

lace trim that was on sale. "What about?" She passed on.

"Oh, the weather. The drought. The new ranch manager," Sheila replied.

They moved out into the mall proper and were greeted by the aroma of freshly baked pretzels. Sheila would have been tempted if they hadn't just finished eating breakfast at Chez Lazar.

"How are your discussions going with that woman at the bank?" Mildred asked.

"Nedra's interested in finding a face-saving way out of the hole she's in with her colleagues. I think she realizes the threat of lawsuits wasn't a bluff. It gives me the upper hand."

There was a gleam in the older woman's eyes. "You're enjoying yourself, aren't you?"

Sheila laughed. "Maybe a little."

Mildred stopped to look at jewelry on display in a window. "What does Adam think about what you're doing?"

Sheila stiffened slightly. "I haven't told him. I've been working out the details with Michael by e-mail. He's offered to talk to his father, but I've asked him not to. I think it's something Adam and I need to discuss face-to-face."

Pinning her with a curious glance, Mildred asked, "So why haven't you?"

Because I'm a coward, Sheila was tempted to say. *Because I don't know if what I'm doing is right.* "With his leg still in a cast, he can't fly here, and… I've been so tied up at the office, I haven't had time to visit him."

"You really can't get away?" Mildred moved on. "Or is that an excuse?"

"Word of my fiasco with Homestead Bank and Trust

spread pretty quickly, so I've been busy on damage control. I've lost several clients." They paused at a shoe store and browsed the bargain counter.

"Fortunately," Sheila continued as she inspected a pair of medium-heel blue pumps with a stylish silver buckle, "there have also been a few new ones. Caleb Hawkins—I did some work for him a couple of years ago—asked me to evaluate a tool company he recently acquired." They walked on. "Maybe bumping into him at the races in Phoenix prompted him to call. Whatever the reason, I'm glad he showed up when he did. It's a good-sized contract."

"I'm thirsty," Mildred said as they approached a sidewalk café at the end of the mall. They found a vacant table, which Mildred tidied up while Sheila went to the counter and bought them iced lattes.

"Has Jonas brought in any new contacts? You were so upbeat when he joined you."

"He's doing his best." Sheila sighed.

Her aunt raised an eyebrow. "But not enough. Is that what you're saying?"

Sheila knew nothing she said would go any further, and sometimes her aunt was able to help her put things in perspective.

"He's changed since I worked with him at C&B. He used to be aggressive and innovative, but the spark seems to have burned out. I thought at first it was part of the adjustment of working for someone he'd once trained, but..."

Mildred sipped her rich, milky drink and waited for Sheila to continue.

"He's been great at tracking things and keeping them in order..."

"Administrative stuff," the older woman observed.

"Essentially." Sheila used her straw to stir her iced coffee. "He brought a few of his old clients with him, which has been a real boost, but I expected him to generate more new business."

"Any particular reason he hasn't, do you think?"

Sheila had thought about it and come to one conclusion. "He's tired, Mildred. I think he's just plain worn-out."

"Because of Catherine?"

Sheila nodded. "Her condition has improved markedly in the past couple of months, but her illness has taken a lot out of him."

Mildred made a sympathetic sound. "It happens. Everyone focuses on the patient and forgets how much it drains the caregiver. Is he pulling his weight?"

"Oh, yes. He's got too much pride to be lazy. He's been a great help on several projects." Sheila sipped. "The person who's turned out to be a real go-getter is Amy. She really clicks with several of our younger clients, and she's full of bright ideas and enthusiasm. Her inexperience requires considerable supervision, though. It's taking a lot of my time."

"Jonas was your mentor," Mildred observed quietly. "Why not make him hers?"

Sheila's eyes widened and she leaned back in her chair. "Now, why didn't I think of that?"

Mildred smiled broadly. "Maybe you're too close to the problem. So when are you going to visit Adam?"

"Next weekend. Michael and I have done as much as we can via e-mail. Now it's time to beard the lion in his den."

SHEILA DROVE the familiar dusty road to gate number five. Michael had e-mailed her the new combination the evening before. Poking it in gave her an uncomfortable sensation of déjà vu. Would Adam be glad to see her? Would he go for her proposal? Or would he take it as another humiliation?

The road to Michael's house took Sheila past the mesa. From below, there was no sign of the house that had stood on its edge. Somewhere up there, in the now-empty air, was the space she and Adam had shared. Gone without a trace. Except in her heart. Was it still his?

Michael's house didn't have a look of wealth from the outside. Had it not been for shade trees surrounding it and Clare's artistic landscaping, the hodgepodge arrangement of modifications and additions might even have been considered ugly. The tangled gables certainly resembled a roofer's worst nightmare. The inside, however, was as warm as the people who lived there.

Adam met her at the door. The full cast was off now, replaced with a walking cast, and the crutches had given way to a single cane. Michael reported that his father was religious about attending his physical therapy sessions. The current concern was that he would overdo his exercises in his eagerness to regain full mobility.

Standing tall and straight, Adam filled the doorway. Her pulse quickened.

"Welcome back," he said. Their eyes met, searched, waited.

"Hey," a man's voice called out from inside, "you two going to shut the door or are we expected to air-condition the whole ranch?"

They laughed nervously. Adam leaned on his cane and moved aside for her to enter.

"I'll be glad when I can throw this damn stick away."

His closeness as she brushed by, the smell of his aftershave, the heat radiating from his tall frame, sent impulses scrambling through her system.

"Actually, I think it makes you look very distinguished."

"Hrumpf." He offered her his arm. "I'd rather be young." They walked through the entryway to the living room. The whole family was present. Michael and Clare, of course, and their children, as well as Gideon, Julie and Brian. Elva was there, a permanent part of the younger First household. Only Kerry was absent. Sheila knew she was still at the Betty Ford Center. Her progress was reportedly good, but according to Michael, it would probably be some time yet before she was discharged.

For the next hour everyone seemed to talk at once. In a few weeks school would be out for the summer, and the children were abuzz with their plans for their summer vacations.

Brian had completed his mandatory public service and had finished overhauling the F150. He was grumbling now because he still had six months to go before Judge Mayhew would even consider giving him back his driver's license, and his curfew was definitely interfering with his social life. He made it sound like a real life crisis. Sheila had to keep herself from laughing. When his probation was over, she ruminated, he'd forget it had ever happened.

She waited until after dinner to tell Adam she wanted to talk to him alone.

CHAPTER SIXTEEN

"Let me get this straight." Adam studied Sheila's face. "You've been negotiating with Nedra Cummings for me to give up my interest in the Number One."

Uneasiness tiptoed in behind her resolve. "In exchange for the home place and—"

"Behind my back."

Her pulse slowed as her heart thudded. "I did it with the verbal permission of Mr. First. Nedra didn't ask which Mr. First, and I didn't volunteer the information."

Adam lowered his brows. "Michael's been in on this?"

She nodded.

"Since when?"

His hard scowl had her fighting the urge to bow her head and avert her eyes. "The day you were released from the hospital."

He sank back into his chair. "This is about my property. Why didn't you at least have the decency to talk to me about it?"

"Adam," she implored, "your home had just been destroyed in a tornado. You had a broken leg and Kerry was in the hospital. It didn't seem like a good time to bring up the subject."

Adam made a sweeping motion, grudgingly conceding the point. "You've had plenty of opportunity to bring it up since then. We've talked on the phone."

The truth was that she was afraid if she told him about her idea he'd quash it. What he didn't know, she'd rationalized, wouldn't hurt her. "I wasn't sure how you'd feel about it." It was a lame excuse.

"Discussing it with me would have been a reasonable way to find out, don't you think?"

Until recently she hadn't thought of herself as devious. On the contrary, she'd taken pride in her straightforward approach to people and issues. No secrets. No hidden agendas. Except in this case. She'd withheld vital information from Adam and intentionally misled Nedra into believing she was representing him.

"I also didn't want to get your hopes up," she ventured.

His expression clouded, then turned dark. "Hopes of giving up what's left of my share of the family ranch? Yeah, I guess that would have been a real bummer," he said sarcastically.

"Get your hopes up about taking sole possession of the original tract of First land."

His features softened for a minute, then he exhaled loudly. "All right, let's hear what you've come up with."

"We call it a *strawman* in contracting," Sheila explained, sensing the first subtle chords of hope. "It's a basic outline of an agreement. Not all the details have been filled in yet, and of course it in no way obligates you to do anything."

Adam impatiently nodded his understanding. "Okay, shoot."

Sheila relaxed marginally. "In consideration for

your thirty percent share of the Number One, you'll be
given clear title to the original 60,000-acre grant of
land awarded to your great-great-grandfather in 1820
by the Spanish government with a right of way in per-
petuity to the property through the Number One.''

Leaning his elbows on the armrests, Adam brought
the fingertips of both hands together and regarded her
coolly over them. ''Sixty thousand isn't thirty percent
of 512,000,'' he reminded her curtly. ''How about mineral rights?''

Without them he had the use of only the top of the
land. The bank would still own all underground resources, including water.

''Full mineral rights,'' she announced.

Surprise showed on his face. ''They know damn well
there's no oil. I guess that's all they care about.'' He
rested back. ''Do they realize it's the head of the Coyote River?''

''I didn't ask and I'm not about to.''

The glint in his eyes and the quirk of his lips sent
her optimism up a notch. He was hardly grinning, however.

''Three vaquero families live on the home place,''
he reminded her. ''What about them?''

She crossed one leg over the other and smoothed out
her skirt. ''As far as the bank's concerned, it's not their
problem. The land and buildings will belong to you. If
you want to let the hands live there and work on the
Number One, fine. How you manage their residing on
your property is your business.''

The irony wasn't lost on Adam. If they lived on the
home place but didn't work there, he'd have to collect
rent, if only to avoid their gaining squatters' rights to
their homes. Of course, the issue could be avoided by

billing them a dollar a year, but the point was, the bank would have won a moral victory: he'd be charging the workers for their quarters.

"And if they choose to work for me?" he asked.

"That's up to you and them. I can tell you this, if they quit the Number One, they probably won't be replaced."

Adam brought his palms together in a prayerful attitude and tapped the tips of his fingers to the cleft in his chin. "Which means if they stay on the Number One they'll eventually be laid off." He hated seeing people used as pawns. "I won't abandon families who have dedicated themselves to the Number One, but we'll get back to that in a minute. You're still not giving me thirty percent value. What about livestock?"

Sheila uncrossed her legs and stretched her back muscles. This was the tricky part. Nedra had been willing to give up several thousand head of cattle, sheep and goats, but Sheila had approached the subject a little differently. "What would you want?" she asked.

"Thirty percent of the livestock, of course."

"How about one hundred percent of competition horses, Thoroughbred and quarter, and ten percent of cattle, sheep and goats?"

His brows rose. "Mares and stallions?" Their earning potential exceeded that of the other livestock combined. He shifted restlessly in his chair, and she knew she now had his undivided attention.

"Remember the board meeting?" she asked rhetorically. "Nedra wanted to sell off the horses, and everyone voted against her. Well, this is her revenge."

The sheer delight in his smile was unmistakable. "Cunning, Mrs. Malone," he grumbled. "Hoisting the imperious VP on her own petard."

Sheila had to stifle the urge to gloat. "Sometimes there is a kind of justice."

"This is all well and good," he said, brushing it aside with the wave of a hand, "but it still isn't enough. My share of this spread far exceeds a few sections of land and a few thousand head of cattle, even with the racehorses thrown in. What about cash?"

"That could be the sticking point," Sheila admitted.

"They paid Kerry $50 million dollars for her six percent," Adam informed her. It hadn't been all that difficult to find out. He had friends. "Which means my thirty percent is worth $250 million."

Surely he didn't think they'd shell out a quarter billion dollars in cash. "Kerry's six percent was critical," Sheila reminded him. "You stock gives them a greater share, but not greater control. They won't recompense you at the same rate. Besides, Kerry walked away with nothing but cash."

"How much do you think they would fork over?" he demanded.

Sheila shook her head. "You'd be taking a 94 square-mile chunk out of the land—"

"Out of 800," he reminded her, "less than twelve percent."

"All the horses and a portion of their other livestock," she continued, undaunted. She had him thinking positive and didn't want to slow the momentum. "They might be willing to match their offer to Kerry."

"Fifty million." Adam's forehead wrinkled, his eyes narrowing. "It's worth a hell of a lot more than that, Sheila." He peered for several moments at a spot somewhere over her head as he considered the implications. "Are they short of liquid assets?"

She pursed her lips. "It's possible. I hear they've

made a few investments that haven't matched their expectations, and of course their payment to Kerry—''

"You seem to have this all figured out."

His bland expression made it impossible to gauge whether he was praising or criticizing. "I've done my research and tried to cover all the contingencies."

He climbed to his feet. "This is important to you, isn't it?"

It was a question she hadn't expected. "To me? No. It is for you."

He came another step closer. "You want me to do this."

"I...I just want you to have options."

"Uh-huh." He leaned against the front of his desk and gazed down at her with an amused smile. It made her squirm and had tiny beads of sweat popping out on her nape. "Have I mentioned that I've missed you, Sheila?"

Unsure where this was leading, she jumped to her feet, but found it only brought her closer to him.

He extended his arms and straightened. "I'd like to think you've missed me, too."

"Adam, I—"

But it was too late for explanations. He latched onto her shoulders. Their eyes met and a second later his mouth was on hers. The kiss was a tender one, the slow savoring of a long-denied pleasure. She hesitated at first, until his tongue nudged hers. Even then, he seemed in no hurry as he gently explored and delightfully tasted.

At last, they parted and he nuzzled the crook of her neck. "Sweetheart, forgive me," he murmured in her ear. "Forgive me for my temper and my cowardice."

"No," she objected, and pulled back, only to see the

glow in his eyes retreat. "I mean yes. That is, I mean you don't have to ask… If only you'll forgive me for—"

He pressed a forefinger to her sweet lips. "Maybe we can call it even, start over. What do you think?"

Start what over? He had her all confused. This conversation? Their affair. "I…"

He grinned happily.

She hugged him then. Hard. "I've missed you so much."

"We can change that, you know." The smile on his face was beatific. "Oh, there is one thing, though." He arched an eyebrow. "I have a counterproposal." He laughed when her expression went blank, as if she was trying to figure out what he was talking about. "About the home place. An offer I'd like you to present to the bank."

He had her so completely off balance she was the one who needed the cane.

"So you'll go for the deal?" She'd calculated her chances of success were fifty-fifty at best. She was sure now the scales had tipped in her favor. Not that it made any difference, now that they were in each other's arms.

"I might." He released her and went over to the wet bat, a holdover from when this had been the game room, and took a bottle of white wine from the small under-the-counter refrigerator. "If they'll agree to my terms."

She followed him and stood a few feet away while he poured two glasses of chardonnay. There was a faraway expression on his face before he offered her a wineglass and held up his.

"We'll get to them later, but first, I propose a toast.

To the home place," he said, adding more intimately, "and to the woman who's brought the word *home* back into my life."

She nipped her bottom lip to keep it from quivering.

He drank deeply of her eyes, but took only a scant sip of the wine.

Her hands shaking, she took his glass from him and placed both of them on the nearby counter. Then she wrapped her arms around him and pressed her cheek to his broad chest. His heartbeat, already loud against her ear, thundered when he hugged her to his body. Or was it hers she was hearing? She had barely a second to gaze up at his strong expressive features before his half-open mouth captured hers.

A warmth, long contained, erupted into heat deep inside her as their tongues capered. Urgency mixed with desperation and produced a fire neither of them could quench.

"Let's go across to the other room," he murmured in her ear as he planted hungry kisses down her neck.

She threw back her head and breathed raggedly as his mouth sucked her skin between his lips and teeth. "I thought you'd never ask," she managed in a whimper of pleasure that had her ears ringing and her knees going weak.

Reluctantly, they separated. His hand holding hers, he thumped his casted leg across the makeshift office and led her to his bedroom. Carefully he closed the door, then twisted the old-fashioned key under the knob. When he turned he found her only inches away. It was still too far. Unwilling to release her, he lumbered to the double bed at the far side of the room.

"I want you so much," he muttered as he resumed his exploration of her skin with his mouth and tongue.

She framed his face between her hands, felt the sand-paper roughness of his jaw and looked deeply into his soul. The need was manifest. Its intensity, the heat of his body, the scent of woodsy aftershave and man had her juices flowing.

"I love you, Adam." Her heart was hammering so loud she could barely hear her own words. "I love you with all I have to give."

His stormy eyes widened, narrowed, melted. The kiss this time was long and raging, sweet and frantic. He pressed himself to her, letting her feel his arousal. He fondled her breasts, found her nipples and skimmed them with gentle insistence.

"I love you, too," he murmured breathlessly in her ear.

Their mouths still locked, they began removing each other's clothes. His shirt, her blouse. His undershirt, her bra. She kicked off her shoes. He tugged off her slacks. He sat on the bed and pulled off his left boot, unbuckled his belt, slid down the zipper and lowered the waist of his jeans. She crouched between his knees and peeled the right pant leg over the half cast.

She gazed up his thighs, past the rigid bulge in his briefs, the slightly concave plane of his abdomen, the gray hair-dusted chest to his face. The smile she found there was boyish and manly, tense with anticipation and eager to pleasure.

He brought his lips down to hers. Their tongues tangled as she traced the contours of his torso, savored the heat emanating from well-used muscles and hard sex.

"This leg cast—" he took her earlobe between his teeth "—is clumsy." He held the weight of her breasts in his hands, his fingers gently rolling their undersides.

"I hope—" he dragged his mouth across her cheeks to her other ear "—it doesn't...get in the way."

She rose to her feet and gently tipped him back against the pillows. "Let me worry about that," she said as she eased his battered leg onto the bed.

His eyes glowed. He breathed through his parted lips in a futile effort to control the passion welling up inside him. His breathing stopped and his heart pounded when she pulled his briefs down, releasing his swollen manhood. After slipping the cotton off, she removed her last barrier of clothing.

"Now I have you where I want you, Adam First," she announced as she straddled him.

"I'm all yours, Sheila Malone," he said in surrender, "body and soul."

EPILOGUE

THE FIELDS SPARKLED with frost as Sheila drove the caliche road along the perimeter of the Number One. Gate five loomed on her right. She didn't slow her new Jeep Cherokee, but proceeded another two miles to a gate that had been installed a couple of months earlier.

She poked in the code on the keypad outside the driver's window, waited for the gate to swing open, pulled through and patiently watched it clank shut.

"Brrr." Mildred pulled the thick cowl of her heavy woolen sweater tighter to her throat. "Jonas and Catherine had the right idea. A Caribbean cruise."

"I don't think they'd want you on their second honeymoon."

Mildred chuckled. "Probably not. Catherine was positively beaming when we saw them off, wasn't she?"

A smile spread across Sheila's face. "Having her hair grow back helped, but yes, she did look wonderful."

"Do you think you'll miss the office?"

Sheila thought about it for a minute. "Maybe a little, but I know Jonas will run the business well, especially with the new help he's put on. Besides, just because I'm only a silent partner now doesn't mean I can't stop in every once in a while and bug them."

The *whop-whop-whop* of a helicopter had her gazing up into the sun.

"Who's that?" Mildred asked.

"Adam's chopper. I wonder where he's been."

The new, unpaved road wended its way among boulders and small stands of live oak and scrub cedar, mounted a long slow rise to a ridgeline, where it descended steeply into a narrow canyon.

The evergreens, dark now in winter's icy grip, were in sharp contrast to the white-laced thatch of annual grasses and dormant weeds. The cottonwoods, pecans and deciduous bur and red oaks were bare, their glorious colors spent. Through their naked fingers Sheila spied the dull gray sheen of a tin roof.

Even in the frosty chill, the shaded porch was every bit as inviting as she had envisioned it almost a year earlier. Adam had supervised every detail of the six-month-long project of restoration—inspecting planking for floors and paneling for walls, ordering custom-made window sashes and overseeing the installation of new plumbing and electrical wiring.

She pulled around the side of the building and brought the four-wheel-drive vehicle to a halt among pickup trucks and vans. After getting out, she leaned back in and removed a gaily wrapped oblong box from behind the seat. She helped her aunt out of the high vehicle, then held Mildred's arm as they trudged the short frosty distance to the back door of the ranch house.

The steamy kitchen smelled of cinnamon and spices. Elva was cutting out gingerbread men while Sally trimmed those already baked with icing, colorful sprinkles and small pieces of candy. Sheila deposited her package against the pantry door and hung her jacket on a peg nearby. Her aunt chose to keep hers on a while longer.

"Mmm. Everything looks and smells wonderful," Sheila commented.

"Hi, Aunt Mildred," Sally called out a greeting.

Mildred patted the eight-year-old girl's shoulder. "You're doing a really good job. I like the cowpoke." Elva had skillfully added a western hat and boots to one of the cutouts.

"That's Daddy. And this one's Uncle Gideon," Sally boasted, pointing to an elongated cowboy wearing a baseball cap.

"You two ought to go into business," Sheila said. "Did you make one for your grandfather, too?"

The girl smiled at her playfully. "Yeah, but you can't see it until later."

Sheila tapped her lips with a finger and winked at her aunt. "A secret, huh? Well, okay." She smiled at Elva. "Where's the rest of the gang?"

"The girls are in the living room, decorating the tree. The men went out hunting." Elva brushed a stray wisp of graying hair from her eyes, getting flour on her forehead in the process. She screwed up her mouth with playful cynicism. "Every year they say they're going to get a wild turkey, and every year I roast a Butterball."

Mildred laughed and settled onto a kitchen chair to watch.

Rubbing Elva's shoulder, Sheila complimented Sally once more, crossed the open country kitchen and entered the living room. This house wasn't nearly as large as the one that had been on the mesa. It contained only three bedrooms, not six, and was single-story instead of two. The rooms were more modest in size, as well, but rather than feeling smaller, they felt cozier.

In a corner of the living room, farthest from the old fieldstone fireplace where oak logs crackled, the Christmas tree, a balled-in-burlap live Afghan pine, sat in a tin washtub. Its wintry scent added to the riot of sensual delights filling the colorfully cluttered room.

Clare and Julie, wearing floppy, fuzz-trimmed Santa caps, were unpacking boxes of ornaments and other decorations they'd brought from Clare's attic. Lupe Amorado, Gideon's friend from the university, and her daughter, Teresita, were stringing popcorn and cranberries for garland. They all greeted Sheila warmly.

"Come on, help us," Julie invited her. "I know you're itching to get your paws into these things."

Sheila tittered. "It's that obvious, huh?"

A conspiratorial grin lit Julie's face. "Yep." She opened a box of fragile glass balls.

"We let the guys do the manly job of putting on the lights," Clare informed her. "Under our artistic supervision, of course. Now we'll make sure each of these ornaments gets placed in exactly the right spot."

Sheila grinned. "Can I hang the tinsel?"

"I'll help," Kristin said enthusiastically.

Beth Ann jumped up, almost knocking over the popcorn. "Me, too," she shouted.

Julie grabbed the wobbling bowl and chuckled. "Go for it."

A CD of Christmas carols played softly in the background. *Home,* Sheila thought, and ached for her children off in other parts of the world.

The sound of boisterous male voices coming from the direction of the kitchen interrupted their work.

"Shut the door," they heard Elva cry as they stole out to see what the commotion was about.

"We got a turkey," Davy shouted to the women. "Brian shot it."

The hero of the hunt stepped forward. "Here you are, Elva," the teenager said proudly, his arm outstretched, a limp turkey dangling by its feet from his gloved fist.

"Never thought we'd bring home the bird, did you?" Gideon asked. His cheeks were rosy from the biting cold. He gave Lupe a bear hug when she slipped over beside him, then squeezed her son Miguelito's shoulder.

Elva looked at the feathered carcass, unimpressed. "You're not through yet. Now you can dress and cook it. I'm still roasting a Butterball."

Gideon threw back his head and guffawed. "Oh, ye of little faith. Come on, guys," he coaxed the others. "Brian and I will pluck and gut. Miguelito and Davy can help Mike get the smoker going."

Adam slipped in the back door, wearing his leather flight jacket and cowboy hat. Sheila shifted around behind the crowd of people and joined him near the pantry. Extending an arm behind the small of his back, she rested her hand comfortably on his lean hip and savored the warmth beneath the outer layer of cold.

He drew her close and planted a kiss on the top of her head. "I was afraid we'd have to send Rudolph out after you."

"It's Christmas Eve," she reminded him. "Everybody's doing last-minute shopping."

He smiled at Mildred. "Enjoying yourself?"

"Oh, yes. Very much, though it's cold as Hades."

He lifted an eyebrow. "I thought Hades was hot."

"At my age, it's the cold that's hell."

He laughed. "I'll have to keep that in mind."

"We saw you fly overhead when we came through the gate," Sheila told Adam. "Where were you coming from?"

"Had a pickup to make in town."

"Uh-huh." So she wasn't the only one leaving things to the last second.

"Come on, you guys," he said to the hunters. "There's work to do."

An hour later the scrawny fowl was hanging in the vertical smoker beside the new garage, the sweet pungency of mesquite smoke adding itself to the other scents of the season.

Brian closed the firebox door. "I'm hungry."

"Hunting's hard work," Gideon agreed. He turned to his father, who'd come outside to join them. "Do you think Elva will let us have something to eat?"

Adam checked his watch, then draped his arms on the shoulders of his son and grandson. "It's almost five o'clock, guys. People will be arriving soon." He ushered them toward the back door of the ranch house and winked at Michael. "You distract Elva so we can filch some grub."

"Only if you snatch something for me, too," Michael agreed.

By sunset, youngsters, mindless of the cold, were scampering about at games in the floodlit outdoors while their parents filled the house, shared mulled wine and eggnog, spiked and plain. Elva served a bottomless cauldron of her special alpine village soup—a creamy vegetable potage—with Aunt Mildred's New England anadama bread—a coarse white bread containing cornmeal and molasses. Visitors brought cheese and crackers, chips and dips, trays of fruits and vegetables and boxes of homemade cookies, fruitcake and other sweets.

Guests pitched in to finish trimming the tree and placed personal gifts under it. A crisp fire blazed in the fireplace and the leisurely goodwill of the season reigned.

"The house is beautiful," Linda Mayhew told Adam. Blond, green-eyed and regal, she was holding hands with the judge. Her engagement and marriage to Ronny Mayhew, the black football running back, had been a scandal thirty-five years earlier. They'd toughed it out and survived stronger. "I can't believe you were able to save the painting from the entrance of the old house." It hung now in a new frame on the wall behind the couch.

"Thanks to Sheila," Adam said with a satisfied smile. "It was in tatters when we found it. I was all set to consign it to the burn pile, but she took it to a restorer in Dallas and had all the pieces put back together." He bracketed an arm around Sheila's shoulders and gave her a squeeze. "She's always coming up with little surprises." Their eyes met briefly, but it was enough to bring a mild blush to her cheeks. He grinned mischievously and kissed her on the forehead.

"How's the leg?" Ronny asked. Adam had stopped using his cane several weeks earlier.

"A built-in barometer." Adam chuckled. "If we ever get rain again, I'll know in advance. Otherwise, it's doing fine."

"I see Brian's here," Linda observed. "He's developing into quite a handsome young man."

"He was so polite when he greeted me," the judge

added, "I wasn't sure he was the same insolent, smart-mouth kid I had in my courtroom a few months ago."

Adam grinned. "He wants his driver's license back."

Ronny chuckled. "Desperately, it would seem."

"He's talking about going to Texas Tech to study architectural engineering," Sheila volunteered. "He really enjoyed working on this place and building the new guest house."

"He's a good worker, too," Adam added.

Linda took a sip of her eggnog, then asked Adam the question Sheila knew was on several people's minds. "How's Kerry?"

"Progressing nicely, thanks," Adam responded easily, as if they were talking about someone on vacation instead of the daughter who hated him. "She may be discharged next month."

The judge fixed his ebony eyes sympathetically on his old friend. "Is she still refusing to see you?"

Adam gazed out across the crowded room, pursed his lips and nodded. Sheila felt the ache the subject always brought to her heart.

"Some things take time," said Linda, "but eventually good people come to their senses."

Adam didn't have to ask where she'd gotten that bit of wisdom. She'd been estranged from her family for nearly ten years after her marriage and still hadn't been accepted by all her husband's relatives.

Ronny shifted his attention to the corner where Gideon had Lupe caged against a wall. Lupe didn't exactly appear to be suffering in captivity, however, as her dark eyes gleamed and her lips curled at the tall blond man whose arm was outstretched to the paneling behind her.

"They make a cute couple, don't they?" Linda observed. "Are they serious about each other?"

Sheila smirked. "Gideon insists they're just good friends and colleagues."

Ronny's snicker was a low rumble. "Uh-huh."

Linda sprinkled nutmeg on her creamy eggnog and scanned the room for Adam's younger daughter. "Julie isn't dating anyone?" When Sheila shook her head, Linda observed, "Maybe I ought to introduce her to Cousin Matt. Oh, there's Penny. Come on, Sheila, we need to talk to her about…" Her last words were lost in the hubbub as the two women snaked their way toward a heavyset woman on the other side of the room.

"I haven't had a chance to talk to you since you finalized the contract with the bank," the judge commented after another sip of mulled wine. "From what I've heard, it was quite a coup."

"Sheila did it all."

"She's quite a lady—and a tough negotiator, by all accounts. Still, it must have been hard giving up the Number One."

"I'm as busy now as I ever was. What I miss is the people. The three families who live on the home place have opted to stay and work for me."

"No surprise there," Ron commented. "Felix Cordero was saying a little while ago that he and the other families would, too, if they could. He mentioned that you convinced the bank to put a five-year moratorium on charging them rent."

Adam nodded.

The judge took another sip of wine. "I also understand you have a provision in your settlement that gives you first option on the sale of any Number One land."

"I don't expect to ever get a chance to exercise it,"

Adam noted. "They have no reason to sell, and while I won't starve on this place, I won't make the kind of money it would take to buy their land—even if I wanted it."

Ronny cast him an assessing grin. "You want it."

Adam snorted. "Yeah, maybe I do."

Someone turned off the music.

"Ladies and gentlemen," Michael called out. "May I have your attention, please." He waited for the din to fade. "On behalf of the First family, I want to thank all of you for coming today and sharing the warmth of this very special season with us. I don't think I need remind anyone that this past year has been challenging, but your generous and unflagging support has sustained us in more ways than you can ever imagine. Without friends with whom to share both joy and sorrow, life would be really miserable."

"Don't get maudlin, big brother," Gideon razzed him.

Michael scowled, then snickered. "For once little brother is right."

A soft chuckle filled the room.

"Gangway." Clare shooed people aside as her three girls brought in a foil-covered cookie sheet. "Sheila, come over here with Dad."

Bewildered, Sheila complied, instinctively reaching out for Adam's hand. Her broad smile lit her face when she saw what the girls were carrying—two oversized gingerbread men. Or rather persons, for they were a man in a cowboy hat and boots and a woman in a cowboy hat and skirt. Their hands were linked.

"This is for you, Grampa and Grandma," Sally announced.

Sheila bit her lips, her eyes instantly moist. "She called me Grandma," she muttered raggedly to Adam.

Carefully, Clare helped the children place their creation on the buffet table.

"You're crying," Beth Ann said. "Don't you like it?"

Sheila knelt down and gathered the girls into a tight embrace. "I love it. And I love you."

"Brian and Davy—" Michael broke off. "Excuse me. Brian and Dave also have something for you."

Brian stood behind his cousin as the ten-year-old brought forth a large pine board. Burned into it were the words *The First Home Place.*

"You can put it over the gate," Davy explained.

"It's perfect." Adam grinned broadly as he accepted the gift and held it over his head for everyone to see. Cheers and applause followed.

"And I've got something for you," Sheila announced. She nodded to Gideon, who was standing in the doorway across the room. He ducked around the corner and reappeared carrying a large box. He held it while his father tore off the gold ribbon and colorful paper wrapping.

"Oh," was all Adam said when he saw the contents—the saddle blanket that had been in the mesa house's entranceway. The newly designed home place brand, a house with a 1 in it, was sewn into the heavy wool fabric opposite the original First brand.

"That's what I went into town for this morning," Sheila explained. "I was afraid it wouldn't be ready in time."

"It's beautiful, sweetheart," he said, and kissed her on the lips. Hoots, whistles and catcalls cheered them on.

There was a momentary draft of cold air as Charlie slipped in through the front door. Nobody paid more than passing attention to the ranch foreman.

Michael raised his wineglass. "Ladies and gentlemen, I propose a toast. To Adam and Sheila First."

"Hear, hear."

Adam jerked up his hand. "Wait," he said. "I've got a present for my wife, too. Charlie?"

"Yep, right here."

Charlie opened the door and ushered in two men, a woman and two small children.

Sheila took one look and nearly collapsed. Her heart beat so fast she was sure she was having a heart attack. "Derek. Melanie." The words were breathless.

For a moment the room was completely silent, then Sheila rushed to her son and daughter. She wept openly as she hugged her grandchildren and son-in-law.

"But how?" she finally managed to get out.

"Adam flew us into Coyote Springs and picked us up—"

"We got to fly in a helicopter, grandma," her elder granddaughter informed her happily.

Surrounded by laughter and tears, Sheila turned to Adam. "You never mentioned anything—"

"It wouldn't have been a surprise if I had." He folded her into his arms.

"As I was saying," Michael resumed in a raised voice, "ladies and gentlemen, a toast." He held his glass aloft. "To Adam and Sheila First. May their lives be filled with bliss."

Adam and Sheila stood amid friends and family, their hands joined. As the toasts were drunk he turned to her. "Do you think you can handle bliss, Mrs. First?"

"Married to you, Mr. First, I can handle anything."

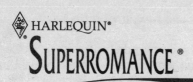

HARLEQUIN®
SUPERROMANCE®

You are now entering

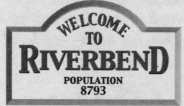

WELCOME TO RIVERBEND

POPULATION
8793

Riverbend...the kind of place where everyone knows your name—and your business. Riverbend...home of the River Rats—a group of small-town sons and daughters who've been friends since high school.

The Rats are all grown up now. Living their lives and learning that some days are good and some days aren't—and that you can get through anything as long as you have your friends.

Starting in July 2000, Harlequin Superromance brings you Riverbend—six books about the River Rats and the Midwest town they live in.

BIRTHRIGHT by **Judith Arnold** (July 2000)
THAT SUMMER THING by **Pamela Bauer** (August 2000)
HOMECOMING by **Laura Abbot** (September 2000)
LAST-MINUTE MARRIAGE by **Marisa Carroll** (October 2000)
A CHRISTMAS LEGACY by **Kathryn Shay** (November 2000)

Available wherever Harlequin books are sold.

HARLEQUIN®
Makes any time special™

Visit us at www.eHarlequin.com   HSRIVER

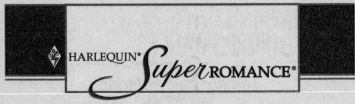

HARLEQUIN *Super*ROMANCE®

They look alike. They sound alike.
They act alike—at least
some of the time.

THE REAL FATHER by Kathleen O'Brien
(Superromance #927)

A woman raises her child alone after her boyfriend,
the father, dies. Only his twin knows that his brother
isn't the real father....
Available July 2000

CHRISTMAS BABIES by Ellen James
(Superromance #953)

One twin masquerades as the other. Now they're both
pregnant. Did the same man father both?
Available November 2000

Available wherever Harlequin books are sold.

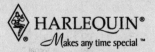

HARLEQUIN®
Makes any time special ™

Visit us at www.eHarlequin.com   HSRTWINS3

CELEBRATE VALENTINE'S DAY
WITH HARLEQUIN®'S
LATEST TITLE— Stolen Memories

Available in trade-size format, this collector's edition contains
three full-length novels by *New York Times* bestselling
authors Jayne Ann Krentz and Tess Gerritsen, along with
national bestselling author Stella Cameron.

TEST OF TIME by **Jayne Ann Krentz**—
He married for the best reason.... She married for the
only reason.... Did they stand a chance at making the
only reason the real reason to share a lifetime?

THIEF OF HEARTS by **Tess Gerritsen**—
Their distrust of each other was only as strong as
their desire. And Jordan began to fear that Diana
was more than just a thief of hearts.

MOONTIDE by **Stella Cameron**—
For Andrew, Greer's return is a miracle. It had broken
his heart to let her go. Now fate has brought them back
together. And he won't lose her again...

Make this Valentine's Day one to remember!

Look for this exciting collector's edition
on sale January 2001 at your favorite retail outlet.

HARLEQUIN®
Makes any time special ™

Visit us at www.eHarlequin.com   PHSM

**COMING IN NOVEMBER 2000
FROM STEEPLE HILL**

Three bestselling authors invite you to share in their

HOLIDAY BLESSINGS
by
New York Times bestselling author
DEBBIE MACOMBER
Thanksgiving Prayer
A young woman must decide whether she is willing
to brave the rugged wilderness of Alaska for
the man she loves.

JANE PEART
The Risk of Loving
During the holiday season, two lonely people decide
to risk their hearts and learn to love again.

IRENE HANNON
Home for the Holidays
A troubled widow finds her faith renewed on
Christmas Eve when she falls in love with
a caring man.

HOLIDAY BLESSINGS
Available November 2000 from

Steeple
Hill™

Visit us at www.steeplehill.com   PSHHB